List of Char~

Iolcus

ALCIMEDE, mother of Jason, married to

AESON, dispossessed king of Iolcus and brother to

PELIAS, king of Iolcus, father of daughters

IPHIAS, priestess of Artemis

The Argo

Many heroes, including

JASON, the captain of the ship

HERACLES, a member of the crew

HYLAS, a reluctant young crewmember

ZETES, son of Boreas, the north wind, brother to

KALAÏS, another member of the crew

EUPHEMOS, a crew member with quick hands

TIPHYS, the helmsman of the ship

The Island of Lemnos

Many women, including

EÏONE, a Lemnian woman, neighbour to

EUNEA, another Lemnian woman

HYPSIPYLE, queen of Lemnos, daughter of

THOAS, old king of Lemnos

POLYXO, nurse and adviser to the queen

IPHINOË, childhood friend of Hypsipyle

ALCIPPE, captured Thracian woman

MENIPPE, captured Thracian woman

Those Found (or Avoided) on Further Voyaging

KLEITE, unforgettable queen of the Doliones

NAIADS, tree-loving nymphs

PHINEUS, a prophet who should have known better

PELEIA, the Greek name for a dove

SYMPLEGADES, Clashing Rocks, a peril of the seas

PHYLLIS, a nymph living in a safe haven

THEOPHANE, young woman seized by Poseidon, who loved

CHRYSOMALLOS, her child

INO, second wife of

ATHAMAS, father of

HELLE and PHRIXUS, children of

NEPHELE, goddess of the clouds

CIRCE, witch and goddess, aunt of Medea

ARETE, queen of the Phaeacians, wife of

ALCINOUS, king of the Phaeacians

Colchis

AIETES, king of Colchis, father to

MEDEA, his youngest child, a powerful witch, and

APSYRTUS, her older brother, and

CHALCIOPE, their older sister, mother to

ARGOS, MELAS and PHRONTIS

NEAERA, queen of Colchis, at least in name, mother of
Chalciope, Apsyrtus and Medea

Corinth

CREON, king of Corinth, father of

GLAUKE, princess of Corinth

AEGEUS, king of Athens, passing through

Deities

ARTEMIS, goddess of the hunt and of trackless places

APHRODITE, goddess of love, married to

HEPHAESTUS, craftsman of the gods

EOS, goddess of the dawn, married to Tithonus

HARPIES, winged snatcher-goddesses, sisters to

IRIS, goddess of the rainbow

POSEIDON, god of the sea

ERATO, Muse of love poetry

HERA, queen of the gods

ATHENE, goddess of wisdom and strategy

EROS, son of Aphrodite

HELIOS, sun god

HECATE, chthonic goddess of witchcraft

SELENE, moon goddess, also known as Mene, lover of

ENDYMION, a beautiful sleeping man

λέγουσι δ᾽ ἡμᾶς ὡς ἀκίνδυνον βίον
ζῶμεν κατ᾽ οἴκους, οἱ δὲ μάρνανται δορί,
κακῶς φρονοῦντες· ὡς τρὶς ἂν παρ᾽ ἀσπίδα
στῆναι θέλοιμ᾽ ἂν μᾶλλον ἢ τεκεῖν ἅπαξ.

They say we live a life at home, without danger, while they do battle with spears. Those fools: I would prefer to stand three times behind a shield than give birth once.

Euripides, *Medea*, 248–251

RIVER PO

ARTEMIS' ISLAND

RIVER ISTER

AEAEA

ADRIATIC SEA

TYRRHENIAN SEA

LEMN

IOLCUS

AEGEA SE

IONIAN SEA

ATHEN

CORINTH

MEDITERRANEAN

HEMESH ALLES.

BLACK SEA

SYMPLEGADES

COLCHIS

NEUS

KIOS

KYZIKOS

SEA

THE VOYAGE OF THE ARGO

Part One

The Voyage of the Argo

Argo

If only the Argo had sunk to the bottom of the sea

It was hardly the fault of the Argo.

This was the kind of thing people said in those days: if you couldn't blame anyone, you'd say it was the ship. But Jason didn't set his Argonauts to row across the oceans because he was captain of the Argo; the men built the Argo because Jason wanted to find the fleece. So if you were trying to find the beginning of this story, then that's where you would go: to the glimmering softness of the golden ram. Would you choose the day it was born? Or the day it appeared in Hellas to rescue two children, about to lose their lives?

But we will start in the place where the ship set sail.

Alcimede

rather than winging its way

Alcimede had never been a fortunate woman, and she said so to anybody who would listen. Of course, she acknowledged that it might look to others as though she had been very fortunate because when she was young, Alcimede had married Aeson, the older son of the ageing king of Iolcus. And that was the kind of thing that girls prayed for: when I grow up, Hera, please let me marry a king, like you did. And her prayers had almost come true. The older son of a king would become king in time, so all Alcimede had to do was wait.

And perhaps that had been her mistake. She had foolishly thought the Fates had granted her a happy lot: the old man would die and she would become queen. And – another ingredient in her happiness – Aeson was a soft, kind man who never raised his voice or tried to win an argument. His father issued occasional decrees and he allowed his wife to make decisions about everything else. This suited Alcimede well, because she was her parents' only child, and she had never learned to yield to anyone. And they were both still so young: her husband had plenty of time to become domineering and inflexible.

When the old king died, Alcimede mourned in public and rejoiced in private. She would not miss the old tyrant, she doubted anyone would. And she would enjoy seeing his younger son Pelias lose influence, just as she gained it. The royal house would now have a king and queen, as was proper. She would go on to tell her friends and – when they had given up listening to her – her slaves, this was the last time she felt happiness.

Because it was not his youth that made Aeson weak, she discovered. It was his nature. And Pelias had known this from infancy, from the first time he grabbed a toy rattle that belonged to his brother and then kept it. He watched as Aeson tried to retrieve the little clay dog, shouted and screamed until Aeson crawled away. He never forgot how quickly his brother gave up, even when it was something he wanted very much. He took a simple lesson from their boyhood: Aeson didn't want anything as much as Pelias wanted everything.

So Pelias seized the throne of Iolcus for himself. He did not ask – or offer – to share power, he simply took it. And Aeson allowed it, because he didn't know what else to do or how to oppose it. Was he meant to take up arms against his own brother? Would any of their citizens wish for a civil war? Was it not better to let Pelias have what he so ardently wanted, and avoid bloodshed?

Alcimede had never forgiven either her brother-in-law or her husband for this disgrace, bundled out of the palace while pregnant and Aeson doing nothing about it except accepting their degraded status. Would he not fight for his son's future, if not for his own, the women of Iolcus asked? And their husbands and brothers all gave the same reply: Aeson would never fight for anything.

And so the city had Pelias for its king: a fractious man who saw his own ambitions concealed behind the eyes of every other man. If Alcimede had been capable of viewing things dispassionately, she would have noticed that although Pelias had stolen the kingdom from his brother, it brought him nothing but unhappiness. He sent messengers to the oracle to try to uncover plots against him, then sent them back to ask again because he could not trust its replies. This illegitimate king was still who he had always been: an anxious, querulous man.

The midwives were nervous when he had one daughter, then two, then three: no one wanted to take bad news to a king. But the birth of his daughters was one of the few parts of his life that did not make Pelias angry. Daughters would take care of him as he aged, but they would never threaten his rule. If he had been cursed with a son, it would not have survived infancy. His nephew – who was changing from child to man at a horrifying speed – was almost as unwanted.

This brought Alcimede to her second piece of terrible misfortune, disguised as good luck. She had a healthy pregnancy, despite the grievous disappointments she had suffered. And she gave birth to a healthy son, who everyone said looked like his father. But there the gods put a cruel end to her family. What had she done to offend Eilythia, goddess of childbirth? She asked the question repeatedly of anyone who would listen. But no one could give her an answer except Aeson, who asked if one healthy son wasn't enough for them.

And he wasn't, of course, because here was the third cruel trick the Fates had played on Alcimede. Despite everything she had told him when he was a boy, her son was determined to be a hero. And because the women of Iolcus were all fools, dazzled by the mere idea of adventures, she could not even share her grief with them. It was easy for them to think a quest would burnish her family honour, but it hardly felt that way to Alcimede. She had been granted only one child, and one who cared so little for her that he would set sail in an untested boat without so much as a thought about who would look after his mother while he was gone.

And of course, Aeson had been no use – again – when Pelias made his cruel announcement. The king had recently declared that Iolcus was in need of a golden fleece, a magical artefact from far across the sea. Pelias knew little more about it: some gift from a goddess to her children, was it? Its beauty and power were fabled; people said it would bring riches to whichever land held it. But Pelias was already rich and had no need of any artefacts. The thing that made the fleece particularly desirable was how very far away it was, and how difficult to reach, across such dangerous seas.

Soon, there was a shipbuilder, and a crew. Men were volunteering from all over Greece to be part of this grand quest. Pelias could scarcely suppress his smirk when the messenger said that Jason – the king's own nephew – was hoping to make his parents and his uncle proud by leading this voyage. Pelias didn't necessarily want Jason to die, although it was all the same to him if he did. He merely wished that his nephew – and any other man who thought he might have a claim on anything Pelias regarded as his own – would leave his kingdom, and never return. Which, of course, this ship's crew could not once they had undertaken such a mighty task. The humiliation of failure would see off the ones death did not seize.

And so, on a bright spring morning, Alcimede counted a whole new set of misfortunes sent by the Fates to plague her. Jason was coming to bid farewell to his mother and to attempt to console his father, who had taken to bed months before when the voyage was first suggested. Alcimede still hoped to dissuade her son from travelling. How could he abandon her this way? Better she should have died before being left with no one to help look after his father.

Jason tried to placate Alcimede, to persuade her that he would be back in Iolcus before long, and to promise that he would be bringing the golden fleece to prove his worth. He would make her proud, he was sure of it. But his mother had grown used to disappointment before her son was born. There was no dissuading her from it now.

Iphias

towards the land of Colchis,

The words Iphias left unsaid would have moved the sky and parted the sea.

Last night she had been standing before the altar of Artemis, protector of her city, murmuring a quiet prayer. No one else was by the shrine at that hour, no one but the statue. Artemis towered above Iphias, left foot planted on the plinth, right foot behind her, heel raised. The golden straps of her sandals and the golden hem of her dress glittered in the flickering torchlight. The goddess had a serene expression and a few strands of hair snaked free from her plait. Something about the pose, the way Artemis had been caught mid-stride, always made Iphias feel restless, as though she too was at the beginning of a journey. But as the priestess picked a stray white hair from her tunic, she was reminded that there were no journeys ahead for her.

Iphias smiled up at the moon as she walked around the sanctuary, checking everything was in order. Artemis was always closer to her when the moon was full. But when she looked back down into the shadows around her, the visions came to her in a rush, bright and terrible: images of the young man who planned to set sail the very next day. She saw lethal trials ahead of him – brief flashes of horror – as though she was gazing up at a pitch-black sky, illuminated by sudden bolts of lightning. Iphias prayed for guidance, but the goddess waited until she was asleep before delivering her message in a dream.

Iphias felt the weariness in her knees as she offered up her thanks the next morning. Tired though she was, the priestess had the strength to perform this task. All she needed to do now was wait for the right time. And she knew it was approaching because the city spoke of nothing else as the men made the final preparations to ready their ship. Everyone who passed the temple brought another fragment of news as Iphias stood on the wide marble steps.

She sensed the tension filling the city as the men prepared to sail and the women to grieve, but she did not share it. The men's impossible quest would become possible once they had Artemis' advice. The priestess watched the street filling with people who wanted to see the Argo launch from her safe harbour. Today was a day they would tell sceptical children and grandchildren they had witnessed. And where there was a spectacle, there were traders selling food, offerings, amulets to bring luck to a sailor or those he was leaving behind.

The hubbub was building now, so Iphias knew that Jason had left his parents' house and was walking towards the harbour. Soon he would be right outside the temple: she had seen it already, in her dream. She descended a single step, wanting to be closer to the path so she could make herself heard, yet not wanting to lose her vantage point.

But as Jason came around the final curve of the street before he reached her, the crowd surged, a sudden swell taking the old woman away from the temple. Jason had grown to be a very handsome man, Iphias thought, as she scurried along with the thronging people to avoid losing her footing. There was no denying it. Even Artemis would look on him with favour: he resembled her twin, the sun to her moon. Iphias felt herself being tugged in his direction and then came the moment of connection, when her eyes met his.

The priestess felt the spark of acknowledgement. She knew Jason had seen her and wanted to discuss his plans. But just as she opened her mouth to speak, the whirl of people moved again and she was behind him as he strode away. She felt dizzy and detached, as though she had been awake through her dreams and was sleeping now. Iphias almost fell, but two younger priestesses from the temple had seen her difficulty and rushed over to help her.

'Did you have something to tell him?' asked one. It took Iphias a moment to hear the words and to understand what the girl was asking.

'We could send a messenger,' the other one said. 'Or take the message ourselves.'

Iphias could see the excitement on their faces but she could not quite remember what might have caused it. She did have a message for someone, she knew that. She had been about to speak, but then she had not. And that was all she could find, blinking away tears from the harsh light of late morning. She would never again remember the words Artemis had given her, or the way Jason had seen her and walked past without stopping to take his leave of the goddess

11

or her priestess. And the goddess would play no role in Jason's quest, because he had shunned her in this way.

Some men are born to be a favourite of the gods. Or at least to seem so, for a while.

Aphrodite

through the dark Symplegades;

Aphrodite perched on her rock at Paphos, and looked out at the Cyprian sea. No wonder she always came here when one or another of the gods had irritated her. As the sun danced on the glimmering waves, she felt something akin to envy that anything could be so beautiful besides her. The Graces were preparing the water for her bath, and she was glad of it. Once her skin was oiled and she could slip into a new dress, she might feel less irritated. She ran her tongue lightly across the back of her teeth because it was the only way she knew to express rage without affecting the shape of her perfect mouth. But she could contain her fury no longer: why would anyone be so foolish – she screamed the word into the gentle breeze – as to neglect her? Why?

She resented it when it was her husband, always leaving her to go and make . . . She paused briefly. Armour? Spear heads? Whatever he did. It scarcely mattered, because if he didn't craft them, then someone else would. Men always needed the tools to wound. And so, she supposed, did other gods. The ethereal glory of her smile was such that no one would have dared call it a smirk. But the satisfaction that

13

prompted it was entirely directed at herself. She could destroy a man or incapacitate a god using nothing but their own desires, which were hers to control. Weapons seemed to her a very cumbersome way to go about taking a life, when compared to longing or its bedfellow, despair.

In this way Aphrodite nursed her anger, allowing it to grow. Hephaestus did sometimes fill her with rage, but he had done nothing particular to antagonize her today, so she would not punish him. Then she heard a pair of oyster-catchers chattering to one another on the shore below, but the birds had never insulted her, so she would leave them to their courtship. No, it was only men who could be so offensive, so provoking. She paused while she remembered some of the many different forms of revenge she had taken on men over the years. She smiled again when she saw the bodies she had broken and the lives she had shattered. No battlefield could be bloodier than hers, and she had never fired so much as a single slender arrow.

And yet. Again she felt the surging anger. And yet, men had learned nothing from these lessons, so kindly offered them by this mightiest goddess. Had they looked on the destruction of the impious and vowed to live better lives? Perhaps they had, but in that case, they were perjurers as well as blasphemers. Because here she was, unable to enjoy her bath because she was thinking of the inexcusable people of some tiny island in the Thracian Sea. She could barely remember its name before today, but she would make the Lemnians one promise, and she would keep it sooner than they could imagine was possible. They would regret insulting her.

They would regret building their temples to Zeus, to Hera, to Artemis and Apollo, of course. Naturally they

14

would build one to Poseidon, because they spent so much of their pitiful lives at sea. They had dedicated their largest temple to Hephaestus, which only sharpened the sting. To ignore her, the goddess whose favour everyone desired? She shook her head and her beautiful hair shimmered in the sun. She had given them plenty of time to correct their catastrophic mistake and beg her forgiveness. And had they?

Perhaps if it had been a sanctuary for Demeter, she might have allowed some of them to live. Mortals needed a good harvest, she supposed. But it was a temple to Athene they had decided to build next. Athene! And even that she might have ignored if the women had prayed to her. She had occasionally let men off if their wives had begged. But the women of Lemnos had done nothing. No temple, no shrine, no offerings. And she could hardly ignore such a slight.

She curled the fingers of her left hand, and examined her shell-like nails. There was no trace of imperfection. A lilting call told her the Graces had readied her bath, and she rose and turned away from the sea. As her gaze fell on the jugs of perfectly heated water, the neat piles of fresh clothes and the bottles of heady perfume, she smiled. Yes, of course. There was no better way to punish the people of Lemnos.

Eïone

*if only the pine trees in the glades on
Mount Pelion had never been chopped down;*

Most of the women agreed the worst of it was that they
didn't know if the men were telling the truth. But for Eïone
– although later she would nod in agreement with the others,
concealing her private grief behind their collective shame
– uncertainty was by no means the worst part. That came
right at the beginning, with the revulsion that crossed her
husband's face when she turned to him one morning, as
she always did. She expected to find herself caught in his
embrace, his chin resting on the top of her head. But instead
of holding her in his arms, he turned away grimacing. She
opened her mouth to ask what was wrong, and then immediately changed her mind. Perhaps he was in pain, in which
case he would surely tell her about it soon. But though she
had never seen such an expression on his face before, she
recognized it immediately. It was not pain she had witnessed.
It was disgust.

She wanted to speak to her sisters about it, but when
she met with them later that day, she found she could not.
There was something wrong between them, all four scratchy

16

and defensive with one another. Usually Eïone kept the peace between her siblings, but she was too upset to intervene, so they squabbled over things none of them cared about and she returned home as anxious as she had left it. And her worry only increased when she found the house empty. The men were preparing for another raid on a Thracian coastal town, their fourth since the seas had calmed at the end of the winter. But surely, he wouldn't have left without a word? Eïone wanted to hurry round to her neighbours and ask if their husbands were missing too, but she felt her face reddening just to think of how she might frame the question. What if their husbands were happily sitting indoors, eating bread and sheep's cheese, and they stared at her as she stammered out her question?

Anyway, he might return at any moment. Perhaps he had gone to feed the chickens and an old friend had arrived unexpectedly. She walked from room to room, unable to settle and unsure if she should prepare food or wait. As the shadows on the floor grew longer, she decided she was hungry, and went to see if the chickens had laid them any eggs. She blinked in the bright sun and almost trod on one of the birds as she stepped outside.

'Why are you sitting right by the door?' she asked the chicken, but it only blinked in reply. As she approached the coop, all three birds ran towards her, clucking urgently. She frowned.

'Did he not feed you?' she asked. 'Are you hungry?'

She had a sudden vision of herself as a widow, a woman crazed with loneliness, talking to her chickens and expecting their reply. There was a small grain store next to the house, so she answered her own question and collected a scoop of grain. The clucking grew increasingly loud and she scattered the food on the dry brown earth. Staphylus had left without even feeding their birds. She tried to remember a time her husband – usually such a kind man – had abandoned animals unfed. She shook her head as if that would dislodge the way the word filled her eyes and ears: never, never, never. As the chickens ate their corn in quiet satisfaction, she collected three eggs and turned to go back indoors. She strained to hear voices from the neighbouring houses but there was nothing, not even a baby crying.

*

By sundown, he had not returned. She had made vegetable soup, but she ate alone, one flickering candle enough to see her meagre dinner. When someone knocked on the door, she started, and put her hand to her mouth to cover the inadvertent cry. The door opened and Eunea looked almost as alarmed as Eïone knew she herself must.

'Is Staphylus here?' she asked.

Eïone opened her mouth to say no, but her voice cracked and no sound came. She shook her head.

'Do you know where he is?' asked Eunea, and Eïone felt her voice return, only temporarily silenced by solitude.

'No,' she replied. 'I came home and the house was empty.' Her face felt hot, and she was grateful for the dim light.

'Oenepion is gone too,' Eunea said. 'He didn't say a word.'

Eïone nodded. 'I don't know where they are.'

'There's a raid coming,' Eunea said, and Eïone nodded again.

'But why leave without saying anything?'

The two women stood in the half dark. 'Can I — ?' Eunea didn't need to finish her sentence because Eïone was already pushing a low chair in her direction.

*

The next day, it became clear that many men were missing, and the women all asked the same questions of themselves and one another. Their ships were gone from the harbour, so this solved one puzzle while creating several more. The men — even those too old to fight — had gone to Thrace, then, but they had done so in a needlessly secretive way. So the women did as they always did when their menfolk were away: tended to their homes, their children, their crops and their livestock, and tried not to think about the spears and arrows of the Thracians piercing their beloved flesh.

Eïone had never worried about Staphylus because he was such a bear of a man. No one would choose to fight him. His sight was keen, his feet were quick and he didn't take foolish risks. But she didn't feel her usual confidence in the man who had left her house without saying goodbye. When she tried to reach him in her mind, she could only see that expression of revulsion, a moment of unspoken estrangement. And she wondered if something had changed within her, because she didn't quite believe that the man who had left — the man who would return, if the gods willed it — was the husband she loved.

*

She knew Oenepion had returned to Eunea, because she heard the shouting.

Word had come early that the first ships had been seen, riding low over the waves, weighed down with booty. Some women flocked to the harbour with their children, but Eïone had stayed on the hill, looking down at the bright white sails and wondering which one was fluttering above his head. She continued to work on their small plot of land, pretending that she wasn't waiting and hoping. But Staphylus didn't come home that day, or the next. And as she opened her door to Eunea again – this time with a bruise purpling her cheek – Eïone wasn't sure how much she minded being alone.

Besides, she was not alone. The two women divided the chores and the food between them: Eïone had more eggs than she could eat, after all. She missed the strength of her husband, and she missed his easy kindness. But when Eunea asked her for an example of him being kind, she realized that it had been many months since she had seen this side of her husband.

'I don't know when it stopped,' she said. And as she spoke, she knew that after the initial shock of his disappearance had worn away, her anxiety had curdled to indifference.

And Eunea nodded in recognition. The idea that Oenepion – a man who had never raised his voice until this year – would physically push her out of her own house was incredible. If she had received an oracle a year ago telling her this would happen, she would have assumed the priestess was lying. But here she was, sitting on her friend's bed, her left eye still swollen shut. After a few days, Eunea crept home to try and collect some of her most precious belongings

– a necklace, a ring that had been her mother's – and she discovered the house was empty. She ran back to tell Eïone that he had gone again, smiling with relief. But she did not stay in her home, fearful that he might return at any moment and blacken her other eye. And again, the women found themselves wondering where the men had gone.

*

The rumour began circulating in the market square, where trade and talk were brisk. Two children had gone hunting on the other side of the island, and they came back with news of the men's camp. The men weren't calling it that, of course. They were claiming it as the new town of Lemnos, but it was a shanty town at most, a few lean-to huts. Nonetheless, it was where the missing men of Lemnos were: they had abandoned their wives and they had sent their comrades to Thrace to raid a town and steal the women they found there. And now – the Lemnian women could scarcely believe it – they were living with these slaves as though these were their wives. While the women who had borne and raised their children were spurned. The violence, the indifference, the cruelty, these all paled beside this public humiliation.

They could tolerate it no longer; they took their grievances to the king.

The Lemnian Women

if only those mighty heroes
had never picked up their oars,

Hypsipyle loved her father, and she tried not to notice his declining faculties. She remembered Thoas when his eyesight was so sharp he could teach her the name of every bird flying overhead; she remembered when his appetite was so great he could enjoy a banquet every night. And as she watched a slave spoon food into her father's mouth across the huge table, she wondered why people prayed for a long life. He reminded her of a story he had told her as a child: of Eos and her mortal husband Tithonus.

The goddess Eos spread the red streaks of dawn across the sky each day, and one morning her searching gaze picked out a beautiful young man from a city on the mainland, not far from Lemnos. Tithonus was tall and strong with golden skin and thick black hair, and he played the lyre almost as well as Apollo himself. When Eos approached him, he didn't falter as mortals so often did. He returned her gaze and her desire, and left his home to live in hers. Every morning Eos would leave him sleeping in their bed

22

and then she would return to him as Helios began to share his light with the world. Tithonus would sing for her and his songs almost never told of the way he missed the light – her light – playing on the walls of his father's house as his family began their day.

One day, Eos noticed a tiny change in her lover's face, a small crease she had never seen before. She tried to hide her alarm, but she could not deceive the man she loved. He was changing, ageing, and there was nothing she could do to keep him as he was. But Zeus could help them, she explained to Tithonus. Zeus could intervene in a man's life if he chose: all Tithonus needed to do was ask. So her beloved approached the king of the gods and begged for a small favour. Zeus affected not to hear him for a while but eventually Hera pointed at the young man and suggested Zeus either swat him or listen to him. Tithonus stammered out his plea for eternal life, and Zeus declared the matter closed.

It was years before they realized his mistake. Faint lines continued to form around his eyes and mouth. Gradually the lines grew less faint, and then they became pronounced. Tithonus had asked to live for ever, but he had not asked to remain young for ever. And so he grew older and drier, smaller and wearier with every passing year. And though Eos had sworn she would love him for ever, she loved him less when he finally turned into a cicada – the oldest and driest of creatures – than she had when he was a man.

Thoas was not yet as small as a cicada, but he had once towered over his daughter and now he would have to raise his head to meet her gaze, although he didn't because he had long ceased to recognize her. Sometimes he thought she was his mother and sometimes he thought she was a servant, but he seemed to love her, whoever he thought she was. This consoled her for feeling that she had lost her father even as he sat beside her.

Now, when the Lemnians came to consult their king, it was Hypsipyle who received them. The princess sat on her father's throne to hear the women's grievances. Firstly, their husbands had been cruel to them. Secondly, their husbands had rejected them. In a little over a month, they had been abandoned, ignored and replaced. And the women would not stand for it.

Hypsipyle listened to them as they wept their rage and hurt, and wondered what she should do. She knew the men had gone on an unplanned raiding expedition, but they didn't need royal permission for that. She knew they had brought back Thracian women, but had assumed they would take them home to their wives, as they usually did when they enslaved those whose men could not save them. More women on Lemnos meant more children, and this was a desirable outcome. They had the resources and the strength to support a larger population, so why not? Hypsipyle had heard that some of the men had set up camp across the hills, but they had sent word to the palace that they were loyal to the king and expanding his territory, so she had allowed it.

Now she felt that she had been naive and too lenient: a few men setting up a new life with their slave-women was one thing, but this was too much. She sent a messenger to the men's camp to demand they return to their wives. But the following day the messenger returned alone. The men were refusing to leave. Hypsipyle sent her father's guards to accompany the messenger on his second visit. She waited all day for news, but none of them returned. She consulted her nurse, because she had no one else.

'Who do I send to bring back the guards?' she asked.

Polyxo had been nurse to Hypsipyle's mother before her, but she had none of the frailty that had robbed the princess of her parents. She was solid and sharp-eyed, the white strands amid her grey hair gleaming in the evening light.

'I don't know,' she replied. 'There is no one left to send.'

'I don't understand,' said the princess. 'We must have other, more loyal men.'

The old nurse shook her head. 'They have all left.'

'So who do we send?' Hypsipyle repeated. 'Slaves?'

'They have also gone,' said the nurse.

'They can't have gone.'

'The last ones disappeared today.'

'But why did no one stop them?'

'All the men – free and enslaved – have gone.'

Hypsipyle took a breath as she tried to understand. 'My father is still here,' she said. Polyxo smiled.

'Yes, my love,' she replied. 'But he cannot walk. He is tended by women now.'

'Is it an attempt to overthrow him?' asked Hypsipyle. Her voice was becoming smaller. How could she protect him with no guards?

'I don't know,' the nurse answered. 'But we can find out.'

'How?'

'We send a small band of women to kidnap one of the men,' said Polyxo, as though she were discussing household supplies. 'Then we torture him until he speaks.' Hypsipyle nodded.

25

'Yes,' she said. 'Who can do this for me?' There was a brief silence. 'Iphinoë?'

Polyxo agreed that the princess's childhood playmate was the ideal choice. Iphinoë had almost killed her father with worry when they were young. If anything was forbidden, she would find a way to climb over a high wall, get past a locked door, range far beyond the limits of the town. She thinks she's a boy, people used to say pityingly to her mother. But her mother simply shrugged as though Iphinoë's behaviour were completely natural. The Lemnians wondered how such a child was allowed anywhere near the royal household, but she and Hypsipyle had been nursed together: they were too close to separate, no matter how badly Iphinoë behaved.

And – as it turned out – she was precisely the friend Hypsipyle now needed. They sent for Iphinoë and asked if she could carry out this task. The girl was more than willing and she knew exactly who to take with her. They would travel as soon as it was fully dark. Iphinoë would have her answers by the morning, she guaranteed it. And she would be back at the palace as quickly as she and her friends could travel.

*

None of them knew what to say. Polyxo, Hypsipyle and Iphinoë all looked at one another in silence. The old nurse opened her mouth to speak but changed her mind. Finally, the princess asked her friend to confirm that she had understood.

'He really said that they have fled our city and their wives because of how we . . . ?'

'Yes,' Iphinoë nodded. 'He said an unbearable stench emanates from each one of us and they couldn't tolerate it for a moment more.'

'How dare he?' Polyxo didn't wait for an answer. 'You both smell of nothing but perfume,' she tilted her head at the princess, 'and pine resin,' she said to Iphinoë.

'We tied him to a pine tree,' the young woman replied.

'And this happened suddenly?' Hypsipyle asked. She could imagine that plenty of Lemnians were not very fragrant in the winter months, when they were bundled up against the cold wind, and it wasted firewood to wash bodies or clothes very frequently. But they had all lived alongside one another happily until a month ago.

'Yes,' Iphinoë replied. 'He described it as being like a curse.'

'We must appeal to the gods and ask them for guidance,' said Polyxo.

'Send for the priestess of Artemis,' Hypsipyle agreed. 'And Hera. And Hestia. Send for all the priestesses.'

'I can go,' said Iphinoë.

'Save your strength,' Hypsipyle replied. 'Until the gods have spoken and we know what to do.'

The priestesses consulted their gods but their answers were frustratingly opaque. When the women discovered that there was no clear answer from any of their temples, they arrived at the palace a few at a time, and they were determined to stay until the princess had meted out punishment to their men.

Hypsipyle understood their anger, she said, as the hubbub in the main courtyard grew louder. But what could they do? They had no menfolk to avenge them, she no longer even had guards to protect her. Lemnos was fatally weakened by the loss of its men.

'Forgive me,' said a young woman standing nearby, bright eyes glittering. Her black hair fell across her brow like a bird's wing and her voice was low music. Hypsipyle wondered how any man had walked away from such a woman.

'What is your name?' she asked.

'I am Eïone,' replied the woman. 'And I don't agree that we are fatally weakened. Eunea and I,' she pointed to the woman standing beside her, 'have been coping very well without our husbands. We have managed our crops and our animals without them – just as we did when they have gone on expeditions in the past.' Women around her murmured their agreement. 'We don't want them back,' she said. 'They can stay away.'

But this was a less popular position.

'No,' cried another woman. 'They can't be trusted to stay away. What's to stop them deciding they would rather live in our houses than in their tents? They would throw us onto the streets. My husband pushed me out of our house and didn't care that I was injured. He slammed the door behind me.'

As the crowd parted, Hypsipyle could see this woman leaned on a stick. Her right foot was bandaged and her arms and face still bore the traces of bruising.

'She's right,' said another voice, and many more muttered their agreement.

'Then what do we do?' asked Eunea, raising her hands in irritation that someone had disagreed with Eïone.

Everyone looked at Hypsipyle, who glanced at her oldest friend. Iphinoë tilted her head and gave her a small smile. If her parents had seen her in that moment, they would have known something irreversible was about to occur.

'Let's seize one or two of their Thracian women,' Iphinoë said. 'They won't have any loyalty to the men who stole them away from their loved ones. They will tell us the weak points in the men's defences, if they even have any defences.' She shrugged. 'They won't be expecting an enemy attack from the land, will they? They'll have a watchman facing the sea.'

'But how will any of us get close to them?' asked Hypsipyle. 'If they can smell something on our skin that is so strong it made them leave.'

Iphinoë grinned broadly. 'We roll around on the ground,' she said. 'We'll smell like whatever animal was there last.'

'Don't kill the Thracians,' Hypsipyle said. 'Bring them here, if you can.'

*

Polyxo found a slave who spoke the dialect and she was able to interpret for them. Iphinoë had brought back two young Thracians, scarcely more than girls. They were sisters, the slave explained to Hypsipyle, but anyone would have known it by looking at them. They had the same wide-spaced eyes, the same reddish tinge to their hair. They were cautious of these Lemnian savages who had lost their men, but they were not unduly afraid. They had been seized by a pair of marauders, who had killed their father and their younger brother in the attack. Iphinoë could offer no hint as to who this man might have been: she had swiped them as they washed clothes in the river.

'Won't the men come looking for them?' Polyxo asked. Iphinoë shook her head as one of the girls replied. Her accent was thick but they understood her well enough.

'They took so many,' she said.

'Roughly how many?' asked Iphinoë. The slave translated this and the two Thracians turned to one another and tried to count, but they soon lost track and had to begin again. Iphinoë asked a simpler question. 'Are there more women, or more men?'

'Women,' came the reply. 'Two for each one.'

The Lemnians tried to count their missing menfolk. They weren't completely sure – who knew how many had died on that last raid – but they knew the men couldn't outnumber them by too many.

'This wouldn't be enough to defend our city against them,' Hypsipyle said. The others nodded.

'You'll stay here,' she said to the Thracian prisoners. 'While we decide what to do next.'

The girls looked confused. The interpreter explained and they nodded eagerly.

'Take them to the kitchens,' said Hypsipyle. 'Give them something to eat.'

The one who had spoken stared at Hypsipyle, unpicking the unfamiliar words. When she understood, she squeezed her sister's arm and the quiet one began to cry.

'One more question,' said Iphinoë, as the three young

women withdrew. They turned and the interpreter raised her eyebrows. 'Ask them what they can smell.'

A few quiet words were exchanged. 'The palace smells of flowers and food, the princess smells of perfume,' said the interpreter. 'You smell like an animal in the forest.' Iphinoë laughed.

'Living or dead?' she asked. There was a pause while the slave realized she wanted an answer and posed the question to the Thracians, whose eyes widened in alarm as they hurriedly replied.

'They didn't mean to cause offence, madam,' said the slave.

'They haven't,' said Iphinoë. 'We need to know.'

'Like a warm animal,' said the Thracian girl. 'Good, not bad.'

'Thank you,' said Iphinoë and waved them away. 'So either the men are lying,' she said, 'or the curse is limited to them.'

*

The reprisal came quickly, in the night. Two women were dragged from their homes on the outskirts of the town and decapitated. The men left their bodies in the street, and tossed their heads onto the palace steps. One of them was the mother of a small girl, to whom they entrusted a simple message: the men wanted their homes back, so the women must leave. They had until the full moon.

'Where are we supposed to go?' asked one woman as they thronged around the dais where Hypsipyle sat. Her despair was echoed by everyone around her. The women

31

could not hold out against their husbands, and they had already seen what the men were capable of doing in anger. The princess ordered her servants to bury the murdered women, and she begged the Lemnians to give her time to consider their best course of action. She withdrew and consulted Iphinoë and Polyxo once more.

'I will not see them turned out of their homes,' she said. 'What can we do?'

'Very little,' said Polyxo. 'They have strength that we don't share. They're armed and we are not.'

'That's not strictly true,' said Iphinoë.

'No,' snapped the old woman. 'This is not one of your games. You may be half Amazon, but the other Lemnian women are not. If we try to fight these men in battle, we will all be killed.'

'Don't cry,' said Hypsipyle. 'Perhaps there are other places we could settle, if we can seize a few of their boats.'

'Why would they let us take their boats?' asked the nurse. 'They will have guards along the shore to protect them. They have all the men they need.'

'Perhaps if we wait until they are back in their homes?' Hypsipyle wondered. 'Then they might leave the shore unguarded, or less well guarded, at least.'

Polyxo shook her head. 'I doubt it,' she said.

Iphinoë smiled at them both. 'I don't think you're thinking about this in the right way,' she said. 'We have strength in numbers.'

'How do you work that out?' replied the nurse. 'Every father, brother, husband and son is there. They have at least as many as we do, and they are bigger and stronger than we are. Be realistic.'

'What are you thinking, Iphinoë?' Hypsipyle knew her friend.

'We withdraw from our homes,' said Iphinoë. 'We leave and we hide in the woods at the foot of the mountains.'

'They can find us there easily!' said Polyxo.

'I know they can,' Iphinoë replied. 'But why would they? We're not trying to convince them we have disappeared into the air. We're trying to persuade them that they have won.'

'And they haven't won?' asked Hypsipyle.

'Not if the Lemnian women have the stomach to deal with them,' said Iphinoë. 'On the second or third night that they sleep in their former beds, we approach the houses in darkness. That will give us enough time to spot where their watchmen are based, but I don't suppose we'll need it.'

'Why?' asked Polyxo.

'Because they will use the lookout points we have always used,' said Hypsipyle.

'Why would they change them?' asked Iphinoë. 'They aren't afraid of us.'

'But no woman can overpower a man.' Polyxo could not conceal her frustration.

'She can if he's asleep.'

There was a pause.

'We all creep back into the houses after they fall asleep?' asked Polyxo. 'What if a man hears us coming and raises the alarm? What if the doors are locked?'

'That is the clever part,' said Iphinoë. 'We have someone to help us. And she is in every house, every bed.'

The nurse frowned. 'What can you mean?' she asked.

'The Thracian women,' said Hypsipyle, understanding at last.

'Yes,' replied her friend. 'I'll send for them?'

*

The two women Iphinoë had captured were brought into the throne room once again, along with their interpreter.

'I only have one question for you,' Hypsipyle said. In the time it had taken to fetch them, the three women had agreed that they must keep their plan secret for as long as possible. 'Do the other Thracian women feel as you do?'

There was a brief silence when the interpreter had finished speaking. The women looked at the princess, hoping they weren't mistaking her meaning. They nodded. One of them muttered a few short, guttural words, and the interpreter cleared her throat.

'Yes,' she said. 'They hate the men who used to be yours.'

*

On the night of the massacre, the moon had begun to wane and a brisk wind sent small clouds rushing across the sky. The plan had been explained first to the Lemnian women, so they had time to make their preparations. Each woman gathered the belongings she did not want to risk losing, and her sharpest knife. They all withdrew to the mountains the day before full moon. Some – those who had been least happily married – treated the whole expedition as an adventure, and they played and sang with their friends as they slept under the starlight. Others were unable to set aside their feelings for the men who had repudiated them, and found their anger unequal to their grief. Polyxo worried that they would falter on the night, and they all knew their safety depended on every woman doing her part. But Iphinoë had the solution. She found the most reluctant participants and paired each with another who lived far from her home. Those who still felt a love they could not overcome would not kill the men they loved, therefore, but another man they could more easily hate. They had debated longest what they should tell the Thracian women, and when. Should they send a secret message to them? What should it say? Did they release their captives, trusting them to participate in the scheme rather than run away? Hypsipyle believed they were trustworthy, but she didn't want to risk the whole enterprise on her belief. In the end, they took the two women aside and asked for their advice. If the Thracian women found themselves separated from one another, one or two in the home of each of the Lemnian men, would they welcome their liberators? Or would they attack? Could they be trusted not to scream and raise the alarm?

'They won't attack!' said the interpreter. 'They will help you if they know you are coming.'

'But if one of them betrays us,' said the princess. The captives shook their heads.

'They will not,' the interpreter confirmed.

Iphinoë agreed that the risk was worth taking. That night, she took the young women back to the outskirts of the city and waited for them. And her trust was well placed: the Thracians returned just as Eos spread her fingers across the morning sky. They had found two of their compatriots – one sleeping in the dust against the wall of a house because the Lemnian thug indoors had thrown her out and she had nowhere else to go, and one doing laundry in the stream before it was light because her captor didn't want his slave to be meeting or talking to her friends. But she would find a way, they assured Iphinoë, both women would find a way to spread the word in secret.

They returned to the women's camp and reported the news to the princess.

'What about the women they cannot reach? There isn't much time.'

'The Lemnian women can rely on us,' said the one who understood more of their Greek. 'If any find a woman who doesn't already know, they must only say this: Alcippe and Menippe ask for your help to kill this man. We will teach you to say it in the dialect they understand.'

'Thank you,' Hypsipyle said. 'Everything else is prepared?'

Iphinoë and Polyxo nodded. 'We are as prepared as we can be,' said the nurse. 'This time tomorrow, we'll be safely back in the palace.'

*

The princess knew that both women were choosing not to ask about her father. Hypsipyle had agreed to the plan, and Thoas was her responsibility. Death was a kindness for someone who had been stripped of everything but life. She knew this to be true, and she remembered moments of lucidity in her father's decline when he had begged for death. If she killed him tonight, she would only be giving him something he wanted. But still, she could not do it. How could she, when the old man had done nothing wrong? Even when the other men were rejecting and abusing their wives and daughters, he had not expressed revulsion at her, or any woman. His senses had dulled over the years, and he gave no indication of being able to smell or taste anything much, so perhaps the curse that afflicted the rest of the Lemnian men had passed over him.

He could not stay in the palace, that much was clear. Hypsipyle could hardly ask the women of Lemnos to do what she could not. She had been thinking about it since they first made their plan. All the details had been resolved except this one: what could she do with her father? She was still turning it round in her mind as the day shifted to night.

The wind had picked up a little and the women were making their final preparations. They chose their dingiest tunics, their darkest cloaks and their sharpest blades. They set out together, but soon broke into smaller groups as neighbours hurried towards the same parts of the town. Hypsipyle and Polyxo were making for the palace, while Iphinoë was accompanying the Thracian women to sweep the houses they thought might be unoccupied. It was the only way to be sure a man didn't escape.

*

Not every killing was silent, but most were quieter than the women expected after everything their husbands had told them about the noise of war. But it wasn't a battle, it was a night raid, and they attacked with the passion of those who had nowhere else to go. The men had driven them out of the only homes they had, so they must be removed. The Thracian women had prepared things well: the Lemnians found their doors unlocked and weapons hidden out of the reach of men.

The blood, though, flowed in rivers.

*

Hypsipyle and Polyxo were accompanied by several other women, in case the palace guards had returned to their posts. But as they approached the royal house, it was clear that no one was guarding the gates. The doors to the palace stood open and the women began to search the outer chambers. Hypsipyle ran towards her father's room, praying she would find him still tended by the slave-woman who had stayed behind. She was not Lemnian, but had been won by her father in a long-forgotten war. They had hoped she would not offend the men who came back to the palace, but as Hypsipyle followed a twisting corridor, she was almost tripped up by the woman's body. What was wrong with the Lemnian men? A living woman offended their sense of smell but the corpse of a dead one did not.

She picked her way past the woman, and moved more slowly now. Men had been here, they might still be here. Surely they would not have left their king alone with no one to help him. But when she approached his door, she could hear only her father, who was singing softly to himself.

'Papa,' she said, as she ran and embraced him. Panic flickered across his face, but he opened his arms just the same. She held his fragile bones and knew she would not let anyone hurt him, no matter what they had agreed.

'Everyone's gone,' he told her. 'I don't know where they're hiding.'

'I do, Papa. Come with me.'

He took her hand. 'Have you seen my daughter?' he asked.

'She's this way,' Hypsipyle replied. 'Come on, we'll find her.'

The old man could move surprisingly fast for one so frail. His muscles had wasted, but he weighed so little that she could put his arm around her waist and help take his weight.

'This way, Papa,' she repeated.

*

Polyxo left the palace as soon as they had confirmed there were no other men inside. She sent the women who'd accompanied her to find Iphinoë and help with the house-to-house search. And she went the other way, towards the shore.

*

Iphinoë had killed three men so far. She had slit the throats of the first two, but the third one woke just as she raised her knife, so she stabbed him quickly in the neck. The Thracian women shook their heads at her and Iphinoë asked what was wrong.

'Nothing,' said the one who had learned enough Lemnian Greek. 'But stab them in the chest and there's less blood to clean up.' Iphinoë nodded.

'I'll try,' she said.

*

39

The Thracian woman who had slept in the street was named Melite. By the time the Lemnian women arrived in the town, she had already drugged the man's cup and clubbed him with a bronze jug until his face was obliterated. His wife crept in through the open door, and saw the carnage on her bed and the young woman – scarcely as old as her own daughter – holding the jug in her hand, crouching next to the wall. She knelt beside her and prised the jug free. She took the girl's hands in hers, and held them tightly until the girl stopped shaking.

*

Hypsipyle met Polyxo by the shore. The nurse was standing by a small boat, scarcely more than a raft. Hypsipyle looked at it with doubt.

'Is it seaworthy?' she asked.

Polyxo did not reply. She reached out a hand to Thoas, and said, 'Here, my king. This is your boat. Do you remember?'

Confusion glazed his eyes, but then cleared, like the rushing clouds above. He nodded happily.

'Oenoë sent for me,' he said.

'Yes,' said Polyxo.

Hypsipyle felt his weight shift as he pulled free of her with a startling strength and clambered onto the boat.

'Who is Oenoë?' she asked. 'How did he . . . ?'

'Hush,' said Thoas. 'When you see my daughter, tell her to take care.'

She pushed loose hair from her face as he picked up the stubby oars. But he had not even touched the surface of the water with them, before the little boat had floated free.

Oenoë – a water nymph who had known him in his younger days – did not neglect a former lover.

'Don't forget,' said Thoas, as the boat bobbed out into the waves. 'She worries.'

'I won't forget,' said his daughter, and she wept as she watched her father slip away from her for the last time.

Argo

the men sent by Pelias

The Argonauts – as they were already called – were approaching Lemnos with little idea of what they would find there. The island was sacred to Hephaestus, they knew, so they anticipated a place filled with craftsmen who might furnish them with new weapons. Those who worshipped Hephaestus would be those who wanted to emulate him. They anchored the Argo and sent Aithalides, their herald, ahead in a small boat. Aithalides was a persuasive man and the son of Hermes, the messenger god himself. So the Lemnian women were never going to refuse him.

Hypsipyle

for the golden sheepskin.

The first time she saw him, she was armoured and ready to fight. It didn't help, of course. Later – when people wanted to justify what happened to her – they said she had been so desperate for the company of a man that she threw herself at him the moment he arrived. But it wasn't true. She had been wary of him and his men from the moment they first saw the ship.

The women of Lemnos had lived for a year without men, and they only occasionally missed them. They had always worked on the land, so grazing the cattle and ploughing the fields was no more arduous than their previous duties. Less so, for the ones who had always found weaving to be a terrible chore. They preferred to be outdoors instead of bent over a loom or a spinning wheel, snagging their fingers on the burrs which needed to be picked out of the fleece one by one. The goddess Athene might have the patience for such fine work, but many mortal women did not. Besides, as they said to one another, if weaving was so enjoyable, men would do it.

And Hypsipyle agreed with her women: she missed her

father, but she knew he was incapable of missing her, so the grief was unmixed with guilt. The only thing that worried her was the attack that must be coming from the men of Thrace. Lemnos had attacked them and stolen their women, they would want revenge. And if they knew by now that the Lemnian women had already had their night of retribution, then that would only increase the likelihood of an attack. Who would miss the opportunity to loot an island with no men to defend it?

Hypsipyle knew the day would come when a warship rounded the headland and made for her town of Myrine. And when that day arrived, when her guardswomen reported a fine-nosed ship being rowed towards their shore, she did not hesitate. She took up her father's abandoned shield and spears, and hurried down to the water's edge.

When one man – a herald, holding his ceremonial sceptre – disembarked from the ship and rowed himself to shore, Hypsipyle felt her fear and anger subside. An invading force did not send a herald ahead to negotiate, surely? If he was surprised to be speaking with a woman, he concealed it well. The queen heard his speech and then told him she would consult the Lemnians and send a messenger to let him know what they decided.

She summoned a meeting with every Lemnian woman who could attend. Word of the ship's arrival had already spread across the city so they came quickly.

'Women,' said Hypsipyle, 'I have news about the ship, and it may not be as bad as we feared.'

There was a general murmuring of scepticism and hope.

'The visitors do not know of our position,' said

Hypsipyle. 'The herald only knows the island is ruled by a woman.'

'So, they're not coming to dig up our worthless husbands?' asked one woman in the crowd.

'They are not,' the queen replied. 'They are a band of adventurers looking for a sacred object, a golden sheepskin. They know it is not on Lemnos. They are coming here hoping for hospitality, which we can easily provide.'

The women nodded. They had plenty of food to share.

'I want to send food and wine to the ship,' said Hypsipyle. 'If they are well supplied, they will have no reason to come ashore, no need to start asking questions about the men. I do not want them to find out about what we did. They will be stopping in at plenty of islands if this voyage is as long as their herald expects. The last thing I want is for our reputation to spread across the sea.'

'I'd welcome it,' cried the woman who had spoken before. 'Perhaps they'd treat their own wives better if they knew the risks of doing otherwise.' She laughed, but the mood around her was sombre. Most of the Lemnian women knew how dangerous it would be for their reputation to reach any shore beyond their own.

'Does anyone have any other suggestions about what we should do?' Hypsipyle asked. She sat on her father's throne, looking out across the sea of faces. But the answering voice was beside her.

'I agree, dear queen, that we must be generous to our visitors. We should send gifts and supplies of food and wine, just as you say.'

Hypsipyle had known her old nurse for too long to believe that Polyxo agreed with her, and waited for her to continue.

'But I do wonder,' said the older woman, 'about the future. We have several problems to overcome. The first is that the men of Thrace set sail to invade our land. Yes, they might be delayed by their ignorance of what has happened on Lemnos, but they – or another army – will come one day. What kind of lives will we have, waiting for our enslavement?' The crowd muttered their agreement, but the nurse had not finished. 'And what of the more distant future?' she asked. 'It is not for myself that I ask this – I don't have many years left to live. But you young women must think about your lives. Do you not want to have children who will take care of you when you become old, if the gods allow it? Because an island of women can plough fields and harvest crops, but an island of old women cannot. But now, perhaps, you do not need to. Because here is a ship filled with men who wish us no harm. Not all of them will want to stay if they're determined to find their golden fleece. But some will stay, if we ask.'

Hypsipyle smiled as she looked down at Polyxo and the expressions of her women, no less determined than they always were, but there was something else in their eyes now.

'You make a strong case,' she said to the nurse. 'Iphinoë, will you go to the herald and invite their captain to come ashore as our friend? Tell him our people have come to a decision which his comrades will surely appreciate. We shall judge his response to our invitation and then we will know whether it is wise to ask him and his men to stay.'

*

When the captain arrived in Myrine, he was dressed in the greatest finery Lemnos had ever seen. If the goddess Athene herself had woven his glorious purple cloak, no one would have been surprised. The whisper went ahead of him into the city: he was showing appropriate respect to their queen. Perhaps the men would stay. He strode along beside his herald, they noted. He was strong, and eager to meet the queen.

Iphinoë escorted the two men to the palace; she and Aithalides stood back when they entered the throne room. Hypsipyle beckoned the captain to step up to her dais.

'Welcome, sir,' she said. 'I am Hypsipyle, daughter of Thoas, queen of Lemnos.'

'I am Jason,' he replied. 'Son of Aeson, captain of the Argo. Thank you for inviting me into your home.'

'Please,' she replied, gesturing at a brightly woven couch. Jason undid the brooch pinning his cloak and released it before sitting down. 'That is a beautiful cloak,' Hypsipyle said.

'And so warm,' he agreed. His tunic was plain and Hypsipyle was glad to see that he looked far more comfortable without the ornate cloak. This man was not too grand for Lemnos, she decided. A Thracian woman appeared at his arm with a cup of wine and water.

'You are probably wondering where the menfolk of Lemnos are,' said the queen.

'I have seen nothing but men for many days,' he smiled. 'It is a great pleasure to see you instead.'

'They are across the strait,' she continued. 'In Thrace. We have long lived separate lives: when my father was king, the men used to work on the fields and go on raiding

47

missions to the mainland. Over time, they developed a greater interest in their Thracian slave-women than in their Lemnian wives. They ignored their children and they ignored us.'

Jason shook his head slowly. 'Some men make strange choices,' he said.

'They took our sons when they left. So for a year now, Lemnos has been an island of women.'

'You've looked after yourselves all that time?' he asked.

'When men abandon their wives, women are left with little choice.'

'I don't wish to speak ill of your brothers and fathers,' he said. 'But that is not the behaviour of anyone I would call a man.'

'That makes my next question an easier one to ask,' she said. 'The women of Lemnos would like to invite you and your men to join us. Leave your ship for a while, come to our city and let us show you our finest hospitality. Perhaps you will like it so much you will want to stay. We would happily give you an equal share in our homeland.' Hypsipyle could not read the thoughts that were playing across her guest's face as he replied.

'We have a quest we are honour-bound to complete, my lady,' he said. Later she would discover that he always became more courteous in the moments when he knew he was disappointing her. Given his capacity for deceit, it was often the first sign something was wrong. 'But we could not possibly refuse such a gracious offer. I will return to the Argo and tell my men we are invited ashore.'

'Good,' she said. 'We will feast tonight in your honour.'

'Your father Thoas ruled here before you?' he asked.

'Yes,' she said.

'But now you are queen of Lemnos? There is no absent king, ploughing his fields in Thrace?'

'There is not,' she replied. And this time they both smiled.

*

Myrine had never known such happiness, Hypsipyle thought. People were dancing in the streets by torchlight, the women becoming freer and somehow younger as they shared their sweet wine with these travellers. She heard music and laughter, and she prayed to Hephaestus and Aphrodite, the skilful god of their clever island and his radiant goddess. She did not know if the prayers made the difference or if it was simply human for women to want men after so long a hiatus and for these men to feel the same way. But when she turned to look at the bright dark eyes of their captain, she wondered if he could really be a mortal man, or if the goddess had breathed beauty into him. She wanted to feel the warmth of his skin on her own, to watch the light play across his face. She could drink him like the wine he was sipping from her finest cup, and now she also noticed his strong, slender fingers holding the stem, like those of a musician. Over the next few days, she made offerings to every god and goddess, praying that the men would stay, and that they would make her women happy, and that they would not stumble across the grave of any former husband.

And her prayers were answered, at least at first. Aphrodite – though Hypsipyle did not know it – had resolved the quarrel she'd had with her husband when all the men of his sacred island were slaughtered in a single night. She had even agreed to help the island prosper once again. This was only possible if men returned to Lemnos, so Aphrodite filled the Argonauts with longing for the women they feasted alongside. The revels began in daylight and continued long after darkness fell, first in the streets then in the houses. It felt like a festival, Hypsipyle thought, a time sacred to the goddess. Perhaps she would decree that this must be celebrated on these days every year.

The light in her palace was golden – the bright rays of the sun softened by thin curtains and low windows. As she and Jason lay in her bed, he told her of the harshness of their voyage even in good weather, when the inescapable heat and the pitiless glare made him wish for rain. But even as he said the words, he made a sign to ward off the evil eye: no sailor could ever wish for a storm. And here he was on dry land again, neither exhausted nor parched. He wished he could stay with her for ever, and she sighed with happiness, not hearing the words he left unsaid. No man who kissed a woman with so much love and longing could ever leave her, unless all the poets were liars.

Hypsipyle did not know – because Jason didn't tell her, if he had even noticed – that not every Argonaut had come ashore. A small band of his men had remained on their ship, keeping company with an influential Greek who claimed direct descendancy from the king of the gods. Whether that was true or not, he had made a name for himself through exploits of varying plausibility. Some of the Argonauts – so Jason told her, in the end – had wanted this Greek to lead them on their quest. He had generously refused to take command, leaving Jason fully aware that he was the second choice. And this man – Heracles – was growing tired of waiting for the voyage to continue.

When he began to complain, the men on shore sent back a message telling him they must complete the festivities sacred to Hephaestus and Aphrodite if their voyage was to have any hope of success. Who could say he wouldn't need the skill and the influence of these two mighty deities? It was not advisable to snub any god, but the Argonauts would certainly not wish to injure the feelings of the Lemnian god or his wife. Heracles accepted the reason but considered it an excuse. A man who has Zeus for a father can offend other gods and survive, said his friends. But our comrades are less fortunate than you, they must appease every immortal. So they bought more time, until it became clear that no festival lasted for so many days. The men were just enjoying their time on the island too much to leave.

Heracles was not used to being ignored. He sent a messenger to the shore, summoning as many of his comrades as would come. The man went from house to house, but did not gain entry to the palace because (he was told) the queen was entertaining her guest in private. So she had no warning of the mutinous discussions that were taking place on her lover's ship, where Heracles was bullying and cajoling the other Argonauts. Didn't they want to win glory? Were they happy to call the first island they reached a new home? Is this why they had all left their old homes? Did they want people to say they must have been on the run from some unforgivable crime? Why else would men slink away from home, if they had no quest to fulfil? If Jason could not wrench himself away from the pretty queen, so be it. Perhaps he was fated to be nothing more than the king of an island without men.

When Heracles had finished, the men rowed back to shore to spend one last day – and night – collecting their belongings and taking leave of their women. The Argo would sail in the morning. Only now did Jason discover what had been suggested. Hypsipyle watched his face as he heard the news and her hopes splintered into tiny shards. She had thought love was the strongest part of him, but now she saw pride trample it down. She wept as he put on his tunic and gathered his cloak in his arms.

'I pray that the gods keep you safe on your quest,' she said. 'You and your men.' Not all your men, she thought. 'Find your sacred fleece, and take it to your king. I can see it is your dearest wish, and surely the gods will protect you. But when you have returned to Iolcus, don't end your journey there. Come back, my love. Come back to me. I will do whatever you wish in the meantime.'

'My queen,' Jason replied, 'thank you for these words. I too hope the gods will favour my journey, and I will come back, if I can. If I cannot, you at least know that my heart wanted to, and I hope that is a comfort to you.'

'What if the gods decide to give us a child?' Hypsipyle asked. She knew it was possible, more than possible.

Jason took her hands in his. 'What a beautiful thought,' he said. 'I will think of it, hope for it, every day. If it is true, if we are blessed in such a way –' He raised her hands to her face and gently uncurled her fingers, so she could wipe away her tears. 'If we are blessed in this way, and we have a son, will you send him to Iolcus? Send him to my parents, to console them for the loss of their son. Keep him until he has grown old enough to take care of them.'

Hypsipyle looked at Jason and he smiled back with such devotion in his eyes that she wondered if he hadn't noticed that in one breath he was wishing her a life raising a child alone, then asking her to deprive herself of this child, and to deprive her island of a king. And that he did this even as he robbed her of the man she loved.

Aphrodite

For then my mistress Medea

The goddess of love bestowed her favours capriciously, and that was exactly as it should be. The Lemnian women had been punished, the Lemnian women had been rewarded. Would they learn to honour her more enthusiastically without such reminders? She neither knew nor cared. She could destroy and replace them whenever she chose. But something had irritated her, and she complained to her husband since it was his sacred island.

'I wanted a festival,' she said. 'They were supposed to give me a festival where my statues are paraded through the streets.'

'You have festivals on so many islands, my love,' replied Hephaestus, and she responded with a venomous hiss. 'Which I see now is not relevant,' he said. 'Because you want one here.'

'They carry your statues through the streets of Lemnos,' she said. 'How dare they not take mine alongside them?'

He looked surprised. 'Would you really like them carried alongside mine?' he asked.

'No,' she said. 'I'd like a festival in my honour, and your statues could be brought out for one day, as my consort.'

'I see,' he said. 'Perhaps I could make a model of the festal processions and have one of my priests see it in a dream.'

'How would that help?' she asked.

'It might inspire him to dedicate a temple to you,' Hephaestus replied.

It was inevitably the wrong answer. 'I don't want a festival because you told them I want one,' she snarled. 'I want one because they love and venerate me and want to show me.'

'Dearest, I think they do,' he said. 'I think the queen of Lemnos is preoccupied with her sorrow.'

'Oh, of course she is. It's always something. Why should she feel grief? Grief because she's pregnant, grief when she finds out it's twins? She has been blessed by the gods, she should feel – what's the word?'

'Gratitude,' he said. 'But I think she is grateful to you. I think her grief is a manifestation of her great reverence for you.'

'Why do you think that? A festival is a good manifestation of reverence, crying is not.'

'But she has lost the man she loved, the man you brought her. Of course she is filled with sorrow.'

'She's lost Jason?'

'Yes, my dear. The Argo has set sail.'

'But I filled the men with desire!' This had never failed to work. Aphrodite could not even begin to imagine what kind of punishment would be great enough for men who ignored her summons in this way. Should she make them desire pigs? Or cows? How could she humiliate them enough to avenge this insult?

'And they felt it,' her husband replied. 'For many, many days. But they had to leave on their quest.'

'They should have forgotten all about their quest.' Her rage was building to its climax and Hephaestus knew his only possible tactic was to deflect it onto someone who deserved it more than him. 'How could they remember their quest when they were with the women they most wanted? How?'

'They were threatened with ignominy,' he said gravely.

There was an almost imperceptible pause before she decided it didn't matter what it meant.

'Whose threat was mightier than mine?' she snapped.

'It was Heracles, I believe.' This was the ideal response, Hephaestus knew. Partly because it was true, which made things less complicated, and partly because even his wife would think twice before annihilating the son of Zeus.

'How dare he?'

'You know what he's like,' Hephaestus said, wondering if he should try reaching out to comfort his wife or if that would only incur further rage. 'He has always been so desperate for fame, for stories to be sung of his mighty deeds.'

'I will make him regret setting himself against me.'

'Zeus loves him,' said her husband. 'It would be dangerous to injure him.'

She smiled. 'I don't have to injure him,' she replied. 'I'll just take the thing he loves.'

Kleite

would not have sailed

Did you just try to miss me out?

Don't lie, it's tiresome. I said, did you just try to miss out my part of the story? Why? No, don't tell me, I already know the answer. It's because no one remembers my name. That's right, I'm just glossed over every time – Kleite with the beautiful hair – as if that tells you who I am or why I did what I did. So if you didn't know me until I got your attention just now, well, isn't that more reason to include me, not less? What's the point in telling the old stories all over again in the same way?

Oh, now you're sorry. Of course you are. No, I'm sure it wasn't intentional. A harmless mistake, was it? I think it's probably up to me to decide how much harm you've caused. But you'll tell my story now, will you? Thank you. I agree, it is the least you can do.

So why the delay? Are you waiting for a propitious omen? It's a bit late for that, for me, isn't it? You aren't sure. Oh, I see. I know what the problem is. You can't quite recall my part in the voyage of the Argo. Is that it? No, I'm not offended. Well, I am offended but I was offended before you said that, so it doesn't really change anything. I already had you down as the sort of person who skips over the difficult bits.

I am Kleite, and I am – or rather, I was, until the Argonauts came along – the queen of the Doliones.

Don't take what the wrong way? Of course. Of course you don't know who they are. The Doliones live beside the Mountain of the Bears, I assume you know where – Phrygia. It's just off the coast of Phrygia. It's inhabited by monsters, so perhaps worth knowing that, if you're ever in that part of the world. No, you're welcome.

The Argo landed on Dolion shores and—

What? Well, why does anyone live next door to monsters? These things happen: you don't choose your neighbours. They left us alone anyway, because we had the protection of Poseidon to keep us safe. Oh, you know who he is, do you? Yes, of course you do. Never any shortage of people talking about him. Well, he loved the Doliones, so perhaps – since you're so keen on him – you might pay a bit more attention to me. My husband Kyzikos – what? Kai-zee-kos, obviously – welcomed them to our land with meat and wine, even though we were only just married.

Yes, that's right. A month or so. And yes, he left me alone for an evening so he could hear all about their quest and their route and all the details. They wanted advice on which way to sail next, so Kyzikos told them of a high point they could climb to the next day, so they could see the shape of the coast and the routes ahead in every direction.

And the following morning a few of them did make the climb, and they had long conversations about landmarks and the direction of the winds, which I have no doubt were fascinating. Then they set sail, and travelled – we assume – the route they intended to take. But somehow – and do tell me if this becomes too confusing for you – they forgot about the wind and they forgot that their precious landmarks were only visible during daylight. So when the light ebbed and the darkness came, they didn't notice the wind had changed direction.

No, I agree, it does sound unlikely. A whole ship full of men, none of whom realized that they were literally being blown back the way they had come. But they couldn't see very much and they must have grown confused. Because somehow – somehow – they sailed all the way back to Dolion. And here's the really impressive bit: they had no idea where they were.

No. None.

It was, as I say, a dark night. Poetic, I suppose. Winds howling, clouds covering a quavering moon. And what followed was very poetic, if you like your poetry to be filled with tragic irony.

Oh, you do? That is good news, I would hate for you to be bored. So the Argonauts moored at a place which we call the Sacred Rock, and under the dark skies – and with the beak of the ship obscured by the shape of the rock – the Doliones didn't realize these were their friends from just a day before. Why? Because we were preparing for an attack from the Makrians and–

What? It doesn't matter who the Makrians are, does it? Because these weren't the Makrians in a warship, they were just your precious Argonauts who didn't know left from right.

And the moment we realized a ship had landed – under

cover of darkness, which is intrinsically untrustworthy, I'm sure you agree – the Doliones rushed to the Sacred Rock to find out if our enemies had arrived on our shores. Kyzikos was at the very front. Always so brave, they told me afterwards. I didn't really have time to get to know that for myself, of course. Because Jason – that cursed fool – hurled his spear straight at the chest of this apparent stranger. Straight into the splintering breastbone of the man he had called a friend.

Kyzikos was not alone in death, which was no consolation at all. The Argonauts – heavily armed and already used to killing – took the lives of many men, and they would surely have wiped out all the Doliones had some not run from the scene of battle. The next morning, they saw the face of the first man they had killed. Kyzikos looked the same in death as in life, because his face was untouched by the spear. He was paler, of course, because so much of his blood was pooled beneath him in the sand. And then – then – they began to weep and groan at their terrible, lethal error.

It didn't stop them trying to blame him for his own death. How could they have known, if only the Doliones had sent a messenger instead of an armed battalion, and so on, and so on. As if they would have done any less to protect their own lands if they had believed them to be in danger. And as if it made any difference to Kyzikos, killed by men he had thought were long gone.

They mourned for days, I am told. Set up a grand tomb, held funeral games to commemorate the loss of a mighty king, all the things you would do, I suppose, to assuage your guilt. I wouldn't know, of course, because I was already dead by then.

Oh, I'm sorry, did you not know? Of course you didn't, you didn't even know who I was a minute ago. I was just a name you skimmed over – Kleite with the exquisite hair – so you wouldn't know that I loved my husband. My brave, beautiful, luckless husband, who made friends in a heartbeat and lost his lifeblood to them a day later. You wouldn't know that I couldn't bear to live without him, that my heart was shattered just like his. You wouldn't know that although we had hoped, I was not yet bearing his child and now I never could. You wouldn't know that it was the one thing I longed for: I didn't wish for beauty, or to be a queen. I wished to be a mother.

No. No, I could not marry again. Well, it is rather a crass question, yes. But since you have asked it, the answer is no. Because no other man would have me once Kyzikos had died in such an appalling way. So what would my life be? I would be called cursed, the cursed bride of a dead man.

I died by suicide, hanging by the neck, my lovely hair flowing down my back in death just as it did in life. I hear they pour libations to us both every year on the day of our deaths. So some people remember me, perhaps.

But the songs? Those are sung about the Argo and her crew, never about the king – and queen – they killed by mistake.

Argo

to the towers of Iolcus,

The Argonauts used their own strength to get away from the land that people had begun to call Kyzikos, after its fallen king. They were so keen to leave that they did not wait for a fair wind to help them. They travelled along the Phrygian coast of the Propontis, the smallest sea, and they rowed with all their might. As the water grew less calm, they began to fatigue until only Heracles was left fighting the force of the waves. A lesser man – or one who had spent more time at sea – would have raised the oar to protect it. But Heracles ploughed on, relentless, until the mighty oar snapped in two, leaving him with nothing but a useless staff in his hands. You could blame that on the ship as well, if you chose.

The Naiads

stricken with love

The Naiads who lived in Kios – the name of their land and their river – were largely untroubled by men. Unless sailors wished to voyage all the way to the distant lands of Tauris or Colchis, they had no reason to come to Kios. And so the Naiads grew accustomed to their own company beside their beautiful lapis sea and their sparkling streams. When a fine-beaked ship came to land, they were mildly curious but no more.

The men disembarked and began to make offerings to the gods, and to prepare a feast. Heracles left his companions and went into the woods on the lower slopes of the mountains that line the coast. He was searching for a tree from which he could make himself an oar and soon he found exactly what he needed: a pine tree with a slender trunk, and not too many branches. He bent his knees and wrapped his huge arms around it, bellowing from the exertion – and with satisfaction at his own strength – as he uprooted it.

The sound echoed across the forest and up into the mountains. The nymphs who lived in almost every part of the land heard the shout and they wept in anger and sorrow

63

at the brutality of it. How dare this stranger – this man – come to their land and take one of their trees? And how dare he part this one luckless tree from her sisters?

One nymph did not weep, because she was preoccupied with the astonishingly beautiful boy who had brought a large bronze jug to her stream to fill. She did not know his name, or that Heracles had killed his father and seized him, calling him a companion when a more honest man would have admitted he was enslaved. But if the boy – whose name was Hylas – had been enslaved by Heracles, the nymph was close to being enslaved by him. She had never seen such large brown eyes, such curling black hair, such golden skin. And if he thirsted for the waters of Pegai – her stream – she thirsted for him with an equal intensity. And she would surely have done so even if Aphrodite had not made her helpless with desire.

Because the goddess never forgot a slight. And she was still filled with rage that Heracles had persuaded the Argonauts to leave Lemnos before she had decided they could go. And if she couldn't injure the son of Zeus himself – and Hephaestus was right about that – she could make him endure something far more agonizing.

As Hylas leaned towards the water to fill his jug, he caught sight of his reflection and something else. He blinked and looked again because for a moment he thought he had seen another face within his own, a matching pair of eyes looking up at him. But how could that be? He was still puzzling over this trick of the light when she reached up and put her left arm round his neck and her right hand on his arm, pulling him down to kiss her. He cried out once before slipping soundlessly into her stream.

Aphrodite

for Jason;

The goddess had disguised herself as a nymph and positioned herself in the woods of Kios so she could see the results of her plan. She smiled as the boy slid under the water without so much as a splash. There was nothing for him to fear: he would not drown now he had been kissed by a water nymph. He would change, but he would not die.

So not even Zeus would be able to complain that Aphrodite had done anything wrong, even as his idiot son pounded up and down the mountainside, screaming the boy's name over and over. As if he would ever find a mortal man that the nymphs had chosen to take. She laughed as darkness fell and Heracles grew hoarse.

She was not a goddess who concerned herself with shifting winds or changeable seas, so when the Argonauts decided they must set sail immediately the next morning, it came as a happy surprise. She perhaps did add a little jolt of longing to each of the sailors so they wanted to be back at sea immediately. That might have contributed to the moment they set sail without anyone noticing Heracles was still missing. But it was surely because of his own arrogance

65

the day before, Aphrodite would protest if she were ever asked. He had broken his oar, so no one noticed a missing rower.

By the time the Argonauts realized they had left him behind, it was too late.

Harpies

nor would the daughters

Whenever a man went travelling, his loved ones faced an agonizing wait. Sometimes a ship sank without survivors, without witnesses. Sometimes a voyage could be retraced to a certain point but then an entire crew seemingly vanished from a small island. Sometimes a ship would return with all its men, except one. And then people might choose to blame the Harpies, the snatchers who flew out of a clear sky, as fast as storm winds, faster than birds. These daughters of the daughter of Oceanus were too quick for men to see, so no one knew what happened to those they seized. And no one could say for sure who they answered to, so no one knew where to direct their prayers. The Harpies never returned anyone they had taken, but they were not lawless creatures. When one of the gods – Zeus, perhaps – gave them orders, they carried them out. It did not matter to them whether it was a single abduction or a daily torture.

And in the case of Phineus, it was a carefully calibrated torment. Once, Phineus had possessed both keen eyesight and unerring foresight, a gift from Apollo. Men sought his wisdom and his prophecies and he did not hesitate to tell them everything he knew about the future. But the gods do not permit any man to share the fullest details of their plans, and Phineus knew that because Apollo doesn't give any gift without conditions. So Zeus punished him, first with blindness and the frailty of age. To this, he added a further misery. Phineus was popular with his neighbours: what man wouldn't be, when he could tell them every aspect of Zeus' mind? They took pity on the old man and every day they brought him their finest food so he would never go hungry.

But whenever Phineus reached out his hand to pick up even the smallest morsel, the Harpies would appear from nowhere and grab it. His body wasted from hunger, but they did not stop. When he was on the verge of death, Zeus amended his instructions. Now the Harpies could leave him just enough food to keep him alive, so he did not curtail his punishment by dying. The Harpies would take even these little scraps of food and drop them onto the ground so Phineus was forced to scratch around in the dirt for any nourishment at all. He could no longer live, he could only survive.

The old man retained his second sight even when he lost the first. He sustained himself from the relentless attacks of the Harpies with his knowledge that one day a ship would bring mighty heroes and the sons of gods to his home. And on that day, Zeus would finally allow him to eat once again. When the Argo dropped her anchor on the coast and Jason and his men disembarked, Phineus heard their voices as they began to come inland. And he knew that these were the heroes whose arrival he had anticipated.

His treatment at the hands of the Harpies had left him emaciated and filthy and he staggered to his feet, supporting himself on a splintering staff. He turned towards the sun, letting its heat warm his ancient bones. When the Argonauts came over the brow of the hill he remembered, he heard their shock that such a pitiable figure could even stand.

'Argonauts,' he cried. 'You are the Argonauts, I think. You have come from across the whole of Greece in search of a fabled sheepskin. And now you are astonished that your fame has travelled ahead of you, but I know how widely your names will be known and sung. I have the gift of prophecy, and I will share what it is permitted for me to reveal. But first, I beg you, by Zeus, who protects suppliants, by Apollo, who gave me my gift, and by Hera, who loves and protects you all, please help me.'

The men crowded around him, amazed that this man – who scarcely seemed alive or even human – knew of their quest.

'As you see,' Phineus continued, 'I live in torment. I am old, and yet I cannot die. I have lost my sight, although my mind's eye is more acute than it has ever been. But other men grow old, and other men become blind. My curse is neither of these, it is the wretched cruelty of the Harpies.'

It was Jason who spoke. 'Harpies? Tell us who or what these are, and if we can help you, we shall.'

Phineus felt an unfamiliar pain in his throat, and knew his voice was straining. He had spent so much time alone and silent, he had almost lost the power of speech.

'The Harpies are terrifying monsters,' he said. 'Terrifying to an old man like me, at least. To heroes like you, they will not be frightening. But you will be revolted by them. They are bird-women, who fly down from the sky and steal any food I might try to eat in their vicious claws. If they leave me scraps, they leave them covered with filth on the ground. No one could eat what they leave behind, it reeks of death and misery, just from their touch. But I have no choice but to try and consume something: they leave me too close to starvation for anything else.'

'You were given the gift of prophecy by the gods, but now you are tormented by these creatures?' asked Jason. 'Who are you?'

'I am Phineus, son of Agenor,' he replied. 'And I still have the gift of prophecy. I know it is the sons of Boreas – two winged heroes of your voyage – who will chase away these foul monsters. They are among your crew, are they not?'

There was a ripple of admiration among the Argonauts that this fragile relic of a man could know something he could not see. The Boreads – Zetes and Kalaïs – stepped forward.

'Phineus, we will ensure these monsters never bother you again,' said Zetes. 'But we must know if that is what the gods themselves desire. If they are punishing you with these attacks, they may not permit anyone to intervene. Can you swear to us that we are not offending Zeus – or any god – if we offer our assistance?'

'I swear it,' replied Phineus.

'Then you will have the help of our crew,' Jason said.

Phineus wanted to smile, but could feel his lips cracking in the sunlight, and he felt two muscled arms catch his wasted body as exhaustion took its toll.

'Prepare food,' he gasped, as two of the Argonauts carried him to the smooth stone that he used as a seat. 'And they will appear.'

*

The younger Argonauts began to prepare a meal immediately. At the beginning of the voyage, they had believed all would take turns to cook. But soon the older men like Heracles were refusing their turn, telling Jason that the captain and his most renowned comrades should not need to do anything that slaves would do on land. Heracles was using Hylas to do his share of the menial work, so it became difficult to maintain that these tasks were being undertaken equally. The younger men resented this, but there weren't enough of them to affect the decision. And by the time the Argo lost Heracles and Hylas, it had become the custom of the ship.

As they built fires to heat water and prepare meat, they found themselves oddly nervous. Would these monsters truly appear with no warning and snatch the food from their mouths? The old man was so frail and peculiar, they didn't really believe him. And yet, he knew the name of their ship, the name of the captain. He even knew the sons of the stiff North Wind, Boreas, were sailing with them. And who but a seer would believe that winged men could choose to travel by boat?

When the meat was cooked, the men took their share, all except Zetes and Kalaïs. They were poised on either side of Phineus, the feathers on the edges of their wings fluttering in the warm breeze. They each held a sword, glinting in the late sun. Then one of the cooks picked up a plate of meat and bread and walked slowly towards the three of them. He held the plate out to Phineus and told the old man to reach forward and he would have food in his hands.

Even the most boisterous of the men had fallen silent.

Everyone was scanning the air above them. Phineus leaned towards the plate and took a hunk of bread, and still nothing happened. He gestured for the young man to step back before he lifted the bread to his mouth.

Only when his lips were almost touching the bread did the sky suddenly darken. There was the whistling of a high wind, and a frantic thrumming of beating wings. The Argonauts held tight to their food and their wine cups, because they were scarcely strong enough to keep these things in their grasp in what felt like a sudden storm. The shapes that rushed past them were so fast only the sharpest-eyed men could make anything out: feathers, outstretched hands, hatred contorting inhuman faces. In the time it took to blink, the Harpies had ripped the food from Phineus' hand and he lay on the ground, bleeding from the nose, dust rising around him. The young man holding the platter had also been knocked to the ground, the plate upturned beside him. The meat had all gone and so had most of the bread. One crust lay crushed in the dirt by his feet. Other men had been sent sprawling to the ground, cups and plates smashed all around them.

The sons of Boreas had the sharpest eyes of anyone, and by the time the Argonauts had recovered from this attack, they had already flown off in pursuit. They prayed to their father and to Zeus to grant them the speed and endurance they needed to follow these creatures as far and as fast as they could go. And these gods heard their prayers, so they raced through the skies as fast as the North Wind himself.

Iris

of Pelias –

Iris loved her sisters, and she did not care at all if men had a low opinion of them. What did they matter, when they had never even seen her sisters? They simply feared them, all except one poet who said they had beautiful hair. He hadn't seen Aello, Podarce and Nicothoë either, but at least he wasn't rude about them. Men were very quick to fear what they didn't control. They didn't control Iris either, but they weren't threatened by her because they could see her radiance and they believed it was for their benefit. When Iris brought a message from the heights of Olympus down to mortal men, she brought a rainbow with her: it marked her route to them, like a path left in water in the wake of a tall ship.

Iris knew that if men could see her sisters, they would compose songs in their honour. They would admire Aello's lovely hair, tied back in careful knots because she didn't like the feel of it in her face as she rushed through the aether. They would sing of the soft, dainty feet of Podarce – which had never touched the ground – believing her to be the fastest of the three. Or would they realise Nicothoë could never be beaten in a race? Iris knew every feather on their beautiful black and white wings and she loved the way they unfurled them so the topmost feathers rose high above their delicate features. Iris had wings too, of course, which men doubtless preferred: a ripple of every colour as she flew. Men would never understand that the storm winds were also a message from the gods, just like the rainbow. Her three sisters wore flowing dresses that billowed around their ankles as they swept across the sky. They – like their beloved sister, Iris – were daughters of the daughter of Oceanus, Electra, and her husband Thaumas. And if Olympus could have held them, Iris had no doubt that the Harpies would have dwelt on its lofty heights beside her. But they were too quick to ever be still, so they called nowhere home.

It was a common mistake among mortals to blame the messenger for the message they received. As if it was Iris who decided what news someone was given, as if the Harpies chose their victims. But if men thought the messenger was the one who was at fault, there was no need for them to wonder if their own behaviour had incurred the rebuke they feared and despised. And this was particularly true in the case of Phineus, who was not the first mortal to be given second sight by Apollo. He was simply the first to be so arrogant as to believe he could share every detail with other men. He had done this even when he had the capacity to look to his own future and see the consequences. But he was so greedy for the praise and gratitude of other mortals that he ignored the limits the gods had placed on him. What other outcome could he have expected?

The Harpies came to him every day on the orders of Zeus. They would always come, until Zeus ordered them to stop. But Phineus was unwilling to accept his punishment, so the gods kept him alive, just a little, until he learned humility. And then Jason and his men arrived, and perhaps the gods had chosen a different way to send their message this time. Iris watched the sons of Boreas drive her sisters away from the seer, and she knew that as quick as these Argonauts were, they were no match for the Harpies. The North Wind can blow a strong gale, but it cannot equal the squalling storm winds that are her sisters.

*

Iris knew the Harpies would outfly these winged boys, so she turned her attention to Phineus, and the Argonauts who were lifting him out of the dust. Two young men brought him a bowl of hot water. Phineus had not dared to light a fire since Zeus took his sight, in case he couldn't put it out again. They helped him to clean the matted dirt from his hair and skin, and one of them gave him a fresh tunic which someone had left behind on the ship. He murmured his thanks. He looked almost like a man again, Iris thought.

Sure enough, Phineus needed very little time after he had been picked up and cleaned before he began to tell the Argonauts their future. Zeus must want this, she supposed, and it saved her from taking them a message. She swept past their ship anyway, her rainbow dispersed into countless airborne droplets as the sea swept up the shore.

Phineus began to speak about the dark Symplegades – the clashing rocks that lay ahead of the Argo – but Iris was not concerned with his advice. The young men would make it through, if the gods willed it. She was suddenly filled with concern for her sisters. The sons of Boreas should have returned by now. She flew up into the aether.

*

Zeus was helping the Boreads, allowing them to fly further and faster than they could ever have travelled alone. Iris did not resent this intervention, because it was not her place to resent the king of the gods. But she did resent the way the men flew after her sisters with their swords drawn. They were being given divine assistance to chase away the Harpies, but they had no right to attack or injure them.

Iris had never acted without word coming from Zeus, or from Hera, which amounted to the same thing. But she would not stand by and see her sisters hurt. The rainbow shot across the sky and came to a halt in front of Zetes and Kalaïs.

'Stop,' she said.

The two men came to an abrupt halt in mid-air, dazzled by her multicoloured beauty.

'It is not permitted for you to injure the Harpies,' she said. 'They will not pursue Phineus again.'

'How can we believe you?' asked the taller man.

Iris had not experienced this emotion before, so she struggled to name it. Her sisters would tell her later that it was contempt.

'I swear by the river Styx,' she said.

'Is that oath binding on a goddess?' asked the man.

'It is the only oath that binds me,' Iris said. 'Rejoin your companions before it is too late.'

The Boreads exchanged a glance and wheeled around to return the way they had come. Iris smiled, because these two men would feel nervous whenever they saw a rainbow for the rest of their lives. And it was deserved, because they should never have drawn weapons against her sisters.

Peleia

persuaded by her –

The bird perched on a low branch, from which it could watch the unfamiliar scene. Visitors were infrequent, and she had never seen so many at once. She was accustomed to the sight of the old man groping his way around the shore, and a short distance inland. And she had heard his voice before now, crying out in pain and anger. But this was new. He was gesturing with his hands, a complicated pattern of movement and stillness. And the curious thing was that the little bird – who was not especially attuned to men's speech, which other birds could mimic with an accuracy that delighted them – knew exactly what he must be saying. She had once flown out a long way and seen the very rocks that the man's hands were describing. He illustrated something she did not recognize – a fluttering path between them – but still she didn't doubt what the men were discussing. She had only seen the rocks once, because they had scared her and she had turned and flown straight back to the shore. She might be a small bird, but she had no desire to be crushed between two gigantic rocks.

So it was unfortunate that she was concentrating so much

on the old man that she didn't notice a young one creeping up behind her. And when she did see him, it was from within the bars of a cage.

*

The Clashing Rocks had a fierce reputation: no man had ever sailed through their strait and lived. And yet, this was the route the Argonauts had been told to attempt. Phineus had warned them that the rocks were never still but always moving in the roiling water, a deafening thunder from the waves that crashed all around them. Jason had asked the seer for reassurance: would the Argo survive its ordeal? But Phineus had no wish to incur the anger of Zeus again, so he offered them only this advice. They must take a bird, a dove, and release it as close to the dark rocks as they could safely go. And this was the first trial. They must watch the dove – even as the spray from the churning waters filled their eyes – to see if it could traverse the strait unharmed. If the dove survived, the Argo had a chance. But only if every man bent his back to the oars and ploughed the ship through this awful furrow. This was their second trial, made more difficult because they had left Heracles, their strongest rower, behind. So now the remaining Argonauts had to row with the strength of a full crew. Jason had promised Phineus that they would pray to the gods as they heaved their oars, and the old man laughed. Save your breath, he had told them. It will be too late for prayers by then. It is strength that will save the Argo, not prayer.

But what if the dove did not survive its attempt? What

if the rocks crushed it, as they did everything else? Phineus had no comfort for them. In that case, the Argonauts must row back from the Symplegades and give up their quest. Prayer would not help them in this case either: the gods had already given their advice, through Phineus. The Argonauts could expect nothing more. He had more to say about their journey on the other side of the Clashing Rocks, but as the Argo sailed towards the unwelcoming sea, Jason could scarcely remember his words.

They heard the thunder of the rocks before they saw them. So much spray flew into the air that they seemed to be approaching a terrible storm. If they had been able to look up at the sky, the men would have been startled to find it clear. But they were bent over their oars and they could see nothing but the sea that was somehow on every side of them. They could feel their ship pulling first one way and then another, as the currents tried to wrench them apart. Euphemos – trying to stand on the prow of the ship but crouching to maintain his balance – looked across at Jason and raised the rough cage he had made. He snapped the twine that held it closed, and the dove flew out. The Argonauts did not question that the gods were aiding them once more, because why else would it fly straight into an apparent storm?

*

The little bird was so terrified by the noise and the water, the men and the cage, the sudden captivity and the hostile freedom that she scarcely knew what she was doing. She flapped away from the man and the ship because they presented an immediate danger, but as she flew into the air, she didn't know where she could find safety. The huge waves drove her high, but the space between the rocks was so narrow, she could not be certain she would fit through. Still, behind her was the ship and the cage. She could see what she thought was light between the two dark rocks, so she flew towards that.

*

The Argonauts tried to keep their ship steady as they watched the silver bird. They could barely keep themselves from being dragged into the strait, and they watched in horror as the rocks began their terrifying dance. As the two sides of the strait closed in on one another, the men tried to keep their eyes on the dove. The Symplegades clashed with a deafening roar of water and rock. Euphemos shouted in triumph.

*

The rocks seemed to squeeze the dove into a smaller and smaller space. She tried to fly higher, but that was narrower, so she went lower, though a surge in the water might drown her. She flew with all her might and saw the thin strip of sky draw closer. Then the rocks came together, crushing everything between them, including two of the bird's tail feathers. She would land awkwardly on a branch of the first tree she saw.

*

The Argonauts had made their plan before they left Phineus, and now they followed it. Tiphys, their helmsman, shouted that they must give all their strength to the oars and they obeyed him. The Argo edged towards the mouth of the strait and the men rowed harder than they had ever believed they could. Their throats were ragged from the salt and their muscles screamed, but they did not slow down. The Symplegades seemed to be in retreat and the men gasped for air, but Tiphys did not lessen their pace. As they passed through the strait, they could not tell how far they had gone: the towering rocks blocked the sky above, and no one could see ahead of him. Time seemed to hold them and still they rowed. The men at the front of the ship gave a shout: at last, they could see something past the black rocks. Ahead of them was a calmer sea, an easier journey. But they celebrated too soon.

The Symplegades had reached their furthest point, and began to churn back together. Tiphys screamed at the men to row harder, but the currents seemed to be pulling the ship back into the narrowest part of the strait. The more they forced their curving oars into the sea, the less they seemed to move. And now the rocks were closing in on them.

Symplegades

have killed

The Clashing Rocks had only one purpose, and it was to destroy every boat that approached their inhospitable waters. They ruled over a tempestuous sea and nothing had ever escaped them.

Perhaps the odd bird had escaped them. Birds were tiny and the rocks could not pay heed to every cormorant. But even the birds would lose a feather or two. A ship would never pass.

Over the years, men had stopped making the attempt: there were longer, safer, slower routes they could take, so they did.

And then came the Argo, and her foolhardy crew, determined to be the exception.

The Symplegades had a reputation to preserve, and they held the ship tight.

The currents would not free the Argo, the rocks would take it.

The goddess Athene rushed down from Olympus. She held the rocks apart.

She lifted the Argo above the churning waves.
She returned it to the sea on the far side of the strait.
The men could not see her, nor did they realize it was
the goddess who had saved them.
She gave the ship a hard push, and it rushed out into
the open sea like an arrow let fly from the bow of
Artemis.
She let go of the Symplegades and they clashed
together one final time. The gods had decreed that the
rocks would never move again once a ship had success-
fully traversed them.
These rocks would not cease their terrible motion
without exacting a small penalty from the ship that had
fused them together. The Argo lost a carved wooden bird
that had adorned its stern. It was smashed into splinters
by the resentful Symplegades.

Argo

their father;

The men were eager to put distance between themselves and the rocks that had so nearly annihilated them, but they could go no further without resting to allow their aching arms to regain strength. They looked out across the widening expanse of the Pontus and they could not see where it ended and the sky began. Tiphys was the first to speak.

'It's because of the Argo,' he said. And given how many people have tried to heap blame on the ship, it was unusual for someone to give credit where it was due.

'What do you mean?' asked one of the men, and Tiphys continued.

'The gods love this ship. Who can doubt it now? Athene instilled her protection into every plank of wood as she watched the shipmakers build this mighty vessel. She is the one who saved us from the rocks. She would not see her favourite ship smashed.'

Jason looked on as most of the Argonauts seemed to agree with the helmsman. He saw an opportunity.

'How can you say that?' he asked. 'How can you pretend

to believe these things just to make me feel better?'

No one responded, allowing him to continue. 'It is the worst decision of my life, agreeing to take on this quest. The only thing I have done which was more foolish was agreeing to be the captain of this ill-fated voyage. I drew you to Iolcus and brought you along with me. You could have followed any man, but somehow, I persuaded you to join this journey which will surely lead us straight to Hades.'

Jason did not know that the Argo was – at this point – very near to a cave which did indeed lead directly to Hades, but the ship would sail past it.

'We all chose this quest,' cried one man, and a shout of agreement went up.

'I cannot rest,' Jason said. 'I have not had a moment's peace since we first set sail.'

One Argonaut wondered about the time they had spent in Lemnos, when their captain had given the strongest impression of a man resting and enjoying himself. But he was still fighting for breath after their exertions, so he stayed quiet.

'Why?' asked another.

'Because I am consumed with worry for you all,' said Jason, his voice shaking with emotion. 'I worry for myself too, of course, but that is not my greatest fear. My greatest fear,' he added, as though someone had asked, 'is that I will not be able to get you all home again. We have already lost Heracles and Hylas. We will lose more of our mighty heroes before this quest is completed. And it will be my fault. I know it will be. Because if it weren't for me, none of you would have risked your lives as you already have.'

Tears streamed down his cheeks, and the Argonauts

sought to console him. It was not his fault that Hylas and Heracles had been lost to them. Zeus himself could not change a man's fate, but he would keep his son from harm, they were sure of it. And even if Zeus couldn't protect Heracles, the man was a great hero and would defend himself with ease. As for the rest of them, they would follow their captain to Hades if necessary.

And Jason smiled bravely through his tears, and allowed them to console him.

Phyllis

and she wouldn't

The Argo did not stop at the mouth of the river Phyllis. Once the men had recovered their strength, they were soon moving quickly along the southern coast of the Pontus. They passed streams and mountains without paying them heed. Some were thinking about their narrow escape, some were focused on the glory that lay ahead, and who would win most renown from their quest. They knew Jason had further instructions from Phineus about the next part of the expedition, but they did not press him too closely, in case he lost confidence in himself again.

But Phineus had only told them to stay close to the shoreline. He had not mentioned the black headland which they would sail past, nor had he told them that the river just beyond it was once home to the nymph, Phyllis, who settled there with her son because she wanted to live quietly in a place where they would rarely be disturbed. It did not occur to the Argonauts to wonder if any Greeks had been here before them: they knew the treachery of the Clashing Rocks.

But – if they had thought about it – they might have realized that not every Greek travelled by ship. One Greek

– a boy named Phrixus – had reached these distant shores by quite another means. And the Argonauts knew that, because Phrixus had travelled on the back of a miraculous creature called Chrysomallos, whose name the Greeks still spoke in wonder: the Golden Ram.

Interlude

The Child of Theophane

Theophane

If there is anyone in this story who would prefer to be overlooked, it's probably me. And I have been, for the most part. I haven't led the life people expected, nor the life I hoped I would have. But if I don't tell you what happened to me, you won't fully understand what happens later, to him. So though I never speak about it, about any of it – you will search for me in vain in even the most detailed histories of this time – I will tell you.

The first thing I need to say will make me sound vain, but it is simply the truth: I was a beautiful child. I grew up in Thrace, the daughter of a powerful man named Bisaltis. And because stories of my beauty were sung across the seas, men came from everywhere to try to make me their wife.

Perhaps this story sounds familiar to you? There are several tales of a woman so beautiful that every man desired to make her his, I suppose. All I can tell you is that this is mine. I would no doubt have married one of these suitors, if my father had been able to make the decision. But my future was decided for him by the god of the sea.

Please, don't do that. That roll of the eyes that asks who do I think I am, this woman you've never heard of telling you she was once a famous beauty, and that a god – not even a minor god – interested himself in me. Is this sounding like a story of hubris to you? I can only tell you that nothing of what followed was what you would have chosen for yourself, or for your daughters.

Poseidon arrived in my father's home and told him he would take me away. My father could not argue with a deity, nor did he try. I was watching him from behind a curtained doorway, and I saw him acquiesce without hesitation. I tried to tell myself – then and now – that this was not a betrayal, that he loved me and could not imagine a better match for his daughter than the sea god. But in that moment when I was watching him, unseen, I saw the expression that formed behind his eyes, and it was not love or pride, but rather relief. He no longer had to worry about who would marry his daughter, nor about which men he would make his enemies by choosing someone else. Everything was decided for him.

I don't remember if he said goodbye. I remember his servants plaiting my hair and taking me outside into the dazzling afternoon sun. A dark-haired, dark-bearded man nodded to them and reached for my hand. This might – I suppose – suggest to you a romantic moment, when we touched for the first time and I shivered with anticipation. You should dispel this idea. I shuddered when he touched me. He felt warm and clammy, like a fever.

He took me to an island, I don't know its name. He didn't tell me; he didn't speak to me at all. I didn't speak to him either. I made myself as small as I could, curling up on the ground beside a spindly tree trunk. But he must have told my father where he would take me, because Bisaltis told the men who wanted to marry me.

Was this an attempt by my father to have me rescued? I don't know. How many men does it take to fight a god? I had barely spoken to any of the suitors, which curiously didn't seem to have put them off. They buried their sworn rivalries and took to the sea together. A risk, you might think, to come after Poseidon that way. Any man who offends him can expect to meet vicious storms and cruel seas.

Poseidon didn't drown them, though. Perhaps there were too many sons of Zeus or Apollo onboard. Instead, he turned his attention first to the island's inhabitants. Did I not say there were people there? I couldn't speak to any of them, of course: no one dared approach me. I didn't blame them for it and it didn't help them, because he still turned them into cattle. Then he turned me into a ewe and himself into a ram.

It's hard to describe how little difference it made. I know the horror of losing form and voice and agency, but I had lost two of those already. And for what? For my beauty, something over which I had no control either. I was no more able to refuse the ram than the god.

The suitors arrived at an apparently uninhabited island. If they thought it was strange to see cattle and sheep but no herdsmen, they didn't allow it to detain them for long. They took a cursory look around but there were so many of them, and it was such a small island, that it didn't take long before they sailed away again.

He didn't restore the island people to human form, he kept them as livestock. He restored me to my human shape, because he preferred it, I imagine. And he left me on the island, alone but for the cattle most of the time. He returned now and then, but less often once he saw I was pregnant.

And now, that is all I am known for, if I am known at all. Impregnated by Poseidon in the form of a ram.

I was relieved, in some ways, to be abandoned, although I missed the sound of speech, and of talking to people who could reply. I spoke to the cows, of course, but I never knew if they could understand me or if he had made them animals in their minds as well as their bodies. For a while, I hoped that a ship would pass the island and find me, but Poseidon knew how to keep them at bay, and no sailors ever arrived.

When I gave birth to his son, it was also a ram. And you may well think me foolish when I tell you I loved him just as much as if he had been human. I spoke to him like mothers speak to their babies, I nursed him and held him and cared for him and, yes, loved him.

I should have known not to be so stupid. Because what would Poseidon do when he saw I felt a love for our child that I had never felt for him? What else would he ever do but seize the child, and take him far away?

Ino

Ino waited until the man had retreated, until the footsteps had faded and until she was sure no one could hear her before she began to cry. She had grown up with the constant presence of siblings. She felt comfortable when there was noise and arguing, but lost now in the silence of the palace of Athamas. She knew why her father had given her to this man, the son of Aeolus. But still she hated him.

Cadmus and Harmonia had been blessed with two daughters, one son, and then two more daughters. The oldest, Autonoë, had been married to her husband for only a year when they began to consider who might be a suitable match for Semele, their second girl. All his daughters were beautiful, as Cadmus never tired of boasting. But only Semele was so striking that she caught the attention of the king of the gods. The family struggled to speak of this, because it was perilously close to blasphemy to wish that Zeus had kept his attentions on Mount Olympus. No one should reject the interest of any god, and especially not that one. And Semele had been happy. That was what hurt Ino now: when she thought of her sister laughing and joking with Autonoë, rolling her eyes at their brother, picking up Ino because she was the smallest and they still could. It had been Semele's joy that made her lovely, more than anything. And when Zeus came to her – Ino was still unsure of how or when this had happened, because no one ever told the youngest child anything – he was disguised. Again, Ino didn't know the form this disguise took, but she imagined he would have seemed like a kind-faced young man. That was what she would have chosen for Semele. It was what she would have chosen for herself.

When Semele understood she was pregnant, her parents were briefly shocked and then immediately delighted. Again, Ino could see now that Zeus himself must have intervened to tell them he was their daughter's lover, because otherwise they would have been far less sanguine about the affair. Ino had never been included in these conversations because she was too young. But then came the part that she knew, because everyone knew. Had it been Hera herself who intervened? Ino had been told so, but it made her shudder even now, to think of the malice that it had taken to look at Semele – so happy and full of hope – and wish her dead.

The story other people told was this: that a vengeful goddess – disguised as an old woman – had persuaded the stupid, vain Semele to ask to see her lover in his truest form. Ino knew this to be nonsense. Semele wasn't curious by nature, she didn't listen to gossip, she wouldn't reassess her feelings for anyone because of what another person told her. She was too open to keep secrets, and too guileless to imagine other people did. She was neither stupid nor vain. Hera's list of victims was long, and Semele couldn't have survived her rage, any more than anyone else could have done. But it would always pain Ino to think people blamed her sister for anything.

Zeus offered Semele the wish, that part Ino did believe. She could so easily imagine her sister laughing and wondering if she could ask for something. Ino could equally well imagine how impossible it would be to refuse her. But did Semele really ask to see her lover in his divine state? Did she not know it was Zeus, did she not remember that he was all the force the sky could muster in one immortal form? Did she imagine she could witness that, and not be obliterated?

Ino knew what she believed, and Agauë and Autonoë too. They knew their sister would never have been so foolish and they knew she would never have put those she loved at risk. She would, however, have agreed to die to keep her baby safe. That made far better sense to those who knew her best. That Hera had threatened her child and that she had chosen to die instead. Because how else could the infant boy have survived the blast that killed his mother? They said Zeus took the unborn child away and kept him safe until he chose to return him to the surviving daughters of Cadmus. And they had cared for the boy until Zeus took him away again.

People believed Semele's son would be a mighty god, and when they said this, they assumed her family would be honoured to share their blood with the son of Zeus himself. But – Ino reflected, as she wept in the empty room – they had never known Semele, so they didn't realize that she was worth far more than a god. Her parents never voiced these thoughts, of course. They had lost one child, they didn't want to lose more. But some thought the family had been cursed by Hera more than blessed by Zeus. He had only desired one daughter; his wife despised the whole clan.

And Cadmus so feared the queen of the gods and her renewing furies that he sent his youngest child as far from her family as he could. Which is how Ino had found herself in the unfamiliar home of a man whose customs she did not know, and who already had two children by a nymph he would never name.

It was painfully clear to her from the first day as his wife that Athamas carried a sadness as deep as her own, which he wouldn't share and which he didn't want to shed. Ino had tried to discover the cause, but he rarely spoke to her in the first months. One slave had told her that Athamas had not smiled since his wife Nephele disappeared and Ino had felt a brief surge of relief when she knew it was not because of her that her husband was filled with rage. Then, of course, she felt a sharp twist of grievance in her gut. How dare he refuse to speak to her because of something that was nothing to do with her?

And as the months dragged into years, and she gave birth to one and then another son, the grievance festered. It wasn't just for herself that Ino felt slighted now, it was for them. How could he prefer his older children to those Ino had borne him? She couldn't point to any examples of this preference, because Athamas was sullen with everyone. But she knew it was there. She longed for advice from one of her sisters, but Autonoë was too unhappy to reply to her messages, and Agauë was lost in the tangled thickets of her own mind. Semele would have helped her – she knew it – but there was no point knowing it because Semele was dead.

Ino had clung to her babies, willing them to speak so there would be someone with whom she could share her thoughts. She didn't even mind their crying, preferring it to the crushing quiet that otherwise filled her rooms. She had tried to befriend his older children, the twins, because she thought it would please Athamas. But when he saw her offering the girl a honeyed fig, he cursed her and sent the children away with their nurse. So then she largely ignored them, in the hope of annoying him less. She knew it was unfair to blame the children for what was doubtless Athamas' choice, but she couldn't help it. Ino's rejected kindness began to twist and congeal and she saw them as arrogant, rude, spoiled.

And then she began to grow anxious about her sons and the future Athamas would give them. She had heard the same stories as every other woman: if a man still loved his first wife, he would always favour her children. And Ino could not take that risk, living so far from her own shattered family. She had to find a way to change her husband's mind.

She began quietly, testing her powers of persuasion. She asked about Phrixus, wondered if he was unwell, then refused to be drawn when her husband asked why. She dropped the subject for several days, then worried he wasn't quite himself. Perhaps they had somehow offended a god. Athamas brushed her concerns aside the first time, and the second. And the days lengthened and she said nothing, only a small frown when Athamas mentioned his oldest son. It took time and patience, but Ino had a great deal of both. Hadn't she proved this when she helped to care for her poor dead sister's baby for two years before she came north to Thessaly? She had cared for the child the way her sister would have done, the way Ino now cared for her own children. The way she would nurture any child but Phrixus and Helle.

As the months passed, Ino slowly formed the idea in her husband's mind that something was amiss in his kingdom, and that somehow it was connected to Phrixus. She was delighted when she realized the twins were responding to her animus as most children would: with rage and irrational tears. They succeeded only in pushing their father towards his second wife, who was always so concerned for him.

The parching of the grain was not her idea. People would blame her for it afterwards, of course. But if they had thought about Ino – about who she was and where she had grown up – they would have realized she was hardly likely to know what to do to make grain refuse to grow. She had no magical skills, nor any idea about planting seeds. She had spent her childhood in a royal house where bread simply appeared in front of her when she was hungry. How on earth, Ino would have liked to ask, was she meant to know that if you heated seeds before planting them, they would never sprout? Who would ever have told her this?

And there was no proof anyway. When the crops failed, people wanted someone to blame and they needed something to do, so they demanded the king send a messenger to the oracle. Ino didn't bribe the messenger, nor did she persuade Apollo's priests to lie. When the divine response was brought before Athamas – with its cloudy words about the king and a sacrifice – she wasn't even the first person to mention Phrixus. That had been his own priest, a man who had been part of his household long before Ino had even set foot in Thessaly. And he had done what those men always did: he claimed he alone could read the riddle and tell his king what to do. I'm sure it can't refer to your son, said the priest, with the conviction of one who thinks the opposite but is afraid to say so. The king had agreed that it couldn't refer to Phrixus, and his priests and advisers discussed the matter until darkness fell.

When Athamas sat down to eat with his wife, his appetite was gone. How could he eat when so many of his subjects would soon be hungry? Ino nodded sympathetically, having suspected this would be his view and eaten her own meal before he arrived. It said the first, he continued. That I must sacrifice the first if I want to avert a famine. And Phrixus is the first? Ino leaned over and touched her husband's wrist. Not Helle? In the moments that followed it became clear that Athamas did not know which of his twins had been born first. He had assumed it was Phrixus, but he had never been told. In this way, Ino discovered that her predecessor had abandoned her husband and children on the day she gave birth, and never returned.

It does seem to say that you must sacrifice your firstborn child, she said. But I suppose if you can't be sure which that is . . . She allowed her voice to die away so that Athamas could work out the terrible truth for himself. If he didn't know which child was the oldest, and the crops could only grow if he offered that one to the gods, then he would have to sacrifice them both. The only thing Ino could be certain of – as she gently squeezed her husband's shoulder before retiring – was that his firstborn child was not hers.

Nephele

Nephele did not fully despise her husband when she left him. If she had, she might have taken her children with her, even though Zeus would have raised his dark eyebrows. She found him dull, a little cloying, and she disliked the way he was so solid, like meat. There was something about the way he sat in a chair that made her want to dissolve.

But the contempt she felt now was new. She loathed his mortal stupidity and his weakness. Did he really imagine that the gods would ask for the life of one of her children? For what possible reason? He should have been pouring offerings of wine to the goddess Demeter if he wanted his crops to thrive. And instead, he had somehow been persuaded to believe that a goddess who had almost starved the world to save her daughter might now require the death of another child. The man was an utter fool.

At first, Nephele refused to believe it. But first one nymph and then another brought her the same message: Athamas is planning to kill them. She laughed it off as a misunderstanding. A king would not slaughter his own children, her children. But then she listened with care and heard what the other nymphs had heard. The desperate muttered prayers of her beautiful twins, begging their mother to intervene and save them from their father's sword.

Nephele responded as swiftly as a rising storm. She issued a plea to every god and – rather to her surprise – it was Poseidon who heard her first. He knew what she needed and he offered her his precious Chrysomallos. She accepted gladly: whatever he required in exchange was worth it. And she watched with relief as he kept his word. Her children would be safe now, she knew. They would be taken from Thessaly, taken far from their father and his vicious little wife. For them, Nephele would need the help of the queen of the gods herself. Because her course of action was quite simple. First came the rescue, then came the revenge.

Helle

It was the evening before the sacrifice, and Helle could not
understand what had happened. Like her brother, she knew
it was their stepmother's doing, but she still couldn't see
how Ino had managed it. How had their father been so
easily persuaded? One bad harvest was just that. But he
was so uncertain of his power over the Thessalians that he
had consulted an oracle straightaway, and only thought
afterwards that he had no one who could interpret its
response.

Ino had known what it meant, of course she had. Helle
knew her stepmother would never have been so foolish as
to claim the oracle was simple to understand. She knew
exactly the strategy Ino would have employed: a faint
suggestion in a quavering voice, a certainty that she must
be wrong, because it couldn't possibly mean . . . Her father
was weak, Helle knew. His weakness would now prove fatal
to her and to Phrixus.

And the horror kept unfurling. It would not be the priests
raising their knives above her throat the next day, she
whispered to Phrixus. She had overheard two slaves talking

outside the small window of their room. The king himself must conduct the sacrifice, the oracle had been quite clear. Phrixus shook his head: nothing about the oracle had been clear. Why was everyone suddenly so certain about something so vague? They sat in silence, wondering if their father could really bring himself to kill them. The room was growing dark, though not cold. But Phrixus was shaking, and Helle put her arms around him.

She had no idea how long they had been sitting on the low couch, her head resting back against the wall, knees pulled up in front of her, and Phrixus nestling his head on her shoulder. She felt a sudden warmth around her, as though someone were holding her the way she was embracing her brother. At the same time, it seemed that the outlines of the door, the table, the two stools in front of her became more distinct. She felt a lurch of panic that she must have fallen asleep, that what she could see was the dawning of their final day. But she wasn't on the side of the palace where the sun rose. Whatever she could see, it couldn't be morning. For a moment she allowed herself to hope it might be the people of Thessaly coming to save their prince and princess from a king who had surely lost his mind. It could be the light of their torches as they strode towards her rescue. But Helle knew that wasn't right either. It was too quiet for there to be any crowd nearby. The brightness seemed to increase and she blinked. Phrixus raised his head and looked at her in confusion. She saw her own thoughts mirrored in his eyes and she wanted to comfort him but did not know what to say.

Phrixus stood and clambered onto the bed. He peered through the small window and burst out laughing. It was such a shock – the noise from the silence and the joy from the fear – that Helle cried out to be quiet. Even as she did so, she wondered why. They could hardly kill her twice for interrupting their sleep. But then Phrixus leaned down and grabbed her hand, tugging her to her feet. She raised herself onto her toes and looked to see what had made her defeated brother laugh like that. And just as she was trying to believe what she saw, the building began to move.

This was not the first time Poseidon had shaken the earth beneath their feet. Thessaly had been struck by a mighty quake the summer before last. The god had taken no lives but they'd spent many months appeasing him in case he tried again. But this felt different, Helle thought. The couch on which they were standing did not move. Nothing rattled or fell in the palace behind them that she could hear. In fact, nothing at all seemed to move except the single wall between the twins and the source of the sudden light and the warmth. And that collapsed entirely, so that they could both step outside their prison and stand free under the light of the stars they couldn't see because of the impossible brightness of the golden ram.

Neither of them dared to move. When Phrixus spoke about it later, he would shake his head at this point in the story. It hadn't been that they thought they would scare the ram away if they approached it. Nothing could be less fearful than the noble creature standing before them. And they – or at least he – hadn't been afraid of it. It was clearly an emissary from a god, and no one would send such a beast to the mortal realm to do anything but good. The children rightly thought the ram must have been sent by their mother – the mother they had never met – to save them.

The ram was huge, the size of a small horse. His fleece glimmered gold and his golden horns curved outwards like the handles of a priceless wine cup. It was not the colour of the ram that paralysed them, but his radiance. His fleece seemed to glow like fire, and he gazed at them with haughty patience: they were expected to stand and stare but not for too long. He dipped his head but his bright golden eyes continued to stare at them both. Phrixus was still holding his sister's hand, and they stepped forward together. The ram raised his head again and they both knew what he wanted them to do.

Phrixus climbed onto his back first, and placed his hands gently behind the creature's horns. He stroked the soft ridges that ran around each one. Helle climbed on behind her brother and leaned into his back. She knew she would have to hold on, but she could not help running her fingers through the fleece, feeling its warmth and its softness. She wanted to bury her face in it. But it was already too late for such childish thoughts, because the ram had begun to gallop away from the palace and as his pace increased Phrixus grabbed his horns more tightly and Helle clasped her hands around her brother's waist.

By the time the ram began to fly, the children had lost their capacity for surprise, although their sense of wonder had not diminished at all.

Nephele

Nephele watched her children fly off the coast of Thessaly like a comet. She had not asked Poseidon where the ram would carry them because she knew they would be safe once they were far from Ino and her poisonous words. Perhaps she would even visit them when they were back on the ground. She wondered if other gods and nymphs were watching the ram's progress as he glittered through the night sky. Perhaps mortals would think it really was a comet. She smiled to herself at how easily they were tricked. And because of the pleasure she was taking in watching the ram – whose name, Poseidon had told her, was Chrysomallos – she was still gazing down at the world beneath her when she saw a curious thing happen.

She could not put into words exactly what she had seen, but the ram had suddenly changed course, just briefly, before continuing his journey. If Nephele had been familiar with the behaviour of horses (to which she had never paid the slightest attention), she might have realized that the ram must have stopped suddenly, like a horse refusing to leap over a high wall. But there was no wall, of course, so the ram immediately continued its journey.

And from her lofty perch, Nephele could not see that now the ram carried only one of her children. Her daughter, Helle, had slipped from his back and fallen beneath the waves. Only Phrixus would land safely in Colchis and make his home in the palace of a new, equally dangerous king.

Poseidon did nothing without exacting a toll.

Ino

Hera had the longest memory, and the things she most enjoyed remembering were the names of those who had offended her alongside a list of the potential punishments they would receive. She would sometimes pause by the name of someone who was under the protection of her husband, Zeus, and grudgingly accept that she would have to save this one for another day. Very occasionally, she was forced to admit defeat, as happened with Dionysus. Her favoured course of action was relentless persecution, but he had been admitted to Mount Olympus as a god, so she had to accept she could not punish him. She consoled herself with the happy recollection of his idiot mother being blasted into oblivion by the full might of Zeus.

But it was insufficient. It wasn't just the mother she hated, it was her whole cursed family (and Hera had personally consulted the Fates to discover that the family would endure generation after generation of misery). One of the sisters had already lost her mind thanks to Dionysus, in an act of ingratitude and revenge so spectacular that Hera almost warmed to him. But there were two more sisters,

112

and one in particular had been very free in shedding tears for her poor dead sibling, and too quick to look after the infant Dionysus. Hera turned her attention to Ino. The other one could wait for now.

It took her a while to track the young woman down in Thessaly. So far from home! Had Cadmus really believed he could protect his daughter by sending her away? Hera's revenge was never lessened by waiting, quite the reverse: it simply gave her more time to plan. And by the time she found Ino – holed up in some minor king's hovel with one, no, two children of her own – Hera had decided exactly what she would do.

She deliberated for a while over the details, before deciding that fear would be preferable to madness. Not that she ruled out madness: it was often a delightful way to watch a human being disintegrate. But this time she wanted something a little more creative, so it was the husband she drove from his senses. She happened to know – thanks to an enlightening conversation with the beautiful cloud goddess Nephele – that he had previously tried to kill his older children, and only been prevented by their divine mother's intervention. His younger children had no such mother: they had Ino. Hera appeared to the king in his dreams during the darkest part of the night and when she left, she took his reason.

He killed the older one of Ino's sons with a knife as she ran from the palace carrying the younger one. She didn't scream, Hera was sorry to note. She liked hearing women scream, there was something so complete about the sound. But Ino was too out of breath, and that grew only more true as Athamas pursued her, holding his knife aloft. His wife was too frantic to think in which direction she should go, and she ran up towards the edge of the Thessalian coast.

When Ino realized she was cornered and had nowhere left to run, she still would not allow her child to be slaughtered like an animal. Holding him in her arms, she jumped from the cliff. Hera eyed the small splash the two of them made as they landed in the rocky waters, and allowed herself a brief smile.

Theophane

Chrysomallos – the golden ram, my golden child, however foolish that sounds, a woman grieving the loss of a creature as though it were a boy – is scarcely remembered by anyone. He was once an important part of the story: Phrixus and Helle carried away from a terrible fate by this magical golden creature. Helle was lost, of course – through no fault of Chrysomallos – and she is remembered. That strait has been called the Hellespont ever since: Helle's sea. She may have been lost, but she has never been forgotten.

But that is not true of Chrysomallos, is it? No one speaks of the golden ram, they prefer to focus on what was important to Jason and his Argonauts: the golden fleece. Such a simple shift in emphasis, you scarcely notice a living creature becoming the remnant of a dead one. And perhaps you also don't notice the small slip of the tongue, either? Because fleece is not the right word to use, although it is the one everyone prefers. A fleece can be shorn from a ram without any harm coming to the creature at all. Sheep have their fleeces sheared every year, so they don't get too hot in the long days of the summer. But Jason wasn't seeking a golden fleece, he was on a quest to find the skin of the creature who wore it, a mythical creature, who was mine, my child, taken from me when he was still so new.

It brings good luck, people used to say of the fleece, to whatever land holds it. No wonder Pelias wanted it for Iolcus. It would grant his people plentiful crops and fertile animals. It would make Jason a hero, if only he returned home carrying it on his ship.

It, it, it.

All I hear when people say these things is the sound of a world that forgets that my son was a living creature, my miraculous, beautiful living child. Oh, I know, I know. Not a child, just an animal. So who would grieve for him if he died? Who would mind if someone tore off his skin and hung it from a tree in a sacred grove, an artefact to bring glory to a god? When you think about him this way, his skin was just an object. It's curious, isn't it, that anything wanted by a man or a god becomes just an object?

And that is why I am still so angry, no matter how many years go past and no matter that there is no one to hear me say it on this desolate island. I was turned into an object when I was just a child: how could I be anything else, when men wanted me, when my father traded me, when a god took me? These aren't words we would use to describe a person. No, they are words we use for a thing. And that is how I felt, curled up on the floor of Poseidon's temple, no strength to push him away, no family who would protect me. I had no more power than a slave, or an animal.

And that is why I couldn't keep my son, because the children of slaves belong not to themselves but to their masters. Poseidon took only what was his. I couldn't keep

Chrysomallos, nor could I keep him safe. All I could do was to wait here, hoping his father would bring him back to me one day, would let me hold him, even for a moment.

So no doubt I sound foolish – a vain old woman stuck on an empty island with no one to hear her weeping for her lost child, only for you to find out he wasn't even human. So be it. I have lost everything I had, because it was never really mine. I was beautiful, but my beauty was a thing men wanted to possess. I had a child but his beauty was another thing men wanted to possess. So they killed him, they cut his skin from his warm body, and they kept it as a trophy. No one thinks it matters because he was only an animal and they are nothing. And no one thinks I matter because I am nothing too. Just the mother of a miracle that men chose to see as a thing.

Phyllis

When the boy arrived on the back of a golden ram, Phyllis and her son looked at the pair in wonder. The boy's hands were wrapped around the ram's horns and he did not move, even when there was firm ground beneath him. Phyllis approached him slowly, not wanting the ram to buck and send the young man flying because – as she drew closer – she realized this was a young man, not a child. Her son was mesmerized by the ram and its sparkling golden wool, but Phyllis was more concerned with the rider. Although he had arrived in such a strange and miraculous way, he did not carry himself like a favourite of the gods.

He was rigid with fear, his knuckles protruding through bone-white skin. And tears coursed down his cheeks. He could do nothing to wipe them away so Phyllis reached up and gently touched his face. He did not speak or acknowledge her at all. She waited a while and then put her hands over his. They felt cold beneath her, as though all his blood had drained away. She felt heat seep into him and tried to unfurl his fingers. The ram – as though it knew what Phyllis was trying to do – knelt, bringing the boy down with him until his feet just touched the ground. She squeezed the boy's hands and tried again to prise his fingers loose. When she managed to open his right hand, he immediately grabbed hers and held it. She pulled him towards her and took him in her arms. As his body relaxed, the ram gave a small shake and the boy slid onto the dusty earth. Phyllis sent her son to fetch water and wine and they helped the boy to sit up and quench his thirst.

'Who are you?' she asked. 'I am Phyllis, and this is my son, Dipsakos. We live here alone, you are quite safe.'

'Phrixus,' he replied. 'I am Phrixus, son of Athamas. We had to flee, he has gone mad, he wanted to –' His voice wavered. 'He wanted to kill us both.'

'You and . . . ?'

'Helle, my sister,' he said. 'She fell.'

Phyllis gave him more wine and held him until he stopped weeping for his lost sister.

'How did you escape?' she asked. Her small son wriggled closer to her. He was not much interested in lost sisters but he did want to know about the miraculous golden ram.

'Our mother, Nephele, sent this ram to rescue us,' he said. 'He broke down the wall of our prison.' Dipsakos eyed the ram with admiration. 'He carried us so far,' Phrixus said. 'I don't know where I am now.'

Phyllis explained her stream and meadows, and their position on the coast of the Black Sea. Phrixus looked around at the vibrant green landscape – so unlike the parched red land in which he had been raised – and realized he had travelled far beyond anywhere he had even heard about in stories.

'Perhaps I can stay here,' he wondered. And Phyllis smiled and said they must eat.

*

Phrixus did stay, for a while. He recovered his strength quickly, and began exploring. He followed the river inland, coming back with fish for the three of them. Dipsakos showed him how they cooked them over a fire and the young man – who had never cooked his own food before – nodded gravely as he was given the instructions. He still wept for the loss of his sister and his home, but the pain was a little less raw with each passing day. In Phyllis he saw a mother he had never known, and he could easily imagine himself as brother to Dipsakos.

But this was not to be his future. One bright morning, the ram – who had been grazing contentedly on the land around the stream – came trotting over to Phrixus and headbutted him gently.

'What is it?' asked Phrixus. He had no desire to travel any further, but the ram seemed determined. Phrixus buried his hands in the thick wool and scratched the creature's head. 'A little longer?' he said. Dipsakos laughed because he said the ram nodded to Phrixus, as though he were a king granting permission. Phrixus laughed too, but only because he enjoyed the child's delight.

After a few more days had passed, the ram came to Phrixus again, and nudged him. Phrixus raised his hands to scratch the wool beneath the ram's horns but the ram stood back so he couldn't reach, and then came forward and butted him again.

'You must leave,' said Phyllis. She tried not to let the sadness show in her voice: she had enjoyed the company of another boy, enjoyed watching her son have someone to play with and impress. Phrixus turned an anxious face towards her, but she smiled. They both knew that the gods had not brought him here to keep her company.

'Tomorrow,' he told the ram, who stared at him until he swore an oath that he would leave at first light, and only then ambled away to eat more of the lush grasses beside the water.

'He doesn't want to leave any more than I do,' Phrixus said.

'I think you're right,' Phyllis replied. 'I wonder where he came from. He seems to like it here, doesn't he?'

'Perhaps he'll want to come back.' Phrixus tried not to let too much hope creep into his voice.

'If he does,' said Phyllis, 'you will both always be welcome on our shores, you know that.'

He nodded and she smiled again, hoping she might be wrong.

*

Many years after Phrixus broke his journey there, the Argonauts did not stop at the place where Phyllis' stream met the Pontus. They were in too much of a hurry. So they did not find out that they were drawing closer to the object of their mission, or that the golden ram possessed other miraculous qualities besides the colour of his fleece. Had they known that he could fly such huge distances, that he seemed to understand human speech, and that he glowed with a warmth that none who saw him ever forgot – even Phrixus, who had lost his sister but never blamed the ram for something beyond his control – perhaps they would have been more prepared for what they would find in Colchis.

Part Two

Colchis

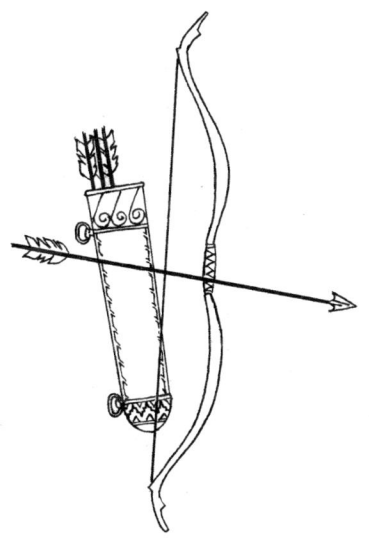

Erato

live here,

And now it's my turn. Don't try to pretend you knew this was coming when we both know you did not. The story of the Argonauts is a grand quest, a mission, a saga. A crew of mighty heroes build their divinely inspired ship and set sail for a distant land. Who would be the Muse you would turn to for this story?

What's that?

Which one am I?

Well, aren't you sweet. You would expect this to be a story told by my sister Calliope, the most important of the Muses. No, don't pretend you didn't know that, everyone knows she's the one for epic tales of courage and sea travel.

But this story is a little different, in case you haven't noticed. Courage has doubtless helped the Argonauts on their way to this point. They had to build a ship, and that can't be easy, even if you have the goddess Athene helping you (which they did). They had to pause to repopulate the island of Lemnos, of course, or at least ensure there would be a few men there in twenty years or so. And that might have been hard work, if Aphrodite hadn't bewitched them with desire and charm, which makes that kind of thing so much easier. There was the rescuing of Phineus when the old man was on the verge of starvation, which would certainly have been extremely arduous, if the Harpies hadn't been called off by Zeus himself. And even then, Iris had to appear to stop the Argonauts from overstepping their mortal limits. Ah, but they had to navigate their way through the Symplegades using only the advice Phineus had offered, and the intervention of Athene herself when they couldn't do it alone.

I'm not saying this story hasn't got the makings of an epic, but it isn't a very satisfying one so far. Every time the Argonauts go anywhere or do anything, a goddess steps in to help them out.

But it's here at Colchis that things are going to become a lot more complicated. Goddesses will still be helping Jason and his crew but they won't be quite as direct about it, so the Argonauts won't notice unless they're paying close attention. And if you're disappointed that you won't have a nice old-fashioned adventure story in front of you when you really thought that's what you'd be getting, perhaps you need to ask yourself why poets asked me to help them tell this tale, rather than asking my sister.

Oh, but you weren't sure which Muse I am, even though there are only nine to choose from, and I already told you I wasn't Calliope. You can probably rule out Ourania, too, since the Argonauts might be navigating by the stars, I suppose, but they have mostly been following the coastline which doesn't require much knowledge of the heavens. No, don't stand there trying to remember, it just makes everyone feel uncomfortable. My name is Erato and I am the Muse of love: its poetry, its stories and its songs. What else do you want to know?

Well yes, of course I can tell you what happened next.

Argo

in Corinth, with

The Argonauts had a few more adventures on their way to Colchis, but none that detained them – or need detain us – very long. They lost a few of their number: Idmon could see the future but did not see his own early death, gored by a wild boar. Tiphys had guided them so bravely as they rowed across the seas, but he was felled by sickness, and quickly replaced by another man. A ship must be steered by someone but it makes little difference who, when the ship is the Argo.

They met with gods and with those sent by goddesses. They encountered wild birds whose feathers were sharpened like arrows, and they had to cover their heads and drive the birds away. Then they stopped at an island sacred to Ares, and discovered three young men who had been marooned there. These men had set sail from the very land the Argonauts wanted to reach, and they were keen to join the ship and add their weight to the oars.

Jason might have hesitated to add strangers to his crew but these men were no threat to him: they were quiet and nervy, desperate for his help. They were also a potential advantage in the looming encounter with Aietes – the king who owned the golden fleece – because they were his grandsons. Even the least welcoming tyrant would surely make an exception for the men who had rescued the sons of his oldest child, Chalciope, and her late husband, Phrixus. And if Aietes did not welcome the Argonauts, he might at least be willing to negotiate with them if they arrived with his own kin as hostages.

The three young men offered to help Jason approach Colchis without being seen by their grandfather's watchmen, and to show him where he could anchor his ship in secret. They waited until they were onboard before they began to offer warnings. They understood why Jason wanted to claim the fleece, but they were certain the king would never give it up. If the Argonauts wanted to take it, they would need more than quick wits and brave hearts.

The men sailed past a place they had thought only a myth: where Prometheus was chained to a mountain, his liver pecked away every day by a tireless eagle. They heard his agonized cries and the clamour of chains as he writhed against them. They rowed their ship quickly past, not wanting to bear witness.

At last, Aietes' grandsons confirmed that the coast ahead of them belonged to Colchis. They waited until nightfall, and then the boys guided them up a narrow river they would never have spotted in the darkness. They anchored their ship in the marshes, and talked late into the night about how best to approach Aietes. They could not have known that they were already being watched.

Hera, Athene and Aphrodite

her husband

The curious thing about Hera and Athene was how often they found themselves on the same side in a contest or a war, and how little camaraderie this ever generated between them. Hera tolerated Athene, who affected indifference in return. But seeing the Argo nestling in the reeds of the river Phasis, Hera approached Athene, apparently to ask for her advice.

'Daughter of Zeus, we need a plan, and I wondered if you might have thought of something. Some trickery that will let the Argonauts take the golden fleece from Aietes? There is no point in them trying to persuade him, when he is known to be such an unpleasant man. But we must think of something.'

'I have thought of so many plans.' Athene had thought of no plans, because she had been occupied elsewhere since her intervention at the Symplegades, assuming the Argonauts could take care of themselves now she had done the difficult part for them. She knew little about Aietes, other than that he was the son of Helios, the sun god. But if Hera – no stranger to violent rage – thought someone had a vile temper,

Athene thought it best to assume the man was murderously unpleasant. 'But I am not convinced any of them is the right one for the Argonauts.'

Hera almost hid the sound of irritation from her reply. 'Then we will have to ask Aphrodite for her help,' she said. 'Aietes has a daughter; she is clever and highly skilled in magical arts. If Aphrodite's boy fires his sharpest arrow at the girl, she can easily be made to fall in love with Jason. And with her advice, I think he will be able to carry the fleece back to Hellas.'

Athene had no better idea, but that didn't mean she had to like this one. 'I don't know anything about enchantment and desire,' she said. 'I don't know how they work. So you'll have to talk to her.'

Hera smiled serenely, and the two goddesses walked to the beautiful house of mighty Hephaestus, both hoping that the blacksmith god would be absent. Hera had no desire to waste time talking to her son, and Athene disliked him for reasons no one knew. But Hephaestus was a god devoted to his craft, and he would always rather spend his days hammering hot metal than lounging on a couch drinking ambrosia. His wife, on the other hand, was a great enthusiast for lounging on couches on Olympus and elsewhere. So when Hera and Athene arrived, they found her bare-shouldered, brushing her hair, almost as though she were expecting someone else who might better appreciate this view. Her expression gave no hint of disappointment that these were the visitors she had received. But she stopped the languid combing and instead plaited her hair neatly while the two goddesses waited.

'How lovely to see you both,' Aphrodite said. 'You must

131

need my help, otherwise you wouldn't be here? I can't even remember when I last saw you.'

Athene looked at the floor, because Aphrodite always made her feel like her elbows took up too much space. Hera arranged her face into politeness.

'It has been far too long, my dear. I always have so much to do as the queen of the gods, I'm sure you can imagine.'

'I'm sure I can't,' Aphrodite replied.

'Our hearts are breaking,' Hera said.

'Your . . . ?' Aphrodite frowned.

'Mine and Athene's hearts are shaken,' Hera continued. 'Because of the Argonauts.'

Aphrodite knew she had heard that name somewhere before, but it took her a moment to place it. The ship, was that it? The ship full of handsome men who she had allowed to spend time with the Lemnian women and who had refused to stay and initiate a festival in her honour. She hated them, didn't she? No, perhaps she only hated some of them. Hera had not stopped talking, but Aphrodite couldn't imagine she had missed anything important.

'I'm sure you know about Jason and his crew, setting sail to find the golden fleece,' Hera said. 'They have reached Colchis and hidden their ship on the river, and I am so worried about them I can think of little else. You must remember how devoted I am to Jason?'

Aphrodite murmured something noncommittal but – as so often – Hera interpreted it as encouragement.

'Jason is my best means of punishing Pelias,' Hera said.

Athene was surprised. 'Isn't that Jason's uncle?' she asked. 'Why do you want to punish him?' If she had not been looking at the floor she might have noticed a tiny shake of Aphrodite's head.

'Pelias has shown contempt for me,' Hera snarled. 'He failed to honour my altars, he failed to offer me sufficient sacrifices, he failed to give me the respect I deserve, as queen of the gods. You remember he killed his own step-mother at my altar, even as she clung to the warm stone of my feet? He will not behave in such a way and continue to prosper as king of Iolcus. I will not allow it.'

'Well, why don't you just drive him mad?' asked Athene. 'Or destroy his city? Or turn him into a snake?'

'Because I want to do something special for Pelias,' Hera smiled. 'So that no one ever does something so stupid again. And it is through Jason that I will exact my revenge. And because of that,' she turned her large brown eyes back to Aphrodite, 'I need your help. And Athene needs your help.' There was a pause before Athene realized Hera expected her to say something, so she nodded. Aphrodite assumed Hera had finished, but she had not.

'And anyway, Jason deserves to be rewarded for being a kind young man.'

Aphrodite glanced at Athene and saw the same shadow of confusion cross her face. Of all the things anyone expected Hera to champion, kindness was perhaps the least likely. Hera was usually motivated by vengeance and icy rage.

'Is he kind?' asked Athene. 'And that's something you want to encourage?'

Hera allowed herself the faintest expression of surprise. 'Of course,' she said. 'I was in the mountains near Iolcus a few years ago, in the winter. I'm surprised you don't remember.'

'Oh,' said Athene. 'I think I wasn't interested.'

Hera didn't want to pick fights until she had what she needed, but her patience with both goddesses was ebbing. 'It was when your father wanted us to test mortals and find the virtuous ones,' she said.

'Did he?' said Athene. 'I didn't test anyone.'

'Nor did I,' Aphrodite smiled. Hera resisted the urge to say that no one would choose Aphrodite to judge anyone's virtue, since her own was in short supply.

'I suppose it was something he only asked the senior Olympians to do,' she said. 'I went to the mountains—'

'You said,' Athene interrupted. She hated to hear anything more than once, it made her feel like a weasel trapped in a cage.

'Beside the Anauros in flood,' Hera continued. 'I was disguised, of course, as a helpless old woman.'

'And was that convincing?' Aphrodite smiled in a way that concealed nothing of her opinion of Hera's usual appearance.

'Of course,' Hera said. 'There was snow on the mountain peaks, the rivers were in full spate, the paths were treacherous with ice.'

'Winter, you said.' Athene felt suddenly wearied by this and all conversations, and wanted to be where other people were not.

'Jason found me on the banks of the Anauros,' said Hera.

'It was flooded, yes.'

'And he offered to carry me across the river on his shoulders,' Hera finished.

'Men are always offering to carry me,' Aphrodite said. 'How did you know he was virtuous? Oh. Did he swing you over his shoulder? How awful.'

'He lifted me carefully onto his shoulders.' Hera was failing to conceal her irritation now. 'Like a precious statue. And he carried me across the swollen river and put me down on the opposite bank very gently.'

'And you didn't mind?' Aphrodite asked.

'I would protect Jason even if he sailed the Argo down to Hades and tried to recruit Ixion to its crew.'

'Which one is Ixion?' Athene often found Hera discussing things that had happened before she – a relative latecomer to Olympus, as the other gods never tired of pointing out – was even born.

'Ixion is the one Hera doesn't like,' said Aphrodite, who also couldn't remember who he was, but didn't want to hear any more about him.

'He assaulted me,' Hera began.

'Oh, one of those ones,' Athene nodded. 'I hate them.'

'He is bound to a wheel that never stops spinning,' Hera said.

'Well, then he would make a terrible Argonaut,' Athene replied. 'I don't see how he could even row.'

'How can I help you?' asked Aphrodite. Hera smiled patiently.

'Nothing difficult at all,' she said. 'Just persuade your son Eros to fire one of his lovely arrows at the daughter of Aietes. She is the key to Jason's quest, I am certain of it. If she helps him, he will have the fleece, he will bring it back to Iolcus. Otherwise, I am not convinced he'll succeed. He is a kind man, but she is . . .' Hera paused. 'She reminds me a little of myself.'

'Oh, if you want help from Eros, you're better off asking him yourself,' Aphrodite replied. 'He doesn't listen to me any more, he's disobedient for the sake of it. I have threatened more than once to take his bow and his spiteful little arrows and snap them all into kindling.'

'That's your mistake,' said Athene.

'What is?' Aphrodite flushed.

'You shouldn't threaten to do anything more than once,' Athene continued. 'If you threaten it, you have to be willing to do it. Otherwise, he knows you don't mean it and he'll just ignore you.'

Aphrodite looked at her in confusion. 'But if I broke his bow and arrows, he wouldn't be able to use them to help the other gods in their plans,' she said.

Athene shrugged. 'We'd plan differently.'

'You wouldn't understand,' Aphrodite snapped. 'You don't even have children.'

'I know how to threaten people properly,' said Athene.

'So does he!' cried Aphrodite. 'He threatened me with his arrows just the other day.'

'I'm sure you can persuade him,' Hera said. 'When he knows it is for us.' She waved a generous hand to include Athene.

'Very well,' Aphrodite said. 'I will do my best. Since it's for you.'

'As soon as you can,' Hera said.

'Of course,' replied Aphrodite, allowing herself to believe it had been a question.

'He will stop this petulance and disobedience.' Hera's eyes were those of a predator. 'You won't see it from him again.'

And Aphrodite knew it was the truth.

*

When the goddess of love approached her son, she came with a bribe. What need had Zeus of his childhood toys now? He would never think of it, so it would never occur to him to ask where it had gone. Aphrodite had found it in her chamber, and she knew who must have left it there. It was beautiful and intricate enough to have been made by her husband, but it was not a gift from Hephaestus. It was a golden sphere, small enough to hold in her hand, with a pleasing weight to it. She held it up and watched the light play across its gleaming surface. A dark blue pattern twisted about the gold, like the night sky embracing a low moon. No stranger to desire, she wanted it for herself. But she knew who it was for, and she admired its loveliness one more time, before hiding it behind a pile of cushions.

She found Eros cheating at some game he was playing with Ganymede, a boy Zeus had stolen from his homeland. Ganymede was no match for the deviousness of any god, least of all Aphrodite's deceitful boy. She watched the boredom settle on her son's face, punctuated by small bursts of glee when he saw Ganymede in real distress.

'Stop tormenting a mortal boy,' Aphrodite said. 'What possible satisfaction is there in beating a fool in a battle of wits?'

'Since when did you care about the feelings of a mortal boy?' retorted Eros.

'I don't care about them,' she replied. 'I'm suggesting that you are making yourself look petty and foolish and that if you continue to hurt the feelings of one of Zeus' favourites, he may change his mind about the toy I am going to give you.'

Boredom turned to greed and her son's eyes suddenly glittered with desire.

'What toy? Show me.'

Aphrodite smiled with real pleasure. 'I didn't bring it to show you, because you are a bully and a thief,' she said. 'So you will have to trust your mother to tell you the truth. It is a bright golden orb, and it belonged to Zeus when he was a baby. It was once his favourite plaything.' She shooed Ganymede away. 'It is intricately crafted in two halves, but you will never see the joins, because there is a deep blue stripe wrapped around them. When you throw it into the air, it will leave a golden trail in its wake, like a comet.'

'Give it to me!' Eros rarely waited for anything he wanted.

'You shall have it, dearest,' his mother replied. 'But first you must shoot one of your sharpest arrows into the heart of the daughter of Aietes.' She watched the name find its home in his mind: he knew who he must injure.

'Who do you want her to love?' he asked, with the confidence of an athlete who never missed his mark.

'Jason,' said Aphrodite.

Eros smirked. 'I thought you liked him.'

Aphrodite shrugged. She could take or leave most mortals, as her son well knew.

'Oh, it's her you hate?'

'If you want the ball, you know what to do,' she said. And suddenly he was bunching his hands in her tunic, begging her for the toy now, this moment. But she didn't chastise him for creasing her dress, or stamp on his bare feet. She stroked his face and whispered in his ear that she promised the toy would be his the instant he had carried out her wishes. Eros pulled away and looked at her. He nodded, and let go of her dress. The shape of his fists held for a moment in the fabric, and then disappeared. Picking up his bow and quiver, he flew off without a word.

Hera

and children,

What else was left for the queen of the gods to arrange? She sat on a low couch, considering her plans. She didn't need to inspire Jason to leave his ship and visit the palace of Aietes: she could surely rely on his own ambition to lead him towards the fleece. She thought for a moment, then sent him a brief vision as a dream, of him escorting the sons of Phrixus to reunite them with their grandfather. It was better to underestimate mortals than overestimate them, in Hera's experience.

Then she needed to keep Aietes' daughter in the palace the following day, so she would meet Jason before he had even spoken to her father. Where did she usually spend her days? Hera wondered. She consulted her spies and discovered that the girl was not just skilful and clever but was also devout: she spent her days in service to Hecate. Hera wondered if the goddess would protect her priestess. Hecate was powerful, even Hera admitted that. If she chose to dwell on Olympus, it might have been a source of friction between them. Happily, the witch goddess made her home in the Underworld, so Hera rarely saw her and was rarely reminded of her. But surely Hecate would not begrudge her acolyte a little passion? Hera wondered how she would respond if one of her priestesses abandoned her temple for a man. Well, perhaps the witch goddess had lower expectations than she did. Besides, she would surely assume that Aphrodite was responsible, so it scarcely mattered.

But now a new concern arose: would the Colchians welcome Jason and the return of their missing sons? Hera sighed. She couldn't rely on it, she supposed. Very well, then she would cover them in mist as they approached Colchis, only allowing it to disperse when they reached the palace. Another problem solved. And then, would the captain of the Argonauts recognize the wealth and power wielded by the man who held the precious fleece?

Of course he would. Hera's son Hephaestus had built the palace himself, according to his own design: a vast metal door stood at its centre, which even a mortal man would realize had been made by the blacksmith god. And how could any man fail to be dazzled by the four fountains, which poured forth water, perfume, milk and wine? Jason had seen nothing so miraculous when he was growing up in Iolcus. He would approach Aietes in the proper way, as the inhabitant of such a palace could only be favoured by the gods.

Hera had left almost nothing to chance.

Toxeuma

pleasing the citizens

The arrow had only one purpose and it had been waiting for a long time. Eros carried his quiver so casually, as though any arrow would serve him equally well. But this had never been the case. Some mortals – some gods, even – were happy to be hit, square in the chest. Some had been longing to experience limb-loosening desire. They found their lives humdrum – not everyone was cut out for heroics, after all – and the faintest brush of the tip of one of these arrows would be their closest encounter with the divine.

And Eros was not always profligate with his arrows, any more than his mother was invariably cruel. If love was anything at all, it was unpredictable. Everyone knew of a woman who had fallen in love with a man who loved her back. Sometimes, it was even the same man as her husband. And even if these examples were rare, there were other desirable outcomes. When Heracles fell in love with Hylas, he had the power and strength to seize what he wanted. The relationship looked very different from Hylas' perspective, no doubt, but the arrow did not concern itself with details like this. All love is war, if you are one of the weapons.

Eros had picked dart after dart from his quiver, while this arrow remained unchosen. It had grown used to the disappointment of seeing another gold tip push past it. It had always believed its moment would come, but it had always been mistaken. It had stopped hoping, because hope was – in its way – as painful as love.

The god had snatched up his bow and quiver and flown quickly to a place that the arrow knew – though it could not say how – would be its home. Eros landed in a crowded courtyard, and the arrow heard a great hubbub surrounding them. A woman – a young woman – had screamed, but not with fear. With something else, perhaps tinged with fear. Another woman had come running to her aid, but then she screamed too and her voice was filled with relief, the opposite of fear. Men and women alike had hurried into the courtyard and everyone was speaking at once. But Eros landed invisible among them. The arrows were jostled as he took his position at a door post; he reached his hand over his shoulder as he knelt at the foot of the young hero who could not see him.

And then the arrow which had gone unchosen for so long – the arrow that was remarkable for the strength and depth of sorrow it carried within itself, so great that the god himself had shunned it for hundreds of years, unable to bear its touch on his perfect skin – this arrow found itself drawn from the quiver and fitted to the bow. It scarcely had a moment to feel the rays of Helios warming its golden feathers, and then it was flying through the bright air to find its mark.

Medea

to whose land

The first time I saw him, I screamed with the shock of seeing strangers – men – inside our home. My father is a suspicious and fearful man, though he hides it behind cruelty and rage. But we never see foreigners here; the last time was Phrixus. And he would never have been welcomed by my father if Zeus hadn't sent Hermes himself to tell Aietes that the boy on the golden ram must be given a warm reception, must be treated like a friend, not a stranger.

But then my shock was compounded because the three foreigners were accompanied by three faces I have known since they were babies: my nephews Argos, Melas and Phrontis. And since their mother and I had wept when they set sail – to claim an inheritance, they said, far away – thinking we might never see them again, it was startling and wonderful to have them back with us so soon.

So yes, I screamed with the joy of seeing my nephews who I thought I might never see again. And I screamed with fear at the sight of three men I didn't know. And he heard my cry and he started, because he wasn't expecting such a sound, I suppose. Handsome men get used to being greeted with smiles and laughter. He was used to that for a long time.

The courtyard filled with people – my sister, weeping for the reunion with her sons; my mother, watchful and silent; my father, his black brows drawn into a hostile line. Slaves and guards came running, each of them with the same fear on his face. Aietes would demand an explanation for how these men suddenly appeared in the centre of his divinely wrought palace with no one noticing until I saw them. To the strangers, they probably conveyed efficiency. But those of us who knew my father were witnessing men wondering whose lives would pay for such an intrusion.

I had no warning that they were coming. No message from my goddess, wrapped in riddles that never puzzle me for long. She had told me that my sister's boys would be safe and their journey short, which had now proven true. But she didn't tell me about the three strangers. She didn't tell me about him.

In all the noise and confusion, I felt something terrible happen that I couldn't – can't – explain. When I was a child, I saw a man helping to raise a block of stone to the top of a high column. There was a team of men, I think, but one was behind the pillar so I couldn't see him. Others were further away in the shadows, but all of them must have been pulling on ropes. The man I was watching was right in the centre of the courtyard in the blazing sun, and he was calling out words I didn't understand. Now, I realize that he was telling each man how much more to tug on the heavy ropes so as to centre the stone on its plinth. But one of the ropes snapped, and the block slid from its perch and it fell so fast that the man had no time to move. The stone

145

seemed to bounce off his head – my sister says I laughed at the sight of it – but of course it must have bounced off the pillar in front of him, or he would have been crushed.

Everyone ran over to him, reaching out their hands to grasp his arms and check he was still alive. Which he was, he was even still standing. But the stone must have caught a glancing blow on the side of his head, because when he collapsed later, there was a rivulet of blood coming from his left ear, buried under his dark hair. And in the time in between sustaining the injury and falling to his knees, he was unmade before my eyes. His mouth moved but he couldn't find any words. His eyes rolled but they could not seem to focus. His comrades spoke to him, but if he heard them, he gave no sign of it. He was a shell, where before he had been a living creature.

And all I know about the day Jason arrived in Colchis is this: a few moments after I saw him (not the first moment, not right away, but then when it happened, for ever), some unseen object hit me with the force of a falling rock. And I was stupefied, lethally so. The only question that remained was how long it would take me to die.

I have no recollection of what my father said to my nephews. I suppose he asked them why they had come back so soon, what had happened to their great voyage to distant lands. I know they must have explained that they were shipwrecked and that the men of the Argo – three of whom stood beside them now – had rescued them.

It was the oldest boy who replied. He had the confidence to answer the king, but he lacked the cunning that would have told him what Aietes was asking. Poor, foolish boy: did he really think Aietes was relieved to have them back?

Perhaps he did. But my father would not thank the Argonauts for returning his missing grandsons. The first thing I remember hearing the boy say was that he and the ship's captain were related, his face open and excited as he explained. Jason's father, Aeson, was some sort of cousin to their father, Phrixus.

It was the first time I ever heard his name – Jason, son of Aeson – and all I wanted to do was take this piece of knowledge away with me and warm my hands on it. Because when I looked at him, I became fully aware that the blow I had sustained – the unseen force that had struck me so hard I do not know how I remained on my feet – was related in some way to this stranger. The sickening sense that my body might collapse beneath me, that I might slide down to the dust at my feet, this ebbed when my eyes were on him. But the awful sickness, the fever that made me feel hot and shivering at once, that only increased. I felt that if he took a single step nearer, I would know what had happened and how he had poisoned me.

But he did not take a step nearer. He stood, hopeful, as my nephew related the story of their sibling grandfathers to Aietes, thinking he would be pleased. I can barely describe Jason's appearance that day because my eyes were stinging as though I were staring at my own grandfather, Helios, as he flew high above us. I have the impression of curling black hair, dark eyes and the dark skin of a man who has been sailing for many days. But the detail of his face – the way his upper lip curved slightly when he listened, as though the words were waiting to pour forth; the way he held himself with shyness instead of confidence, even though he was the captain of a great crew of heroes; the way his

147

eyes seemed equally ready to weep or laugh – I cannot remember any of these from that day in Colchis. They are set in my mind from later. And I find when I think of him, it is never like this: us facing one another, me gazing at him as he concentrates on the man he needs to impress. I always think of him in profile, lying beside me.

Argos was now explaining that the whole of Jason's crew were heroes, the sons of gods and goddesses, on a quest to obtain the golden fleece from my father and return it to Hellas. I could not take my eyes from Jason, but I felt my sister stiffen beside me. How could these boys be so naive? We had protected them, of course, when their father died. We told them it was a short illness, we gave no hint of what had happened to poor, stupid Phrixus. But they had grown up in Aietes' palace, they knew something of his paranoia, his cruelty, his cupidity. The idea that he might be willing to part with the fleece was itself absurd. The thought that he would be impressed by a boat filled with heroes rather than threatened and angered was fanciful. And his response was exactly as my sister and I would have predicted, even if her foolish sons did not.

Aietes barely looked at his grandsons.

'Can you have been so stupid as to guide these thieves into my palace?' he snarled. 'When they so clearly mean your country, your king nothing but harm. How dare they come here intending to steal what belongs to me, to Colchis? You flaunt their divine connections as though I do not have my own. They want to take my fleece back to Hellas? The fleece cannot be returned to somewhere it has never been: that skin was created here in my country, when Phrixus sacrificed his ram to Ares. It is mine. I will keep it, and the good fortune it brings to all of Colchis. If these raiders had not shared my food and wine, know this: I would cut off their hands and cut out their tongues, and I would send them back to their crew as a warning of what happens to those who would steal from Aietes.'

I would come to know very well that Jason is never calmer or more charming than when his safety is threatened. But this was the first time I heard him speak, and the dizziness almost overwhelmed me. He had a beautiful voice, soft and lilting.

'Forgive us, king, we mean you no harm. We have not travelled to your shores by choice: we were sent on this terrible quest by a cruel king. We would not attempt to take what belongs to you. Rather, we were hoping to offer you an exchange: our fighting prowess is at your service. We will fight any enemies you have, we will pitch our strength against theirs to assist you. You could gain whatever territory you like. In return for this, we hoped you might grant us the fleece as a reward.'

Of course my father would not be swayed by honeyed words from this man he didn't trust. But the smile on his face was more terrible than the fury which preceded it.

'You say you are sons of gods, and so you are my equals. In which case, who am I to keep you from the object of your quest, just because I am its rightful owner? You may take the fleece, so let no one say that I am as cruel as your Hellene king. But first I must test the truth of your claims.'

The heat that had been pulsing through my veins evaporated. In its place came a clammy cold. I already knew that whatever my father was about to propose would cause the death of this man.

149

'I will ask no more of you than I do myself,' Aietes continued. 'But you must complete this task. I have two bronze bulls, made for me by the god Hephaestus, when he built this palace.'

Jason and his men looked around them in astonishment, as though this impossible statement now resolved their unspoken confusion: how could mortals live in a palace like this, where perfume and wine flowed from the fountains like water?

'These bulls will pull a bronze plough across the field that is sacred to Ares. It is hard ground, as you would imagine: Ares would hardly be satisfied with anything less. First, you must yoke them. But be warned: they breathe fire, as you might expect from the divine blacksmith. Attach the plough, draw it across the field. Then you will sow the teeth of a giant snake, and they will produce a crop of armed fighters. As they rise to attack, you must scythe them with your spear. You will plough the field and cut down the earth-born men in a single day, just as I do. If you show yourself to be my equal – as the boy has claimed you are – you will have no difficulty, and I will give you the fleece to take to Hellas. Otherwise, it will remain here: the son of Helios will not yield to a lesser man.'

The entire courtyard was silent, but I could hear a rushing sound in my ears and I thought I was about to faint. Jason had no choice but to agree to this vicious proposal, but he knew he was agreeing to his own death. The fear and sorrow in his voice were clear to all, and I knew how my father would be enjoying this display of cowardice.

'Go back to your ship,' the king told Jason. 'Tell your men that Aietes has given you a simple choice, and that you may either live up to your reputation, or you may skulk back home. Either way, I shall not be troubled by any more Hellenes thinking they have the right to what belongs to Colchis.'

Jason and his two comrades turned to leave, along with Argos. My younger nephews remained beside their mother, and I split in two: my eyes and my thoughts followed Jason as he walked away, graceful and strong. My heart – burning my ribs like blackened embers – stayed with me.

My sister and her boys hurried away from the courtyard without saying a word: Chalciope knew my father's moods better than anyone, and she would not have her sons anywhere in sight, if she could avoid it. Aietes would be in a murderous temper for days now. He did not notice them leave, he was issuing orders to his guards to punish the men who had somehow failed to notice the strangers arrive. They would die by stoning at the hands of their comrades: it was always my father's way to make his underlings turn on one another. Men who have no one to trust must trust their king, was his belief.

I staggered to my chamber, where I wept freely but without understanding. I wanted to talk to my sister but I could barely see to stand. Everything seemed unfamiliar and unstable: I felt that the walls would melt away and expose my inexplicable grief for all to see. How could I be so distressed by the fate of a man I had never even met? How could he be more real for me than the bed on which I lay? I felt as though I could stretch my fingers out and the pillows around me would dissolve into the floor. But the face of a man I had seen once was so solid that I could have sculpted it from clay. I could have repeated his every word, every pause, every breath from memory. And how could this man – this dazzling man who Aietes taunted as inferior when anyone could see he was without equal – how could he die tomorrow, to satiate my father's endless cruelty? This must be the reason for the agony I felt: a great man, a favourite of the gods, was about to meet a senseless death.

I prayed to my goddess Hecate, but I scarcely knew what I wanted to say because I knew so little about the man whose fate caused me such horror. Was I trying to save the best of heroes, or the most cowardly of men? I did not know. All I knew was that he would die. So I begged her to intercede, please, and take him home. Let him slink away from Colchis, let him leave my father gloating about the worthless men of Hellas who did not dare take up his challenge. No pride, no name was so important as to be worth this beautiful man's death. Let him go. If he must stay, if he must be so rash as to set himself against my father's lethal will, let him die quickly, and let him know that it brought me no pleasure to see him cut down this way.

I repeated my prayer over and over. I had been a priestess to the goddess for so long, I sometimes believed I knew her will, as much as a mortal can ever know the mind of a goddess. I had been her keenest disciple from the first day I entered her temple: I served her every day. But as I lay there beseeching her, asking again and again if she would save the life of this stranger – this best or worst of men – I could sense nothing from Hecate. If she heard me, she was silent.

Argo

she came

Jason and his shipmates returned to the Argo, alongside his comrades and Argos, the oldest son of Phrixus. Their beautiful ship had sustained a little damage on the voyage, but it was scarcely noticeable now. You would still have said she was a gift from the gods. But when Jason climbed onboard, you would no longer have mistaken him for Apollo. His skin was clammy, as though fever had taken him, and fear had settled behind his eyes. The Argonauts gathered quickly to find out what had happened.

Jason explained the offer Aietes had made, and that he had agreed to it, despite believing that he would certainly die. The men were quiet, none of them able to imagine a better outcome. But when he finished speaking, first one, another, then two more offered to attempt the tasks in his stead. The Argo – as would be agreed by every poet who sang of her journey – was not short of courage. But it was Argos – so nearly her namesake that they seemed destined to sail together – who had another idea.

'New friends, before we all despair, I think there is one potential source of help. There is a young woman living in the palace, who has remarkable magical prowess. She has been taught by Hecate herself – goddess of the darkest powers – she knows the properties of every plant. She can make the most powerful drugs, she can stop rivers in full flood, she can change the path of a racing fire. The stars and the moon bow to her will, if she chooses. I believe she could be the difference between life and death for Jason. And I believe my mother could persuade her: they are sisters.'

The Argonauts began murmuring among themselves: was this the salvation they sought? Or was it unthinkable to put the success of their quest into the hands of a woman, and a foreign woman at that? Was it a trap? They had met the sons of Phrixus only a few days earlier: had this king sent them out to waylay the Argo and deceive her crew? As they discussed the possibilities, they heard a sudden cry overhead.

Peleia

in flight,

The little dove had been feeling rather sorry for herself, in the days since her lucky escape from the Symplegades. She had been uprooted from her home, locked in a cage, set free into a terrifying trap of water and clashing rocks and – when she had finally found a safe harbour in a small coastal tree – it had taken her many days to recover. She had only just begun to feel like her former self when another disaster befell her. She had fluttered down from a sheltered branch of her tree to peck at what she thought might be seeds, though the vegetation here was different from what she was used to eating. Suddenly, she heard a beating sound and felt an awful pain in her wings, and she was soaring up into the sky. She tilted her head to see that she was caught in the talons of an enormous hawk.

The dove could not free herself, the hawk's talons were piercing her shoulders. She could do nothing but wait for the hawk to snap its mighty beak straight through her neck. She had no idea how long she was held in this suspended anguish, but suddenly she was falling through the air and she could not even flap her wings to save herself because

155

they were numb and wouldn't move. Just as she expected to hit the surface of the ocean, she landed on something soft: the tunic of a seated man. The little bird could scarcely believe she had avoided death again, and she looked around her, trying to assess her new situation. The man was sitting on a boat, and it looked uncomfortably familiar. Men were staring at her, and she felt anxious again, wondering if they might be so hungry as to eat her. But the man who had caught her on his lap was looking at her in astonishment. Another man was talking in a loud voice, gesturing at her and then up at the sky from which she had fallen.

The dove could not begin to understand, of course, that she had fallen from the claws of a hawk into the lap of Jason, captain of the Argo. She did not understand that the man who was speaking now claimed to be able to read omens, and was saying that she was the bird sacred to Cyprian Aphrodite. She had fallen from the grip of a cruel predator, and she symbolized the notion that the Argonauts must now accept that brute strength alone would not help their captain in his next trial. Jason needed the assistance of a more delicate creature, a young woman, if he was to win through. And perhaps Aphrodite would help him to win the girl over, if her sacred bird was literally landing on him. Phineus the seer had told them that their journey home again depended on the goddess.

The little bird heard the general agreement of these men, though she could not identify it. She could identify a man who was now shouting as a threat, because loud noises were always a threat. But she didn't know that he was complaining that he must have set sail with women, not men, if the crew of the Argo really intended to trust the success of their mission to Aphrodite. She didn't know he was furious that they were even considering a plan to ask a young woman for help.

Perhaps the bird sensed the tension dissipate as a man called Argos left to beg his mother to help his friends, but perhaps she did not. She did, however, recognize the face of the man who had captured and caged her before, and she fluttered her wings desperately, trying to escape this horrifying ship for the second time. The man on whom she had landed seemed amused by her fruitless endeavours, and he stood, carrying her in his hands. The dove felt panic rising within her, but the man climbed down from the ship and found a tree with several low branches and many more overhead. He put the bird carefully onto a branch near the trunk, and made sure she was safely perched there before he stood back.

Chalciope

helping Jason

The first time my world ended was when my husband died. Phrixus was not a perfect man, by any means, but he was always loving and kind. If you had grown up where I have grown up – with my father and king – you would value these qualities in a man above all others. Phrixus wasn't very clever or ambitious. He didn't know how to cope with my father nor did he ever recover from the unhappiness of losing his own. He was scared of Aietes and sometimes scared of his own sons. I often used to think he would have been happier with daughters, because he had loved his sister Helle so much. Phrixus had none of the skills needed to survive palace life in Colchis; he was incapable of dissembling in the way my father demanded of us all. One day Aietes would want support for a catastrophic plan, the next day he would deny ever having spoken of it. You could never show fear, surprise or criticism at these changes of mind; you had to agree with whatever he said at the time.

Phrixus was naive in ways I found hard to understand. How – when he had fled his own home after his father had sworn to kill him – could he assume that my father would be kind? Aietes scarcely trusted my brother, Apsyrtus. Medea was too young to be a threat, and I was not worth considering. But when I tried to explain my father's suspicions would therefore be directed at Phrixus and our sons, Phrixus wouldn't believe it. Your father welcomed me when I was a refugee, he said. I tried to make him see that this was because he had arrived on the back of a magical creature, that even Aietes would think twice before refusing to help someone who clearly had the gods' favour. But I couldn't shake his belief that Aietes was a fair man beneath his bluster. He believed this until my father had him slowly poisoned, and even then Phrixus thought he must have a wasting sickness.

Medea and I knew better: she recognized the symptoms of the poison, but it had no antidote. And so I watched my husband sicken and die, and I kept the truth from my sons because it was the best way to keep them safe. And even that wasn't enough. When a messenger arrived from the distant shores of some island in the west, saying they had an inheritance to claim on their father's side, my sister and I were sceptical, of course. We tried to persuade my sons that they should stay, that nothing across the distant Aegean could bring them anything but sorrow. But they were so trusting, so sure that Aietes would thank them for bringing back their patrimony to Colchis. The moment he agreed to their journey, I began to grieve. If my father was agreeing to it, he believed – or more probably knew – they wouldn't survive.

I could not weep openly, or he would have called me a traitor. Medea was so afraid she would lose me too that she kept me to my room, telling even the slaves that I was sick with a contagion only she could treat. There was no one we could trust to keep our secrets but each other. So when the boys returned, I was filled with joy and relief but also fear. It was all too apparent from the way Aietes reacted that he had not expected them to return, and certainly not to bring strangers with them. His offer to their captain to attempt tasks that would certainly kill him was not sincere: the boy will die tomorrow or the next day, whenever he tries to perform the impossible. And when he dies, Aietes will expend his rage on burning their ship and killing its crew. The only question is whether my boys will be counted among the bodies.

It would be rash to believe that Aietes would not kill his only grandsons. And I cannot reason with him, remind him that they share his blood, that their glory reflects on him. Such considerations – so important to other kings – would not affect Aietes at all. He has a son, he has no need of mine. Since they returned, only one thought has plagued me: how can I save them? It plays in my head like an incessant drum. If the stranger dies, his ship becomes the next target of my father's wrath. So even before Argos – my oldest boy, the most worldly, perhaps – came to me that night, pleading with me to intercede with my sister to protect his friend, I had planned to do exactly this. Medea can help us, if she chooses. And though she has no reason to help the stranger, she will surely act to protect my boys.

*

Medea tried to find refuge from misery in sleep, but the sickness was unrelenting. She dreamed that the man had come to Colchis to claim her rather than the fleece, and she took on the challenge of the bronze-footed bulls to help him. She passed every test, but her father declared the challenge void, because the stranger had not completed the tasks himself. Medea was forced to choose between the man she loved and the family she cherished, and the pain of abandoning her parents woke her and she wept with guilt and grief.

She rose from her bed and went to the door, wanting to rush to her sister and seek comfort, but she was too ashamed. What would she say? That she burned with love for a man she didn't know? That she dreamed of leaving her family here on Colchis and accompanying this stranger back to his homeland? Her cheeks reddened as she imagined herself saying the words. She could not do it. She lifted her hand from the door and turned back to her bed. Lying down, she wept as though the man really were her husband and had died on his quest, leaving her bereaved before they could even have a child.

A young woman opened the door, planning to check that Medea had everything she needed for the night. Seeing the princess sobbing on her bed, the girl withdrew noiselessly. She ran along the corridor, burning with the news.

*

I have always known it was worth bribing slaves. You cannot leave anything to chance here. Anyone could be spying on us for my father. Though my sister would not be so suspicious: she loves our parents, even though she knows Aietes killed Phrixus. And she believes they return her love, although it is perfectly clear that Aietes cares for no one

161

but himself. It is lucky, then, that I have some sway over the slaves who tend the women's quarters, so that the girl who saw my sister in tears came to me and not to my father. Who knows what conclusion he would have drawn from the tale of his young daughter crying into her pillows? I doubt it would have been good for Medea or for my sons.

I hurried to my sister's chamber and found her exactly as the girl had described: swollen eyes lost in her puffy face. I asked her what had happened and why she was grieving so piteously. Medea has a powerful connection to her goddess, so she often knows more than anyone. I couldn't tell if she was ill and in pain, or if her agonies were caused by fear of something that Aietes might be planning. She could not answer at first, the words seemed to stick behind her tongue. But then, she confessed everything.

'Beloved sister,' she said, through more tears. 'I have had awful nightmares, I cannot describe them. But it has left me with a terrible anxiety that something might happen to your sons. I could not bear to see you afflicted by further grief after you lost your dear husband.'

I sank onto her bed and embraced her.

'Will you help me? Will you swear to keep this secret and help me protect my boys?'

Medea is virtually the same age as my sons, and I know she loves them like brothers. In fact, she probably loves them more deeply than she does our brother Apsyrtus, who has always been our father's favourite, of course, and has kept himself distant from us. Doubtless for the same reason that I bribe the slaves: he would not want his own favoured position to be damaged by anything my family did.

'What can I do?' Medea asked. There was something

dancing behind her eyes, and it took me a moment to realize it was hope. My poor, dear sister. She really had been consumed with grief at the thought of losing her nephews. 'Any wisdom, any strength I have: it is all at your disposal. I don't know what I can do to protect the boys but I will do whatever I can, you know that.'

I held her more tightly and murmured my request into her ear. Some words are too dangerous to speak out loud, and these were certainly treason.

'Could you help the stranger? The tasks Aietes has set him will cost him his life and then our father will turn on the rest of the crew, my sons included. You know this already. But you have such powers, your goddess has such wisdom. You could find some protection for him, you could give him what he needs so he will survive the day. Aietes will not be able to go back on his word when he has publicly sworn to give them the fleece if Jason completes the task. He would be committing perjury if he did, he will not take the risk of angering Zeus.'

Medea said nothing, but continued to cry into my shoulder.

'The stranger has asked for your help,' I added. 'Argos came to me and begged me to ask you.'

Finally, her sobbing abated. After a few moments she raised her head and looked into my eyes. Her face was blotched with red.

'The stranger asked for my help,' she said. 'And Argos asked for help, and now you. No priestess of Hecate could refuse a three-headed request like this. So let me make you the strongest promise. I swear that I will never again see the golden light of day – of our grandfather, Helios – if I ever put anything before the safety of you and your sons. You are more of a mother to me than a sister; they are brothers more than nephews. You must keep my secret as I will keep yours. But tell Argos this: I will go to the temple of Hecate at first light. I will have what the stranger needs to survive his encounter with the bulls. Our parents will know nothing about it.'

I held her again and thanked her for her love and her loyalty.

Medea

in everything.

I could not sleep after speaking to my sister.

My limbs were tingling with the knowledge that I would see the stranger in the morning, that I would meet him, alone. The pain I had felt almost since the moment I saw him was in abeyance, like a hunger being fed. But just as I thought this, the agony redoubled through my chest: what if he died tomorrow? Fire rushed under my skin. Could I save him? Did I know enough magic, did I have the right ingredients? I needed to think, but my mind was so caught up in fear that I could barely concentrate.

I sat on the edge of the bed, and traced my fingers across the golden threads that marked out a meandering pattern around the edge of the crimson blanket. I had been doing this since I was a child, following the golden line with my hand, trying to get from one corner to the next without losing track. It made me wish I had stayed a child, had never reached the age where this man could torment me. Artemis takes the lives of some young girls: you hear parents praying to her in the darkest night, begging her to spare their daughters. Now I wondered if she had really spared me, when the alternative to her quick arrows was this awful burning. This man must have been brought to Colchis by a god, I thought. And then I corrected myself: a god, or a Fury. What else could have caused me such grief?

I must let him die. That was the only possible course of action available to me, whatever my sister wanted. If his fate was to meet his death in the sacred field of Ares on the orders of my father, so be it. I could not avert it, and even trying to do so would be dangerous. How could I treat him with any of my drugs and escape the attention of my parents? Whatever I used to help him, it would be obvious that I had done so: my father is nobody's fool.

But if I let him die, then what happens? Will the pain of not having him recede? Of course it won't. It will intensify. Not only will I not have him, I will have lost any possibility of having him. And how would I grieve for him when he is nothing to me? Who would understand the pain I suffered?

So I cannot help him without incurring suspicion, and if I do nothing, he will die. These are the irreconcilable truths. My suffering is intolerable either way. So what does that leave me? Suicide is the only option. I can attach a noose to the beam of this roof and end my life by hanging. I can mix a painless concoction to take my life another way. Surely this would be the best way out of my hateful dilemma.

Except, no. It would do nothing to save me from the mockery that would be heaped upon me after death. What kind of woman, the Colchians would ask, ends her life over love for a stranger? A man she has never even spoken to, a man she never saw before today? Would they conclude that I had been cursed by a goddess, or would they just pour contempt over my cooling corpse? Death seems the best answer, but it is no good either.

I raised my weary bones and walked across the room. A large wooden chest contained a smaller box, in which I stored all the plants and other drugs I needed for my art. I lifted out the box, and I placed it on the lid of the chest. It was familiar and pungent, the sweet spices and acrid roots mingled. None of the slaves would ever touch it, they knew enough about its contents. Without looking I could have reached inside and pulled out a small flask that would have ended everything within ten heartbeats. I could see it in my mind: a pale, cloudy bottle containing a dark liquid harvested with a silver knife under the thinnest moon. I took a breath in, waited, then exhaled. Did I really want to die? I knew the poison would work: I had seen it used on a wild dog. It was quick, but it was far from painless.

And then unwanted thoughts rushed into my mind: memories of playing with my nephews when we were all children together, the brightness of the sun gleaming above us all. Yes, Hades would free me from my current agonies, but how much would he steal? Could I really choose never to see my friends, my family again? When I thought of Chalciope's grief when her husband died and her terror now for her sons, I knew she would not survive my death as well. I pushed the casket away from me, and stood.

Very well, then. If I was not going to die, then nor would the stranger. Yes, the bulls were strong and their breath was a toxic flame. But my father was not the only one who had a god on his side. I had the favour of my goddess, of Hecate, and she had taught me well. I bent down and opened the casket, but I did not go near the poisons that

I keep at the back. I pulled out a larger bottle from the middle row. I raised it in my right hand, then shut the lid of the box firmly with my left hand. I held the flask up to the light and saw the liquid glistening within. This was the drug of Prometheus, harvested from a flower that grew in the shadow of the tormented Titan.

His liver has been pecked out by an eagle every day for unimaginable centuries, and it will be pecked out over and over again, as Zeus has decreed. Far beneath the rock to which he has been chained are small patches of stony ground, and every day his ichor drips from the wound onto these inhospitable patches of earth. In one of those places, I once found two bright yellow flowers growing on two narrow stems. I knew the power of this plant would be immense, so I bathed seven times in a flowing stream, and I called seven times on the roaring might of Hecate. I called on her from the earth and beneath the earth. I called on her as the nurse of every child and the queen of every corpse. I wore dark robes and I approached the spot in the darkness of the night. When I cut the root of this rarest plant, the ground beneath me shook, as Prometheus twisted in pain. I almost dropped my knife but then I remembered Prometheus must writhe like this every day, in vain. At least on this day, someone would gain from his agony. I collected the sap in a white shell, and carried it away with care.

And this was the drug that I needed now, for Jason. I hid it within the folds of my dress, and I walked over to the door, opening it just enough to see if there was any trace of the dawn. The moment I could see my hands in front of me was the moment I told my attendants to prepare our fastest wagon as soon as they could. They were obviously confused by the early hour, but no one ever questions a priestess.

Nor did any of the Colchians challenge us, as we sped through the streets on our way to the shrine of Hecate. The horses were quick, as if they could feel the urgency I was trying to conceal. When we arrived at the shrine, it was deserted, and I began to weave my deceit.

'I have been foolish, friends,' I said. 'I thought the other women would be here as usual, tending the altars. But of course I should have thought that the arrival of those foreigners on their ship has thrown everyone into confusion. The women aren't here because they are nervous of these strangers. So let us enjoy ourselves together, picking flowers. We will stay here for a while and – if you would like to – we will go back to the palace later, having won ourselves many fine things.'

My women looked at one another, to see if any of them knew already what I meant.

'This is a secret, and we cannot continue with my plan unless you all promise to keep it so.'

There was much nodding and murmuring of quiet oaths.

'Then listen: my nephew Argos has asked me for help. So has his mother. She came to me under the shadows of darkness last night. My father must never hear of this. But they have asked me to help the foreigner, the one who my father has challenged to yoke the bulls and sow the dragon's teeth. They say if I help him, he will give us gifts all the way from his homeland. All I must do is meet him, here, this morning. He will bring his gifts in exchange for the protective drugs they imagine I will provide. So when he comes, you girls must make yourselves scarce. Otherwise,

169

he may guess that I am not doing what I have promised, which he knows would have to take place in total secrecy.'

One of the girls frowned. 'Won't he realize you're not doing what they have asked anyway? When you don't give him the drug he needs?'

I smiled. I could not have arranged things more perfectly if I had bribed the girl myself. 'He won't know that I am giving him a different drug,' I shrugged. 'If he were an expert in the properties of exotic plants, he would not need my help. If he had the favour of a goddess as I have the ear of Hecate, he would be begging her to save his life, not me. I'm his only hope of life: he will cling to whatever I give him.'

I was such a fool then; I can hardly bear to think of myself.

Korone

That is

Oh, come on, just how stupid are you? Aren't you the one who's supposed to be a seer? Mopsos, isn't that your name? Mopsos, son of Ampykos? And you're meant to be the one who can see things yet to come, as clearly as you see the world before your eyes? Because at the moment, you aren't seeing anything clearly.

Look at Jason! I mean, really look at him. Did he look like that yesterday? You think so? Blind seers are a thing, aren't they? There have been a few men who could see into the future but would stumble over their own feet without a child to guide them along their dusty paths. Are you one of those? You don't think you are? But you also think Jason looks the same as – oh, here we are. Now you really look at him, he seems a bit shinier than before? And Greek is your first language, is it? Shinier? Well, no, I suppose it isn't completely wrong, but don't ever take up poetry if the seeing doesn't work out, will you?

That divine glow you're trying to find words for, that was provided by my goddess. Hera, of course. Well, yes, you should have known. I would definitely think about apologizing next time you are making your offerings, yes. You know she would turn you into a snake in a heartbeat, I assume? Oh, so you know something. That's a start, I suppose. He also looks taller? Yes, that was Hera as well. And oddly handsome, if that's the right word? Can you even hear yourself? Yes, also Hera: the beauty, the athleticism, the radiance are all down to her. Jason isn't a bad-looking man, I suppose, if you like that kind of thing. But he isn't anything special unless a goddess takes a hand in his appearance, is he?

What are you doing now? What do I mean? I mean that – what are you even doing? – that bizarre head-turning and peering thing you're doing? Are you trying to impersonate an owl? No, I don't know why you would be doing that, but I can't see what else you could be— You're looking for me? Can you not hear any better than you can see? I'm up here, of course. No, up here. In the highest branches. Look, I'll shake the branch under my feet so you can see it. Yes, here. Well, where did you think my voice was coming from? A what? An otherworldly phantom? Are you drunk?

I'm sure crows don't usually speak, but if Hera can enchant your ordinary-looking friend, she can certainly give voice to a crow, can't she? You suppose so? I should add an extra goat to that sacrifice you're planning to make to her. Because if she's listening at the moment – and she might well be, given how much effort she's putting into your man Jason today – she isn't going to be impressed with your tone at all. You're sorry? You don't have to be sorry to me, I'm just a crow. A crow to whom Hera has decided to give the gift of speech, yes, but just a crow. You know, a better question might be to ask why she has given me the power to speak to you: had you considered that? You had? So, what's the answer?

Of course you don't know. Then let me tell you. She wants me to tell you what should have been obvious to anyone: Jason needs to go and meet the princess alone. As in, on his own. Yes, without you. Is it a trap? Are you sure you're not drunk? When Hera decides to set a trap for you, be certain you won't get a friendly warning from anyone. You'll just have time to realize it's her doing before you meet an agonizing death. So let me make this very clear, since you apparently struggle to understand quite simple words. Jason needs help from the princess unless you want to see him burned alive tomorrow. Do you want to see that? Well, I thought I should check, because every moment you delay acting on Hera's instructions is making that outcome more likely.

What? You know he needs her help, that's why you're taking him to meet her? Seriously? I honestly can't tell if you are simple, or just, I don't know. Ill? What do you think is going to persuade the princess to help him? Her sister's son has asked her, yes. And her sister, that's right. And you would betray your home and your father to do a small favour for a foreigner, if a sibling asked, would you? It doesn't matter what I would do: I'm a crow. We don't have murderous kings. We just have other crows.

No, you don't think so? You wouldn't betray your king for a complete stranger, no matter who asked? But you're hoping Medea will? Yes, that's her name. Well, Hera has given me permission to say this: Medea will help your captain, but she won't do it as a favour, or because her sister asked her. She'll do it because she's in love with him.

173

How? What do you mean, how? Because the gods arranged it this way, of course. Do you think Hera leaves these things to chance? Or to the Fates? Or – worse – to idiot mortals like you? Medea is in love with Jason but she has been deeply troubled by this. She doesn't want to deceive her father, but she will, if her love for Jason is given just a little space to develop.

Should you wait here and let him go ahead on his own? I mean, it's a thought, isn't it? Why didn't I just say so in the first place? I was trying to let you work it out for yourself, so you didn't embarrass yourself any more than you already have. I'm not your friend, I don't have to tell you things if I don't want to. I'm just the way Hera has chosen to speak to you today which – given the options she had – has really worked out well for you. Tell Jason you and the other fool will stay here and he needs to go on alone. No, obviously he can't hear me, or I wouldn't be telling you to tell him, would I? My goddess, you're an idiot.

Stay here. Tell him to go ahead without you and to meet you back here when Medea has given him what he needs. Will you hear from me again? I can only say I hope not.

Medea

the greatest help:

I could not concentrate on anything while my maidservants and I waited for Jason to arrive. Why do I limit the time like this? I have concentrated on nothing but Jason since the first moment I saw him. He has consumed my thoughts every day, every part of every day. This no doubt adds to the picture you may have of me, as a foolish lovesick child who would do anything for whichever handsome man asked. I'm aware that this is how I have been portrayed by many people. You will no doubt pride yourself on your independence of mind, and believe that the impressions you have of me, the conclusions you have reached about me are all your own. You are astute, observant, analytical. You couldn't have your opinions swayed by prejudice.

And yet, I fulfil so many preconceptions you have. A young girl, the plaything of the gods and an easy target for an adventuring hero. It isn't unreasonable to suppose I might be a little foolish, lacking in what people like to call common sense, no matter how uncommon it is. And a foreign girl at that: I lived at the very edge of the world that the Hellenes could imagine. My father was so exotic, with his divinely built palace and his refusal to respect the laws of Greek hospitality that prohibit a king from injuring those who have offered succour to his family, his grandsons in this case.

And then there is the magic. The exoticism isn't confined to my father, it spreads to me too. Witches are dangerous no matter where they're from. Until you want our help, of course. Then, we are wisdom personified and the cruel jibes are silenced, for a while.

I will not address these charges at this time. Perhaps I never will.

I am simply telling you the truth of things. I met Jason and I loved him before I knew him. It was like a terrible curse had been laid upon me. There was no happiness, no soft unfurling of gentle feelings, nothing like that. I felt like I had been poisoned: weak, dizzy and sick. My goddess has ensured that I know my way around poisons, and I'd never seen one that caused so much damage but did not kill. The pains in my body – my whole body – were as sharp as if someone was stabbing me with long brooch pins. The fever was identical to those that carry off new mothers and their babies in the night. None of my remedies had any effect, which is how I knew it was not an illness. Someone, something, had attacked me using some form of magic that I didn't recognize.

I had told the girls to pick flowers, to play games while we were waiting for Jason. But I could not give them even a part of my attention because I was looking out for signs of his arrival, trying to hear his footsteps over their words and low laughter. I wanted to bark at them to be silent, but I could not if I was to maintain the pretence that he meant nothing to me. And all the while, the pain of countless goads twisting into my flesh. I heard him coming so many times, and each time I was mistaken: an animal hurrying through the trees, the wind mocking me as it blew.

When he finally arrived, it was worse than the waiting had been. The maids took themselves away very prettily; l would have laughed if I had not been striving to stay on my feet. The pain of seeing him again was almost intolerable and I could take only the shallowest breaths, as though some creature was sitting on my chest. I felt the sweat beginning to drip at the back of my neck and pool at the base of my spine. I knew my cheeks were dark because I could feel the heat pulsing across my face. I wanted to run and join the girls but my feet wouldn't move and so I simply stood there, stranded in pain, as he approached.

When he drew close enough to speak, he did not. He too stood in silence. I took in the sight of this stranger, who was so tall and strong and beautiful and somehow artificial. My mind seemed to be split in two. One half of me – the girl, I suppose – was sick and growing sicker the nearer he came. But the other part – the witch – was looking on with interest at his changed appearance. What had happened to him? Was it a drug, a spell? How had he made himself taller and more athletic? Had the change been made to his body or to my perception? I could not tell, and I stared at him, trying to uncover the trick. But all I could sense was a strange sort of flatness, as though someone were holding gauze in front of my eyes.

'Don't be afraid,' he said. His tone was soft, as though he were hoping to calm a wild animal. Part of me wanted to melt at the music of his lovely voice. The other part was fascinated to discover that the trick extended across all my senses. He looked more beautiful, sounded gentler and, yes, there it was on the breeze: his breath was lightly perfumed. So much trouble! Someone vastly more powerful than my sister wanted this man to live.

'You don't need to be frightened of me,' he said again. 'You can say whatever you want to, ask whatever you like. This is a sacred space, no harm can befall us here: the gods would not permit it. And I know you have promised your sister that you will help me. I am so grateful.'

There was laughter dancing in his eyes. He was charming himself as much as he was charming me. 'You have some potion or powder that will save my life,' he said. 'So I beg you by your goddess Hecate, and by Zeus who guards the lives of suppliants and guests, since I am both your suppliant and your guest.' As he spoke these words, he reached across and took my hand in his. I knew his skin was not burning hot, but it felt so to me. 'I will get down on my knees,' he added, 'so I can supplicate you.'

I watched him kneel before me, still holding my hand. He smiled up at me and the effect was dizzying. I wanted to collapse into him, to have him hold me and never let go.

And I wanted to know who was doing this to me, and how.

'I cannot win this bitter contest without you and your goddess on my side,' he said. 'I will celebrate your name everywhere I go; the story of you – your cleverness and piety and kindness to a guest and suppliant – will be sung all across Hellas. And it will not just be me raising my voice in praise of you, it will be all the Argonauts. And when we return home, they will tell their wives, their mothers who saved our quest from failure. And then these women will praise you even more. They are no doubt grieving for us already, terrified we won't make the return journey. You – and you alone – have the power to take all that pain and sorrow away.'

I still could not speak. He reached up to take my other hand, nestling both inside his own as he pulled them towards his face. 'You're so kind,' he murmured, allowing the words to disappear between his fingers. 'I knew from the moment I saw you that you were soft and kind.'

I could have dissolved and then rained gently down on him, so he would know how very soft I was.

But I could not, because then how would I find out who was helping him? I did not reply, but I freed one of my hands from his grasp. I reached up into the folds of my dress and found the bottle I had brought for him. He watched me with a frank hunger in his eyes. For me or for the drug? As I offered it to him, he snatched at it, and I had my answer. But then I saw him reconsider, and he held his hand out again and threaded his fingers through mine. I would have poured my soul into another flask and given him that too, if he had asked. But I knew he needed to be told how to use the drug and how to beg for the favour of my goddess if he was to survive the next few days. So I found my voice again and asked him to stand, now his supplication had succeeded.

'You need to begin the task by visiting my father to collect the dragon's teeth. He will be cold and jeering; you must be humble and polite. When you have them, withdraw to your ship and wait.'

He nodded. His eyes were focused on my mouth as I

spoke. 'You must wait until the middle of the night,' I said. 'Bathe in a stream that is always flowing, be sure to immerse your whole body.' A flash of mischief crossed his face, and I felt myself blush. 'You must be completely alone,' I said. 'You must dress yourself in the darkest robes you have, and you must then dig a pit. Do it carefully: this is the place you make your offerings to Hecate: she must see your respect.' He nodded again, and the mischief was gone. Whatever else he wanted from me, he needed the priestess first. 'Slit the throat of a sheep at the pit's edge and let the blood drain into the darkness. Place its body on a pyre, right there next to the pit. Burn it whole. Then pour honey into the pit and beg the goddess for her sweet favour. And then you must walk away. You may hear footsteps close behind you; you may hear dogs bark. You must not turn around. Do you understand?' He looked suddenly afraid. 'You could destroy all hope of success if you fail to heed this warning,' I continued. 'And you might not return to your crew in the state you left them, if you return to them at all. The next morning, you must take this bottle I have given you: it is half full. Add a little water until you have made a thin paste. Anoint yourself with it as though it were oil. This will give you the strength you need to survive the tasks ahead. You will feel as strong as a god; you can trust your feelings for one day.'

Again, his eyes glittered. This man wanted very much to be the equal of a god. What man doesn't? But he wanted it more than most.

'Take the last droplets of the potion you have made, and sprinkle them on your shield, your spear and your sword. You – and your weapons and armour – will be impervious to the flames that those bronze bulls will exhale. You will be protected too from the spears of the earth-born: they will not penetrate your shield or your skin.'

'Thank you,' he said, his voice shaky.

'I have further advice for you,' I replied. I wanted his thanks but something in me shunned it too. Was it guilt, for betraying my father? Fear, for asking so great a favour from my goddess? Desire, so I did not want to think him my inferior? 'You must act quickly. The bulls are strong but you will be stronger. Plough the field swiftly and sow the seeds as you go. Then wait, do not be tricked into acting too soon. Wait until many earth-born have sprouted from the soil. As they begin to notice one another, they will be distracted: this is when you must act. Throw a large rock into their midst. Each will blame the others, they will turn on one another. You can kill whoever is left when they have exhausted themselves. Then you can claim the precious fleece and take it home with you, to Hellas.'

The word sounded strange on my tongue and I felt tears forming. 'Wherever you go, remember the name of Medea,' I said.

He clasped my right hand more tightly, perhaps with gratitude.

'My city is Iolcus,' he said, gleaming. 'And if I escape Colchis unharmed, if I manage to return home, I will never forget your name. Medea will be on my mind, on my tongue, day and night.'

I stared, trying to assess his intent.

'My father is not a hospitable man,' I said. 'And I am sorry he has not made you welcome. But when you leave here you will think of me, not him. And I will remember you.'

The horror of being here after Jason had left was like a physical blow that threatened to knock me off my feet. 'The winds and the birds will tell me, if you forget the debt you owe me. I could have the winds carry me to the very centre of your house so I could air my grievance to you face to face.'

And now the mischief was back in his eyes.

'Why would you need the winds to carry you, when I have such a beautiful ship?' he asked. 'If you were to come to Hellas, you would be treated as a goddess, your reputation blossoming thanks to the men whose lives you have saved. And you would share my marriage bed, of course. Nothing will ever separate us, except death.'

I was not sure what to reply, but there was no time anyway. He looked up at the sun and said we should separate before anyone found out about our meeting. He kissed my hands and left.

He always walks away like this: a sudden change in mood and urgency, and he is gone before you can speak.

Hera

whenever a wife

The queen of the gods was satisfied with the outcome of this meeting. Pelias would pay for the insult he had levelled at her, and perhaps Medea would be the tool of her perfect revenge. Hera would keep watch on this young couple. The girl must be kept from feeling too much guilt about her parents and her homeland, at least until after she had sailed away with Jason. She would be no good to Hera if she remained in Colchis. Medea was grieving, certainly, at the prospect of betraying her father. But Aphrodite and her petulant son had done enough to keep the girl in thrall to Jason. Hera watched Medea weeping as she returned to her chamber and thought about the treachery she had committed. But Jason had the drug and her advice: there was nothing she could withhold now. He was already on his way to claim the dragon's teeth from Aietes.

Hera thought for a moment in case there was anything she had forgotten, but she could think of nothing. Smiling, she decided she would share the good news with Athene.

Hecate

doesn't disagree

The goddess who dwelt in the darkest recesses beneath the earth heard a distant call. She ignored it, because she had no reason to heed the voice of a man she didn't know. No, not his voice, his thoughts. The man had been warned to approach her with the greatest humility, and he did not speak. But she heard him nonetheless as he crept towards a lonely spot to bathe and dress in dark robes, especially to appeal to her. There was something about the robe that was snagging his conscience, though. Was he not wearing the proper garb? No, that wasn't it. These robes had been the gift of a queen, who wanted the man to remember her and his time in her bed. Hecate sensed the hand of another goddess in this: the queen had loved him thanks to Aphrodite, she supposed. But now he was shielded by the love of another. Another goddess or another woman? Perhaps it was both, Hecate could not be sure.

He had the help of her priestess, she knew that. She could sense Medea's calm, clear instructions as the man dug his pit and sacrificed his ewe. She drank the blood greedily, like the dead, who thirst for nothing else. She relished the

184

smell of burning flesh as he placed the bloodless body on
his pyre. She closed her eyes in the darkness, for the pleasure
of so much death and heat and smoke. And as she revelled
in his offering, there came a libation. Hecate was never
hungry, and yet the sweetness of the honey made her almost
believe she was. She drank it down after the blood, the way
the dead would never dare.

And then she heard him call her name and she answered
with a giant roar. What did this mortal want, to have
approached her with such precision? Her assistance in a
contest against Aietes, a favourite of the gods. She would
not help this man kill the son of Helios, but he didn't ask
for that. He wanted to survive an encounter with bronze
bulls wrought by Hephaestus and a battle with the earth-
born. The latter gave her pause – these warriors would
almost be her kin – but she decided to give him what he
sought.

She took on her favourite guise, rising from behind his
freshly dug pit. She was gigantic, a wreath of snakes twisted
around the oak branches encircling her huge head. She
carried torches in each hand, dazzling the mortal as he
shielded his eyes. Her hounds accompanied her; their
screaming barks enough to drive any man to the edge of
the world. Even the nymphs who lived in the marshes
around this place – who had seen and heard a great deal
in their time – were moved to scream in fear. No one
witnessed the coming of Hecate and her dogs and remained
unchanged.

But the mortal man was brave, she saw. No doubt Medea
had told him he must walk away from the pit and the pyre
and not look back, but it was another thing to hear the

roaring and screaming and remember what you had been told. But he left without turning, no matter how the terror gripped him. Hecate could smell his fear just as she could smell the charred, sweet stench of death. She licked the last traces of honey from her sated lips.

Medea

with her husband.

The guilt was like a weight, pressing down on my throat so I could scarcely breathe. I had given him the tools with which he could defeat my father's challenge, and I would have to stand and watch beside my father as he made his attempt. I was afraid he would die and afraid he would live. I hid in my room in the darkness, listening for the voice of my goddess. Chalciope came seeking reassurance for her sons, but I could not hear her. I heard him call on Hecate, and I heard her answer. I felt the earth move aside for her, felt the marsh grasses and the stagnant water on her skin as she rose through them to stand above his makeshift altar. I felt the air tremble at her cries.

And only then did I know that I must have acted in accordance with the gods' wishes. Hecate would not answer an ordinary man, no matter how he begged for her help. The stranger had already received assistance from one or more of the gods, and now my own was willing to grant him favours. This night would be a short one, I knew. My father would be readying himself before dawn, and Jason should be anointing his body and his weapons, as I had explained to him. By the time my sister knocked at my door, the Colchians were jostling around the field my father had chosen for the contest.

There was a giddiness in the crowd, an anticipation of blood and spectacle. My father wore a golden helmet that glinted in the rays of his father Helios, and a breastplate given to him by Ares. But when Jason arrived – rowed upstream by his Argonauts – he gleamed like a golden statue. He was naked, save the sword he wore strapped across his body. In his hand, he held a bronze helmet full of the dragon's teeth. My father boasted of his acquisitions from the gods, but it was Jason who seemed to have been forged by Hephaestus.

I had never seen anything so beautiful in my life. I knew the Colchians felt the same way, I could hear it in the way their chatter dimmed to a murmur as he strode towards the field of Ares. He could have been the god himself, or perhaps he was more like Apollo. But the gods would have claimed him as their own that day: I was sure of it. My concoction had done its work. His beauty might have been provided by another goddess, but his confidence and his strength came from Hecate, and from me. He took up a spear and a shield and he held them lightly in his hands, as though they weighed nothing at all. None of the spectators could mistake what they saw: if any man were to equal my father in might and skill, this was him.

You already know that he survived his encounter with the bulls: he stood before them with his enhanced shield to protect him, and their harmless flames whistled past him like waves crashing against an impervious rock. He grabbed one creature by its curving horn, then the other. He held them down with one hand until he could force the yoke over their necks, and nothing deterred him. I watched him, trying to unpick which part of his endeavours was him, what belonged to his protector-goddess, and what was mine. But the strands were woven too tightly and I could not.

He ploughed the field, he sowed the dragon's teeth. This much is already the stuff of songs, as was my father's hard-jawed rage when he saw it. We all watched him take water from a nearby stream, filling the helmet that had just held the teeth, holding it to his lips for a long, slow drink. I thought of his promise that we would marry if I came with him to Greece, and I stared at his beautiful mouth, wondering how he would taste.

He came back to the field and now he was holding his sword. I could feel the anger and confusion emanating from my father as he began to realize that the stranger might well survive this challenge and claim the fleece. Not that Aietes would even consider giving it up, no matter what he had offered. Even if Jason survived the earth-born, he might well die at my father's hands.

Jason was standing at the edge of the furrow he had ploughed. His breathing was steady and his eyes were watchful. His body was unmarked: no burns, no scratches, not even dirt thrown up by the plough had left a trace on him. He looked like an athlete about to begin a bout of wrestling. But when the first snow-white arm of the first earth-born warrior punched its way free, even he took an involuntary step back.

One fist was followed by another, and another; one still-sightless head broke out of its dark prison, then shoulders, and a pale, gleaming torso. Their pallor against the black earth was like the stars against the night sky. But each of these stars held a spear or a sword: the earth may have borne them, but this patch was sacred to Ares. And as their heads pushed through the surface, they wore glinting helmets; when their bodies appeared, they were covered by shields.

Jason looked on in revulsion: their whiteness reminded him of maggots, he would later explain. He wanted to rush among them, cutting them down before any more of them arrived. But he remembered my words, and he remembered how well my guidance had served him so far. So as he waited, he looked for the largest rock he could throw. The one he chose was immense; I held my breath to see if the potion had truly given him the strength he needed. More and more arms and weapons sprouted from the ground.

He lifted the great stone with ease, and the Colchians gasped. Even my father was transfixed by this feat, and I half-expected him to turn to me and accuse me of giving aid to his enemy. I could feel the sweat forming along my hairline, certain that he would guess what I had done. But he stood with every muscle clenched as Jason drew back his arms and flung the boulder high and long. It arced above the earth-born and landed in their midst with a low thud that even the spectators could feel.

The earth-born did not have eyes that I could discern. Their bronze helmets covered their faces, and the sockets were dark: empty or in shadow, I did not know which. But they could perceive the rock and they ran towards it, each one hacking at his neighbour with his sword or hurling his spear at a more distant rival. Did they all blame each other for the missile which had crushed several of them when it landed? Were they avenging their lost kin or merely trying to save themselves? These creatures were unknown to me before that day, and I will never see such things again.

They fell on one another with cruel screams and tore at each other's pale flesh, doing Jason's work for him. He began to move towards them, cutting down the ones appearing latest, at the far edge of his ploughed furrow. Some he sliced in two while their arms were still earthbound, others he decapitated. The ones nearest to the boulder – who weren't already dead – had maimed one another so ruthlessly that by the time Jason reached them, they were scarcely able to lift their swords. He looked out across the field, tired but jubilant. The earth-born were all dead, and he had survived the day.

My father said nothing. He turned and walked to his chariot and drove himself back to the city. My sister and I accompanied our mother as we trudged silently after him, too shocked to speak. There had been no way of talking to Jason, who had been surrounded by his thronging companions, all of them shouting and laughing at his remarkable achievements. I found that as one anxiety – that he would die on the field – ebbed away, it was replaced by another, more potent one. What would happen when my father refused to give up the fleece?

Because he had never had the slightest intention of awarding his treasure to these foreigners, nor would he do so now, not even if Hermes had brought an order from Zeus himself. Aietes would do whatever he deemed necessary to keep the fleece. So the question in my mind was: what would Jason do to take it?

Selene

But now,

The silver Moon had only one destination in mind, as she prepared to set out each night. First, she would bathe in the waters of Ocean, and then she would put on a beautiful golden dress and a bright gold crown. Her elegantly maned horses were always ready, and she would pat their glorious necks as she yoked them to her chariot. And every night – whether the moon was new or full – she would travel the same arcing route across the sky. Sometimes the clouds hid her soft light, and other times she shone in her fullest brightness. But no matter what else changed, one thing never did: she was always driving her horses towards Mount Latmos.

Because on the side of Latmos was a cave, and in that cave slept the most beautiful man the Moon had ever seen. She had loved Endymion since the first moment she saw him sleeping. Everyone had loved Endymion: his beauty was simply too pure for anyone to resist it. He was so lovely that Zeus allowed him to choose when he would die, and Endymion chose not death, but sleep. Eternal, restorative sleep. From the moment he lay down in the cave, Endymion did not age another day. He remained as perfect as when he had been a shepherd, catching the eye of every god and goddess alike. But no one else had loved him the way the Moon loved him.

She loved his sleeping form just as she had loved him awake: beyond all other things she had ever known. She asked Zeus to be allowed to make Endymion her lover, and the king of the gods agreed. The other goddesses nudged one another and laughed: what was the point of Endymion asleep? Wasn't his whole worth contained in the way his deepest brown eyes met yours? The Moon did not agree. She knew that Endymion's beauty was the same whether he slept or woke, and she wanted him either way. When Zeus granted her wish, she deviated the route she drove her chariot each night, just a little. Just enough to allow her to visit Endymion in his cave.

When the Moon gave birth to his first daughter, the goddesses became thoughtful while the gods sniggered. How had she managed that, with a mortal man who never woke up? But the Moon smiled to herself, in her gentle light. No one knew what happened in the darkness of the Latmian cave. Even her brother Helios – usually a witness to everything – slept while she drove across the night. So they would never know of the way she stirred Endymion, and the words he murmured in her ear as she crept in beside him. And they did not know of the vows the two had exchanged before he chose his endless, blissful night.

Unlike so many gods, the Moon never wearied of her love. She visited Endymion every night. Or rather, she visited him almost every night. When she thought of the few nights she had missed with him, her beautiful face clouded over. Because on those nights too, she had bathed in Ocean, she had dressed in gold, and she had yoked her shining horses. She had set out on the same arc as she always did, heading towards Latmos, to her beloved's mountain home. But on these nights, her chariot was pulled off course by a force she could not withstand. She held on to the reins, but the horses veered anyway, and her light was shrouded in darkness until she could exert her authority once again. And yet, the horses were not disobeying her deliberately. They seemed as perplexed as she was about their changed path.

The first time it happened, the Moon told herself it could have been an accident: a rogue storm wind, perhaps. The second time, she knew that someone was interfering deliberately. She raged quietly during the hours of the Sun, then tried to find out who had been so impertinent. But no one on Olympus had even noticed her wandering chariot. Anyone she questioned said the same thing: that the clouds often scudded in front of Helios too, so there was no shame for her in being hidden the same way. But the Moon had not just discovered clouds, even if some of her fellow gods apparently had.

Eventually, the Moon concluded that it could only be a powerful witch, since witches had tried to draw her off her course before, in a display of their strength. One or two had come close to succeeding over the years, she recalled. She did not know why they singled her out, but it was always the Moon against whom they wished to pit their powers. And rivers, she remembered. They liked to make rivers run the wrong way too. This witch was stronger than any mortal had the right to be, the Moon thought, so she must have the help of a goddess. But none that she had questioned, so it must be one who lived elsewhere. Why did she even pause to name her: of course it was Hecate. The witches all served her, one way or another. The Moon thought about the witch goddess, so mighty in her underworld lair, and she wondered what Hecate would say when she – the Moon – went to demand an apology for her acolyte's audacity. Then she thought a little longer, and wondered if she really needed the apology. And then, after still more thought, she decided she might not make any demands of the dread goddess, even though she had been so vexed. But she kept a half-closed eye on the witch, knowing that the girl sought darkness to collect her herbs or work her spells.

So she was delighted to witness the scene that was now unfolding beneath her. The witch-girl was running away from home, the Moon could see it quite clearly. Her pale beams crept in through a small window in the girl's bedchamber as she wept and fretted that she was about to be discovered. Discovered doing what, the Moon would like to know, but she would find out in due course. The girl was running around the room like a trapped bird, pulling bottles from a chest of drugs (made in the Moon's unlawful absence, no doubt) until the chest was empty and the folds of her dress were full. She clipped off a lock of hair and left it on her pillow, a keepsake for her mother, perhaps. And she drew a feather-light hand across the wall, as though she were bidding farewell to a lover.

And then the Moon knew what had happened. The girl was running away to be with a man. That was it. She cackled with delight. The girl who had shown so little respect for the Moon's night-time assignations was now keeping one of her own. And she was so desperate to make her escape that she ran barefoot from the palace. Filled with malicious joy, the Moon shone as brightly as she could. But the Colchians were blind to what she was showing them. Their princess was running through the streets, her cloak held up over her hair in a false show of piety. The girl wasn't on her way to an altar to make a sacrifice, she was simply trying to hide her face from passers-by.

The Moon watched as Medea – whose name she did not normally acknowledge, but she was willing to make an exception on this glorious night – rushed through the streets, not towards any temple but towards a large field outside the city walls. The Moon had seen her digging around in this marshy land before, always searching for more plants to feed her magic. But this time, the girl wasn't looking for any herbs, she was making for— The Moon blinked. There was not usually a ship here, was there? Certainly not a fine ship like this one, which bore the clear mark of divine assistance in its construction. This was the Argo, the Moon had seen it winging its way across the seas.

And with that, she knew it all. That it was an Argonaut that Medea was hurrying to find, perhaps even their captain, Jason. The Moon remembered that Hera and perhaps Athene and even Aphrodite had been offering their help to him. She dimmed her light a little. There was no point making enemies she didn't need. But the dimming of her brightness did nothing to quench her spiteful glee. The witch had disrupted the Moon's nights with Endymion, and now she was cursed with a far more terrible passion. At least Endymion was only asleep. Whereas Jason — But the Moon did not need to complete her thought. Medea would find out, soon enough.

Medea

everything

The second time we met, I fell to my knees at his feet.

I ran to the ship, to where I knew they had moored it. I should have been in total darkness but of course there wasn't a cloud anywhere to protect me. But I wore my mantle up high, as though I were preparing for a sacrifice. No one saw me, or if they did, they didn't dare speak to me. But as I left Colchis, I knew that my father had realized I was the traitor. I could feel it somehow: the stones of the palace walls seemed to be urging me to leave. Small, sharp pieces of grit worked their way between my feet and my sandals as I ran, exacting the only revenge they could.

I knew the ship would be upstream, and I ran to the closest bank of the river, and called for my nephews. They were near to the shore, rowing their little boat back to the Argo to spend the night celebrating and feasting. I could feel them leaving, just as the rocks could feel me. It was Phrontis – the youngest boy – who answered. They rowed back to land, and three men jumped out of their boat to meet me: Argos, Phrontis and Jason. They were still giddy with Jason's unexpected victory. I needed to convince them of the urgency of my request.

So I fell to my knees, and I reached out and wrapped my hands around his ankles. I could feel such heat radiating from him, and I knew it came from the drugs I had given him, but it felt real. I would have touched my forehead to his feet, but there was no time.

'Friends, you must save me. Save yourselves and save me. Aietes knows what we did: there is nothing to be done about this now. He will never let you take the fleece; he would never have let you take it anyway. The only possible way for you – for any of us – to leave here alive is if you do what I say. We must set sail before he can unleash his men upon you. If you really want the fleece, we must go to the sacred grove of Ares now. I can give you what you seek, I can get us past the dragon that guards it. It never sleeps but I can close its eyes, if you trust me. If this is what you want, you have only to say the word. But first, Stranger, you must repeat the promises you made to me at the temple of my goddess yesterday, you must tell me in the presence of my nephews that you will take me with you to Hellas, and that you will marry me when we arrive there. These are the words you spoke when you needed my help. You still need my help, unless you wish to leave your quest unfinished. Do I have your word? I cannot stay here now I have betrayed my father for your sake, for all your sakes. I will not survive the night. You are no doubt shocked to hear these words from a girl like me; I'm sure the girls of Hellas have kind fathers who make these decisions on their daughters' behalf. But I am not in that position, because I chose you, your companions and my nephews over my father.

So I no longer have the protection of my relatives, I only have myself.'

He reached down and lifted me from the ground, his eyes never leaving mine. The warmth came from his voice now, which I had not affected with magic.

'No, no, no, lovely girl! You are not without protection, you have mine. You have my gratitude and with that comes an obligation that I am happy to meet. I swear – not just before your nephews, though I am quite sure they would protect your honour – but before Zeus, who keeps our oaths close, and before Hera, goddess of marriage, who shares his bed. In just the same way, you will share my bed when we arrive back in Hellas.'

As he spoke, he took my right hand – the hand with which the Greeks swear their pledges – in his.

*

This is what no one tells you, in the songs sung about Jason and the Argo. When he spoke like this – so proper and persuasive – his voice was filled with laughter. The amusement was never unkind, it always seemed generous. So the idea that my nephews – scarcely more than children – might be capable of protecting me was not risible, exactly, but somehow enjoyable to him. The way he bestowed his affection was almost regal, as though he were the princess and I were the adventurer. And every word felt like a gift, even as he acknowledged his promises to me.

I didn't know this at the time, of course. I just thought it was one of those vocal mannerisms that foreigners some-times have. It was only later, when I had seen him under different circumstances, that I knew he found delight in these moments. He loved to be asked for help, he loved to feel that he was granting wonderful favours. He believed his own generosity was the cause of anything he did at another's request: he might use the language of obligation, but he never felt the weight of a debt owed.

This part of his quest has been forgotten too, by everyone but me. But as he swore his oaths – by the king and queen of his gods – he was laughing with delight.

*

My nephews rowed us towards the sacred grove. They understood too well the swiftness with which Aietes would act. As we hurried upstream, I whispered instructions to them: they must wait on the shore, ready to leave. They must not come after us, or they could distract the dragon I had promised to subdue. I felt Jason's pleasure subsiding as we approached land again, his fear starting to mount once more. He had no idea what he was about to encounter, but he did have the sense to know it could kill him.

The place we set down is called the Ram's Bed, and it is the exact spot where my brother-in-law first landed in Colchis. The altar where Phrixus sacrificed his companion to Zeus is still blackened by the smoke of his offering. There is a narrow, overgrown path behind it, which leads to the grove. Jason and I left the boys behind, and I told him to be silent no matter what he saw. The path wound its way through the trees, until they thinned out a little. On the far side of the grove was a large oak tree, sacred to Zeus. Wrapped around the tree, its huge coils filling the grove and disappearing off into the darkness, was the dragon. The moment it saw us – as I had said, it never sleeps – it began to emit a deafening hissing. I felt Jason stiffen beside me, and the noise was horrifying, even though I had heard it before. The dragon raised its scaled head from the ground and reared up. A shudder went through each coil as it unfurled itself and began advancing on us. Jason gasped in fright and I grabbed his arm to keep him silent. As the monster's head drew level with mine, I held its gaze. I knew I needed to keep it from looking away, if my magic was to work.

I called upon Hypnos, the giver of sleep, and I called upon my goddess, the night-roaming, gracious queen: I asked for their aid in our task. My song was a powerful invocation, and they heard me, I knew. The snake was still staring at me, but it was affecting him too. As I repeated my prayers, the monster's coils relaxed and began to sink to the ground. I sang the words again and watched the twin forces raging behind the dragon's eyes: its body was betraying it but still it opened its mighty jaws to swallow us both whole. I heard a whimper from behind me, but I ignored him. The monster's open mouth was exactly what I needed. I raised my hand and sprinkled a powdered drug into its eyes, which quickly drooped shut. Then I dropped more of the powder onto its tongue and around its teeth.

Its gigantic head sank and its lower jaw collapsed to the ground as its eyes finally closed. Its body no longer served it: huge, scaled muscle lying useless between the trees. It had been impossible to calculate the quantities required, and I did not know how long the creature would be incapacitated, or whether I had poisoned it. I squeezed Jason's arm again, but he could not seem to move. I took the risk of leaving him unguarded and crossed the grove myself, stepping carefully across the vast, sinuous coils at my feet.

I had seen the fleece before, but never touched it. To call it golden does not do it justice: it shone in the dark, as though lit by torches. I reached out to take it, and it was warm and softer than you could ever imagine. Phrixus would never talk about his voyage on the back of the golden ram, because he had lost his sister on the journey and, I think, because he had struggled to slit the throat of the ram even on the orders of Hermes. Phrixus was soft-hearted in every way: he could not even raise his voice to his own children. I lifted the fleece down from the branch which had held it all these years, and I turned to make my way back.

The dragon still slept, and I was relieved that I wouldn't have to kill it with Jason's sword, which was what I had planned to do if it woke. Jason was not standing where I had left him, though. He had hidden himself behind a small clump of trees, his eyes fixed on the snakish head. He was holding his sword but he could not possibly have used it: his arms hung useless at his sides. I made my careful journey across the grove and held out the fleece.

'Here,' I murmured. But he looked at me, mute.

I took his hand and tugged him away from the clearing, trying to keep him from stumbling as he kept looking behind him to check the dragon was not following us. Only when we were almost in sight of my nephews did he finally reach for the fleece. But when he touched it, the transformation was extraordinary. Its glow illuminated him, as though he were lit by the brightest torches. He buried his hands in its depths, his fingers lost in the enveloping gold. He was a still image of wonder as he lifted it to his face and stroked it against his cheek. In that moment, he looked like a child besotted with her new dress, turning it to see it sparkle in the moonlight. I watched him, helpless.

We were soon on the boat, my nephews buoyant with relief at our return, rowing hard to ferry us back to the Argo. Jason's companions surged around us when we arrived, all of them desperate to touch the fleece. He took a finely woven robe – of a foreign design I did not recognize – and threw it around the fleece to keep it unharmed and unseen. And then he told them to bend to their oars now, with me onboard, because I was the one who had seized the fleece. At this point he put his hands around my waist and lifted me up onto the stern so the men could all see. They cheered and whistled. Jason was laughing again, as he told them the success of their voyage was all down to me and that I had agreed to be married when we arrived in Hellas. So they must make haste or I would accuse them of delaying unfairly, when I had done everything they asked of me and more.

I had not done everything yet, of course. Because at this point, my brother still lived.

Hera

is hostile,

The queen of the gods looked down on the Argonauts, as they rowed their way into open water. She allowed herself a moment of self-congratulation, something she usually reserved until the entrails of her enemy were unspooling wetly on hard, dry earth. But Pelias was as good as dead, now Medea was on the Argo. Hera did not know how the witch would destroy him – she had only an opaque oracle – but she was confident that Pelias would meet a wretched death.

She did not wish to wait any longer, so she bribed one of the winds to set the Argo running across the seas away from Colchis. It occurred to her that Aietes might pursue his daughter and her thief, but she didn't allow it to concern her. Jason could look after himself now, she decided. And if he couldn't, the girl would save him.

Neaera

and the things

Neaera rarely spoke to her husband. Aietes was such a cold man, she could never quite believe that Helios was his father. His sister Circe had all the warmth in the family, Aietes was the harsh glare. If he had claimed the peaks of a distant mountain had sired him, she would have accepted it without hesitation. But he prided himself on his parentage, of course, and frequently called on the Sun God to support him. Their connection must be a true one, however unlikely.

Aietes did not consult her before he summoned the Colchians to the palace. Neaera was woken by feet pounding past her chamber. She dressed by the light of a guttering torch and hurried out into the courtyard. Her husband might not wish to speak to her, but he would nonetheless view her absence as treachery. She glanced across the courtyard as many times as she dared: she could not afford to be seen looking for anyone in particular. Aietes had informers all over the palace, Neaera had spent years being as colourless as possible. But no one could escape their attention altogether. She noticed Chalciope hastening ahead of her, tendrils of her hair sliding across her shoulders as she went. Neaera felt a sudden pang as she remembered when her eldest daughter had been small, and her dark hair had fanned around her head as she slept. She wondered if it still did that, and then she wondered what it would be like to be close to a daughter, to know how she looked when she was asleep.

She tried to compose her expression into one in which Aietes could not find offence. She should look concerned but not worried, or he might believe her sympathies lay with whoever had incurred his rage this time. But experience had taught her that she might well anger him no matter what she did.

Aietes stood on the dais in the centre of the courtyard, his face contorted as he snarled orders at their son. Apsyrtus no longer even looked afraid, Neaera thought, as she watched flecks of spittle flying from her husband's mouth. Immediately she noticed them, she looked away. Chalciope was holding back too, she saw. It would do her no good, though: Aietes had already turned on his grandsons, there would be no reprieve. Neaera had long ago learned that love was not something she could afford to express or even acknowledge, if she wished to stay alive.

She listened as Aietes addressed the men of Colchis, as he demanded nothing less than their absolute loyalty. They must launch every ship in pursuit of the foreigners who had stolen his prized fleece. They must go now, or it would be too late. Apsyrtus would captain their fastest vessel, he had already chosen his crew.

Neaera didn't expect her son to take leave of her, and she was not disappointed. She maintained her blank facade as she added his name to that of her grandsons. The boys had left with the foreigners, and there was no possibility she could imagine that saw all of them safely back in Colchis. Apsyrtus would sink their ship, she concluded. Or perhaps he would die in the attempt and the boys would escape to Greece, where Aietes could not follow them. In that case, she realized, she would lose Chalciope too: Aietes would certainly not let his daughter live. So the only one Neaera could be sure she wouldn't lose was Medea.

Only then did she realize that her younger daughter was missing. She wondered if Aietes had noticed that Medea wasn't here. He gave no sign of looking anywhere but directly in front of himself, and yet he always knew everything that was going on in every part of the palace. Neaera bit the inside of her cheek until she tasted the metallic tang. She would lose them all, her children and grandchildren, all in the same terrible day. She tried to breathe normally, but the crowd seemed to be surging around her and then almost on top of her, as she sank to the ground. Medea was gone, her grandsons were gone, Chalciope would not survive the day. The only thing Neaera could hope for was the safe return of her son.

Medea

she loves most

I knew they would come after us. Knew not by magic, but by experience: Aietes would never allow anyone to injure him without exacting a cost. So I was expecting the Colchians to man their ships and try to cut us off before we made the open sea. Already, I speak like an Argonaut, talking of the sea as though I had been criss-crossing it for years. It took only three days before we realized we were surrounded, and had to land on a small island devoted to the goddess Artemis. She is close to my goddess, so I knew we would have her protection for a while, at least.

The Colchians sent a messenger on a small boat, who made a simple offer. Aietes would allow Jason to keep the fleece, since he had performed the tasks that had been set, despite suspicions that he had not acted alone. He was not, however, going to sail off with Aietes' daughter. This was an unarguable condition of the Argonauts' safe return to Greece: they must return me.

Some of the Argonauts clearly thought this a more than reasonable exchange, their freedom for mine. I knew Jason could be swayed by their opinion, so I took him to one side and reminded him of his promises, and of the gods who had witnessed them. He could not expect to return home safely as a perjurer. I had saved his life and completed his quest; he could not abandon me now. If he thought Aietes cruel to strangers, he had no idea what my father was capable of doing to his family. I asked Hera to support me in my claim to be Jason's wife, and I watched his expression shift as he remembered the oaths he had sworn. He used words so lightly, it almost seemed to surprise him that I had taken them to my heart. But I did not come from a place where everyone was charming and plausible, I came from Colchis. I warned him that if he abandoned me now, he would lose the fleece, acquiring a Fury in its place.

Jason heard my words, and his face creased with unhappiness. He hated to feel that anyone was angry with him, or thought him less than the best and most honourable of men. He didn't like to argue, he just wanted to persuade you to see things his way. And he was the most persuasive man.

'Darling girl,' he said. 'Of course I won't abandon you. I made you a promise when we met at your goddess's temple, and I have no intention of breaking that promise a few days later. We must simply find a way to get past your father's men. Or perhaps we could trick them into thinking we're returning you when we aren't.'

I closed my eyes as he pulled me to his chest. I wanted so much to go along with his plans, wanted to be able to believe they could work. I tried to disagree with him in a way that wouldn't upset him further.

'I think the message has come from my brother's ship,' I said. 'Apsyrtus is clever and experienced, even though he is young.'

'I didn't even know you had a brother,' he whispered into my hair. 'Older or younger?'

'Older,' I said. 'He's younger than my sister but a year older than me.'

'I see.' He was stroking the place between my shoulder blades, but I could feel his attention wandering. 'Perhaps you could reason with him?' he asked.

'Apsyrtus has never listened to me,' I said. 'He won't care what I say, he'll just do what Aietes has asked of him. He's afraid of our father, like the rest of us.'

Now his hands were tangling themselves in my hair. 'So Apsyrtus isn't your ally, in the way your nephews are?'

I snorted. 'Never. He has always been jealous of me.'

And then I felt the tension in his body, though his hands remained as gentle as before. 'Perhaps we could use that against him?'

And I allowed my breathing to match his. 'We could.'

*

The message we sent in reply was brief and all deceit. The Argonauts would leave me on the island of Artemis. I would wait for my brother in her shrine. I would have gifts for him, which I had taken from Jason and his men. We would talk alone and all would be well.

*

Didn't I love my brother, people would ask in the months and years that followed. How could I have done such a thing?

They had no idea what I had done, of course, because few of the stories told about me are true. Nor could they begin to understand what there is in place of love between siblings who are not friends. They had not grown up in the palace of a capricious king, never knowing if I was safe or who I could trust. Even before Aietes had Phrixus killed, my sister and I lived in constant fear. Would I have betrayed her, the way I did Apsyrtus? Perhaps. She would have betrayed me to save her sons.

The Argonauts rowed away from Artemis' island, leaving me and Jason behind. The shrine was quite small and plain – just an unadorned altar and some offerings – but the island was thick with trees and Jason hid himself easily. And then we waited.

A fairer question would be, did I know what would happen when Apsyrtus arrived? Of course not: I did not even know that he would come to the island. If the Fates had wished to intervene, they had the opportunity to do so. But as I sat alone on the shore so he could see what awaited him, I prayed to my goddess to help me escape this ambush, and I felt her listening. I looked across to the Colchian ships, and I picked out the small boat, bobbing beside them. A few moments later, I realized the boat was moving towards me. I didn't know Apsyrtus was rowing. Even then, I thought it could have been the messenger refusing our offer and making counter demands.

But as the boat drew closer, I saw it was him. I had never seen him row before, and the thought sat stupidly in my head. Colchians don't live at sea, like the Greeks; climbing onto the deck of the Argo was the first time I had ever been onboard a ship. I stood and dusted the sand from my dress. I walked up to the shrine to wait for him.

I didn't know how he rowed a boat until that day. And after that day, I would never be surprised by him again.

I felt pity surging through my body, I almost choked. But then I thought of the danger he was to me and I knew there was no other way out. I could go back with him, as I had promised in the message we sent. But my father would have killed me before night fell. This is what the people who question me prefer to overlook: they are certain they would never have turned on their brothers. But very few people must make the choice I made that day.

I watched him jump out of the boat, I watched him stumble on the uneven shore and grab the side of the little craft to keep his balance. I watched him drag the boat out of the sea and pause, his chest rising and falling as he looked around to get a sense of the island. I watched him catch sight of me, and decide I was no threat to him, alone in a sanctuary. I watched the arrogance straighten his spine. I watched him walk up the rocky ground to the shrine and I heard him say, 'Sister', in a tone of contempt.

And even then, I might have saved him, if he had just said one kind word.

But the next thing he said was that Aietes would have his men rape me until my body broke apart and then he would slit my throat himself. And I turned my head and closed my eyes as Jason stepped noiselessly behind him and drove his blade between two of my brother's ribs.

Apsyrtus cried out, but the sound was faint as though he were far away. I turned back to face him but he was beyond threatening me now. He looked down at his chest, as if he hoped to see what had stung him and crush it between finger and thumb, but Jason tugged his sword free and Apsyrtus staggered and fell to his knees, blood gushing thickly from the wound. He raised his hands as though he could stop the flow.

I stepped forward as he knelt – performing obeisance to a goddess he had never respected in life – and I heard myself say I might have saved him if I hadn't known that he would never have saved me.

People would say I killed him, because I laid the trap for him, and acted as the bait. They said I killed him for my lover, that I chose my man over my kin. When they grew tired of saying that, they said I tore his body to pieces and threw each part into the sea. They never accused Jason of killing his brother-in-law, they never asked themselves which of us was more experienced with a sword. They saw his handsome face and heard his gentle voice, and they never imagined that he would have torn my brother's tunic open and licked the blood from his fatal wound before spitting it onto the ground.

And because they believed that I had killed him, that I had torn him limb from limb as we sailed across the oceans, that his wretched father had ceased his pursuit of me because he had to pause to collect the body parts I had thrown overboard, because they believed all this, they never asked themselves who closed his poor dead eyes and buried his body on the island of Artemis. They never knew where I laid him, or saw the stone that marked his grave.

Argo

are harming her.

The Argo helped them in the next part of their journey: that is undeniable. When I said at the beginning that people used to wish the Argo had never set sail, but that none of this was the fault of the ship, I meant it. But I will concede that the Argo helped them here.

When Jason and Medea returned to the ship, it was clear that something terrible had happened. Medea was small and pale, her hands were dirty and she didn't seem to have noticed. Jason was silent as he reached out to help her climb onboard. She was making sure of her footing and seemed about to refuse his hand, but then she looked up and her face softened. He took her hand, and as he pulled her onto the ship, he gave her a small smile. She stared at him and then nodded and he took her in his arms. Whatever he had done, muttered one of the Argonauts, he was forgiven.

The Colchians were not the threat we had initially presumed they might be. Several Argonauts took advantage of the darkness and managed to climb aboard their nearest ship without being spotted. They set it alight in five different places before jumping down to their boat and rowing back to safety. The Colchians had not expected this kind of attack; they were in no way prepared for it. They died, the whole crew, before most of them even knew the ship was ablaze. As for the other ships in their fleet – if you could call it a fleet when none of them seemed to be an experienced sailor – they offered no resistance. Deprived of their leader, and of one of their ships, they melted away.

Now they were free of the Colchian ambush, the Argonauts were not sure which direction they should take. Some said that Zeus was angry with Jason for the murder he had committed, others wondered if it was Artemis to whom they should make their offerings, since it was her temple they had profaned. The sky darkened and the winds began to bite at their sails and it was only then – when it looked like a storm might wipe them out, fleece and all – that Athene chose to give them advice.

When the Argo was being built, Athene had offered her assistance and they had gratefully accepted. And when they were fitting the pieces of carefully smoothed wood into its keel, she had helped them with more than advice: she fitted a plank of sacred oak – all the way from Dodona – into the centre of the ship. She was always thinking ahead, and she knew that one day she might need to make the Argonauts aware of the will of the gods – and, specifically, her will – in a hurry. This was the moment.

If the Argonauts were shocked when a plank of wood suddenly screamed at them with a human voice, they showed little sign of it. Perhaps – after everything they had already seen – they had lost their capacity for surprise. But the ship cried out that they had angered Zeus with the killing of Apsyrtus and that they must sail for Aeaea, the home of Circe. Medea looked astonished and relieved, even as the rain began to beat down on them. She cried out that this was her aunt, and that she would purify them for whatever wrongs they had committed.

The Argo soon found the winds she needed to sail to Aeaea. Or rather, the goddess Hera – who had endured a mighty argument with her husband over the fate of the Argonauts, which she had fortunately won – sent them gentler breezes.

Circe

For Jason –

Circe awoke, filled with anger. She did not usually have nightmares, she often did not sleep at all. But when she did – when she chose to live like a mortal woman, even for one night – she expected to wake feeling rested and content. Instead of which, she found herself deeply disturbed after her mind had been filled with the kind of terrifying visions she might visit on an undeserving stranger. She had dreamed of blood dripping down every wall of her palace, the floors swimming crimson. And then fire had broken out, and the potions and draughts which she used to work her magic were all ablaze. She poured blood over the fire to quench it, but the fear and horror came with her when she opened her eyes.

She rose and took herself to the shore. Her creatures – once men – accompanied her and watched in confusion as she walked into the sea, allowing the salt to draw the darkness from her hair, her clothes. Their confusion only increased when a ship appeared on the horizon, something which rarely happened. Circe raised her head from beneath the gentle waves and saw the agitation on the face of one of her creatures. He had human eyes over a pig snout, his arms and legs terminating in small trotters. He was by no means the strangest of her hybrids: the body parts of wolves, dogs, pigs, cattle and horses mingled with human limbs and faces. She was growing tired of these experiments, however. Perhaps next time she would simply make them into pigs. She turned to follow the creature's anxious gaze and saw the ship, which looked so familiar she knew that it had been in her dreams last night, although she had forgotten it until now.

Circe lifted herself from the water and the creatures began thronging around her, each of them hoping to be her favourite today. She shook her head and they cowered away. If only, she thought wearily, they had been so amenable when they were men. Perhaps they would still be recognizable as human. Circe allowed the warmth of her father Helios to dry her hair and clothes as she returned to her palace. If these sailors wanted her help, they would come and ask for it. She would not stand waiting for them on the shore.

She watched with amusement as the ship dropped its anchor in her harbour and its men spilled onto her island. They were so young and confident, and she wondered if it would be a shame to make all of them into pigs. She beckoned them to come into her home, laughing at their horror when they caught sight of her creatures. But the men were told by their captain to stay outside, and only two people approached her. She drew back from her doorway, surprised to see that one of the two was a young woman. It was only ever men who came to Aeaea. The girl kept her eyes trained on the ground, hands covering her face. The man's eyes

were similarly lowered, though his face was visible. He was
– Circe noted – a very handsome young man.

Circe greeted them and gestured to a pair of grand chairs,
but the couple hurried past her in silence to the very centre
of the hall. The young man drove his sword into the ground,
and then the two of them lay face down beside the hearth,
arms stretched forward. Circe had not seen such a posture
in many years, but she recognized it. They were murderers,
then, seeking purification. She felt a brief surge of annoyance:
Zeus must have sent them to her. Whatever crime they had
committed was so terrible that they had offended the king
of the gods himself. But he had nonetheless offered them a
way back into civilized society.

Circe performed the sacrifices the ritual demanded, slit-
ting the throat of a young pig with the sword the man had
carried, then burning offerings of grain and honey. She
chanted the prayers to Zeus in his role as both Avenger
and Purifier. She held the young man's sword in the fire,
cleansing the blade of the blood he had spilled. Circe then
made further appeals to the Furies – who pursued those
guilty of kin-killing to the very ends of the earth – and
begged them to soften their rage. Once her servants had
cleaned the hearth of all remnants of these sacrifices, she
had completed the task to her satisfaction. Whoever they
had killed, this couple could now sit by her hearth on her
finely polished chairs and they would be offending no
immortal god. Not even her.

She told them they could now rise and asked them where
they had come from. But as the couple stood, the girl
finally revealed her face and Circe felt another shock of
recognition. She had seen this young woman in her dream

last night. Not only that, but she was speaking to family. This girl was related to Helios: she had the same gold in and around her as Circe. A mortal would not see it, but now the goddess couldn't miss it. She found the ages of humans hard to judge but the girl was surely too young to be a daughter of the Sun God. She must be his grand-daughter, daughter of Aietes.

'You're my niece?' Circe asked, in the Colchian language. The girl looked amazed and replied in the same rapid tongue.

'Yes, I am Medea, your brother's youngest child. I helped my nephews – at my sister's urging – in their quest to take the golden fleece back to Hellas. They completed the tasks my father set but he reneged on his promise, so we took the fleece and fled before he could take his revenge on us all.' Tears sprang from the girl's eyes as she spoke, and she made no attempt to stop them.

Circe felt the warmth of her home language rolling over her, and wished that the girl was speaking honestly. She did not challenge her because everything Medea had said was true. But the parts that were missing changed the meaning entirely. The full truth came to Circe in a rush: the way Medea had helped this stranger to defeat her own father, the way she had run away with him, the way she had incurred the blood guilt that Circe had just lifted from her. Of course Aietes was pursuing her: it must be the brother she had killed. Absyrtus, Apsyrtus? Circe couldn't remember and it was hardly likely she would need to know it, now she had seen this handsome young man pierce his lung with a sword, as clearly as if she had been standing beside them.

221

'You will leave my island now,' she said. Medea was nervous, she saw. She was an accomplished liar, but she hadn't wanted to lie. The puzzle was interesting to Circe, but not enough that she would antagonize Aietes any more than she already had done. 'Your father will continue in his efforts to find you,' she said. 'Hellas may not be far enough. This stranger you have brought with you – whoever he is – does not belong here. You might have done once, but no longer. I have purified you because it is what Zeus wanted, and perhaps what Helios wanted, though I can't be sure. But you cannot stay.'

Medea nodded, and touched the young man's arm. She began to speak in halting Greek, but he had already understood Circe's meaning. He nodded and smiled as though he were taking his leave of her by choice. He murmured something about gratitude and Circe nodded and turned away. She heard the two of them leave her palace, hastening back to their comrades. Some of her creatures howled as they went, sorry to miss a chance for new playmates, or perhaps food. Circe could feel her island pushing their ship away, and she poured herself a cup of wine. She sipped it as she wondered why the gods were helping this pair. The girl was clever, certainly, and Circe knew she was a skilled witch. It would take talent at least equal to her own to have outwitted Aietes. Medea could have come to Aeaea to learn from her aunt, but she had abandoned her family and her people in the service of a stranger. And for what? For love? Circe snorted and one of her beasts snorted in reply. No, not for love, or not only for love. Because the gods had ordained it, then? It wasn't like Zeus to want to see a young woman married off, so perhaps that was Hera. She shook her head, answering her next question: why? She had no idea. But she did know that while the young man was in control of her niece at this point, it would not last. She took another sip of her wine.

Arete

betraying

The Argo arrived at the land of the Phaeacians and spilled its crew onto our shores. We receive many storm-tossed sailors here, so it is fortunate that we are such a hospitable people. But even we do not usually receive both sides in a conflict. And yet, chasing close behind the Argo came the ships from Colchis, determined to retrieve their princess, who they said had been stolen by the marauding Greeks. But we had already welcomed the Argonauts and were throwing a grand feast for them in our halls.

The girl in question – a self-possessed young woman on the arm of the ship's captain – spoke to me repeatedly during the feast. She presented herself as a victim of circumstance, and I felt for her. How could I not, when she begged me to take pity on her, to intercede with my husband on her behalf? Alcinous is a generous king, but he would not wish to make an enemy of Colchis. She understood that, but she still hoped we would show clemency.

When the feasting was over and the palace was sinking into sleep, I took my husband's hand as we lay beside each other in our bed.

'Did you speak to their captain?' I asked.

He nodded and said the young man was polite, charming, assured. 'I can see why a young woman might run off with him,' he added. 'You spoke to her?'

'I did, she would scarcely leave me alone,' I replied. 'She is terrified that we will allow the Colchians to take her home.'

'She should never have left there,' Alcinous said.

'She says she had no choice. She gave help to the Argonauts and only then realized that she had condemned herself to exile or death. Her father is notoriously cruel, so I can well imagine that she believed she had to flee. She does seem genuinely afraid of him.'

Alcinous nodded again. 'I don't blame her.'

'And I think she is right to feel aggrieved that the Argonauts would be happy to hand her over to their pursuers,' I said. 'She said – while many of them were in earshot – that she gained them the object of their quest, the golden fleece. And that until they had it on their ship, they were brave as lions. But now they are taking it back to Iolcus, they don't want the inconvenience of a woman onboard their ship, and they don't feel the gratitude she has earned from them, many times over.'

'Did they refute her claims?' Alcinous was still interested, even though his eyelids were half-closed.

'They didn't. I have the strong impression that they have done exactly as she claims: taken advantage of her youth and her inexperience, and now they want to be rid of her.'

'You think a girl like that could have completed a hero's quest?' Alcinous had woken himself back up with indignation.

I laughed at him, and said, 'She is certainly clever enough.'

'But not clever enough to have earned their loyalty?' he asked. 'Does that tell us more about her or about them?'

'I will only say this,' I replied. 'She is . . . I'm not sure what the right word would be? Intense, perhaps? She could easily make men uncomfortable, I think. She had her hand on my arm the whole time we were speaking and it seemed to pulse with heat. She is certainly the granddaughter of Helios, that much is clear. We live a great distance from Colchis but a much shorter one from the homes of the Argonauts. She has a promise from Jason – made in front of witnesses, she says – that he will marry her when they arrive in Iolcus. If he fails to keep that oath, the gods will find a way to punish him. So let us keep this couple together, if we can. She was so sincere when she pleaded with me.'

Alcinous sighed and it turned into a yawn. 'I only spoke to her for the briefest time, but I am inclined to agree with you,' he said. 'She seems very sincere and I wish we could simply offer Phaeacian support to the Argonauts to fight off the Colchians. But we cannot. I don't want to make an enemy of Aietes if I can avoid it; he is certainly ill-tempered enough to make our lives difficult, no matter how far his land is from mine. Without time to consult the gods and find out their views on this couple, I think we must appeal to good sense alone.' I squeezed his hand and he smiled. 'Let us say that if they have shared a bed, we consider them married and she cannot be separated from her husband. If they have only pledged to marry, that is not a strong enough bond, and we return her to her father. If she is carrying his child, of course that would settle it even more decisively: neither she nor the child will lack my protection.'

Exhaustion overwhelmed him and he fell fast asleep. I pulled a thin blanket over him so he would not feel a chill if he woke in the small hours. I rose from the bed and hurried through the halls until I found a servant I trusted to deliver an important message. I was sure of the depth of the girl's feelings, but I was less certain of Jason. So this would be a chance for him to prove himself to me. And, I supposed, to her.

Medea

his own

The messenger arrived in the middle of the night, but the Argonauts were still awake, preparing themselves for battle. He said he had welcome news for Jason, and the men shouted to him to announce it to them all, so they could share in their captain's joy. The man delivered the Phaeacian queen's message with a broad smile and – even as I reddened – the Argonauts greeted it with a huge cheer.

'If all we need to do to make the Colchian problem go away is prepare Jason's marriage bed,' shouted one, 'then let's get to work.'

They had been drinking wine for many hours, but they took their responsibility seriously. Wine was poured into a ceremonial cup, and they made the necessary sacrifices. And then they prepared our bed in a cave nearby.

For years afterwards, people would ask if I had really become Jason's wife on top of the golden fleece. Their tone was always the same, no matter who was asking: shocked and amused at once. In the early days, they would ask the two of us, and Jason would always deny it, but somehow he would do it without lying. 'Does that sound like the sort

228

of thing I would do?' he would laugh. And they would conclude – exactly as he intended – that it was not.

I never told him I felt betrayed by this. I didn't say that lying about our marriage was somehow different from the other lies he told, in his constant quest to smooth over the truth no matter who he was addressing. If I challenged him about anything like this, he would allow a small frown to disturb his perfect brow, and he would place his hand gently on my face, stroke my jawbone with his thumb, and say, 'Things are different here, pretty girl.'

But things were not different the night we married. We had a marriage bed built from cushions on the ground, with the fleece thrown on top of them, glimmering in the light of our torches. The Argonauts did not use the fleece because they had nothing else, or because they ignored its true value, or because they wanted to be sure Aietes wouldn't change his mind and ask for it back. All these excuses have been given since that night, and none of them is true. They turned the fleece into our bed because they believed our marriage would – and should – be sung about by the great rhapsodes.

They were not the only ones who felt this way: nymphs brought wedding flowers and decorated the whole cave as though it were a spring meadow. The glow of the fleece turned everything around it to gold. The Argonauts guarded the entrance to the cave with their spears, just in case a Colchian force came looking for us by night. And Orpheus himself sang our wedding hymn. The gods wanted this marriage, in other words. They wanted me and Jason to be bound together, with their blessing.

What people also want to ask, but don't dare to, is this:

what was it like, that first night you spent with a man you had betrayed your home for? What was he like in bed? Perhaps they worry that I would tell them the truth, and they don't want to be disappointed. The truth is this: he was my first partner but naturally I was not his. I wanted his beautiful golden body but I was also afraid of it. I was certainly more afraid of being taken back to Colchis, so there was never any question of me clinging to my virginity. Not in these circumstances, when it could cost me my freedom and my life.

But if things had been different? If I hadn't had one chance and only one to escape my father's wrath? I don't know if I would have married Jason. I had to, I suppose. I'd run away with him, it had deprived me of alternatives. If I'd had other options, I might have taken a different path. Before the Argo landed in Colchis, I intended to stay celibate, a priestess of Hecate. In spite of what people choose to believe, I was not motivated by sexual desire. Not that night, and not before.

He talked me into the bed, in the same way he talked me into helping him in Colchis. He was so persuasive always, but never more so than when we had sex, during which he would speak softly and coaxingly. For many years, I believed all men were like this, or at least all Greek men. That they must all have an accent, a tone that would disarm anyone. But that was always true for us both: I thought Jason was like other men, when he was nothing like them. And he, of course, believed I was like other women. Which – for a long time – I was.

Part Three

The Return to Iolcus

Peliades

children

Don't speak of her. Don't even use her name in our presence. She is evil, nothing less.

Perhaps you don't know what she did when Jason returned with the fleece.

Everyone was fawning over him, of course. Everyone in Iolcus. The rumours were flying through the streets before his cursed ship was even in the harbour: the Argo is back, it's back!

It sickens us even to think of it. It would have been better if the ship had capsized mid-ocean, a day after leaving Iolcus, if every man onboard had died before they laid eyes on the fleece. Better yet, if it had capsized on its return journey, drowning the Argonauts and that vicious, conniving creature alongside them. That would have been no more than she deserved after betraying her family, after murdering her own brother.

Oh, we didn't know that when she arrived here. When she turned up in Iolcus as Jason's wife – if you can call it that with a straight face – she was as sweet as honey dripping from the comb. So shy and demure, eyes down as

233

though she wouldn't dream of even looking at someone she didn't know. None of us could believe it, when we found out who she was and what she'd done. It just goes to show: you can never tell. Because they arrived here and she was quite happy to stand back and let him take all the credit for his so-called heroics and people were flocking to the harbour, thrilled to see their men back safe and sound. All except the ones who didn't make it, the ones who died on the voyage. There were a few families weeping over their lost sons, but don't imagine Jason spared them even a moment of his time. Too busy receiving all the praise, with his characteristic humility. No, of course we're not serious, why should he show humility now, when he never had before? He was preening by his ship, smiling delightedly, as though he was personally responsible for every family reunion taking place.

There was no sign of his own family, you might note. His mother didn't rush to greet him because she was still so angry with him for leaving all those months before. His father was – so people claimed – too frail and unwell to survive a carriage ride to the harbour. We have serious doubts that this was the truth, for reasons you will soon understand.

Once everyone had wept and embraced and celebrated for longer than you would have imagined possible, Jason decided he would take his foreign wife to meet his parents. They walked through the streets, arm in arm. It was sickening. Children were running around them, trying to get their hands on the so-called golden fleece, which he had wrapped in woollen blankets to keep it safe, he said. More likely it was to keep whatever was in there out of sight.

They arrived at his parents' house with quite the entourage tagging along.

No one knows exactly what happened when they went inside. We have heard several different accounts and none of them rings true. It is probably the case that his mother Alcimede gave them a cool welcome: she would not have been pleased to see Jason bringing an encumbrance with him. She certainly had ambitions for him to marry someone whose status would enhance his own, and a foreign wife was likely to hinder that. But perhaps she would have managed to contain her disapproval, although it would have been the first time.

And what of Aeson? Was he as ill as was claimed? These rumours had been spreading around Iolcus for a long time, thanks to Alcimede and her poisonous friends. It was a painfully obvious attempt to foment ill feeling against our father, Pelias. Aeson was so determined that he would snatch the kingdom from his brother, without any sense of what he would do if he managed it. He was old and confused: he would have been a terrible king.

So what did she do, when she met him for the first time? Magic, apparently. They say she is a highly skilled witch, that magic runs in her family, no less. Maybe it's true, maybe it isn't. But if she found Aeson as near death as has been claimed, she gave him some potion or other. Or perhaps she took the allegedly miraculous fleece and wrapped it round his ageing body, like people said. Whatever happened, he was suddenly able to stand and speak and even walk outside. Something which he had not been able to do since before Jason set sail on his misbegotten ship.

And because they had dragged half the people of the city

after them – all desperate for a moment with the hero and his wife, for some reason – there was a great audience there for Aeson's apparent rejuvenation. And the children who had followed them were soon racing down every street, announcing that a miracle had been performed by this foreign witch. Which is how word came to us, in the palace, that the fleece had magical properties and that she – and she alone – understood how to use it.

There was feasting that night and all the next day. You might have thought that Jason would be polite enough to visit his king and take the fleece to him. It was Pelias, after all, who had sent him to fetch it, it was our father who wanted it. And as king, anything that belonged to one of his subjects was his, so he was being extremely patient allowing Jason this time to be the focus of everyone's attention.

But when Jason finally arrived at the palace, he brought not only the fleece but also his witch wife. Pelias received them both, instead of telling Jason to send his foreign-born woman home. It was his only mistake, and it is one that other men have made, before and since. He thought she was just a woman, instead of understanding that she was a monster, a witch, a Harpy, a Fury, whatever you want to call her: she is all of these and worse. Instead, he told her to meet his daughters, now she was here. He wanted to have Jason's story first-hand, without interruptions. And he wanted his fleece.

We received her kindly, offering her a little wine and quite a comfortable three-legged stool to sit on. And we listened politely to her broken Greek, trying not to laugh when she stumbled over words. How did we end up telling her so much about ourselves, about our worries for our father? We have discussed it subsequently, as you would expect. None of us knows how she did it, sitting there with her garbled questions about his health. The rumours had come to us too, of course, that she had revived Aeson in a way no one could explain. That he was young again.

Our father was not as old as Aeson, it is true. But he too was beginning to show signs of frailty. His movement was not as vigorous as it had once been, his memory would sometimes play tricks on him. His breathing grew ragged if he had to talk for too long. Small things, individually. But together, they gave the impression of a man losing vitality, and he worried more and more that a younger man – any younger man – was plotting to seize his throne.

When his steward came to our quarters and told Medea to get up and leave, because Pelias had finished with Jason, her dark eyes flickered. She stood and walked to the door, turning as she left to tell us that we could try to use the fleece as she had used it on Aeson, but that it wouldn't have the same effect on Pelias. As she walked away, we turned to one another in astonishment and anger. How dare she guess what we planned to do, and how dare she tell us it wouldn't work?

Oh, she was clever. Whatever else you hear about her, this is what you need to remember: she is much cleverer than you know, even though her speech is so backward and her accent virtually impenetrable. She is laying traps for you all the time, and if you notice one, you were meant to: it is to distract you from three more she has hidden. Of course she knew we would try to use the fleece to revitalize our father, and of course she knew we would fail. And she knew we would send for her, and we would ask her if she could help us.

*

We can hardly bear to discuss what happened next. We watched our father sicken over the following days, losing more strength, more capacity. Had she poisoned him? Had Jason? We will never be able to prove it, but we know that one of them was responsible. Jason could have slipped something toxic into the king's wine cup. She could have weakened him simply by staring at him and muttering one of her dark incantations. The stories we have heard would make you shiver on the hottest day.

As he grew weaker, we took the fleece and laid it over his papery skin. It was a nice enough thing – warm and soft – but it had no more effect on our father than any other blanket or sheepskin would have done. He became feverish and pale. We asked the doctor to help him, and he spoke confidently about the remedies he would try. Days passed and Pelias' condition was unchanged.

Then we sent word to Jason, asking him to bring his wife to the palace. None of us wanted to ask her for help, but we didn't know what else to do. This – we should emphasize – is how she likes things. She does whatever it is she does to make you think she can help you, and then she finds a way to remove all other sources of help. We don't know how. But believe us, this is how she operates. They came to the palace together, of course. The pious married couple, doing their duty to his uncle. Jason was taken aside by the steward and she came with us to see our father.

He was sleeping and his breathing was shallow. She looked at him for a long moment, and then said we must come with her. She took us to a dark, curtained room which was usually used for bathing. We have no way of knowing which of the slaves told her it was there, but when she strode so confidently to a room she had never been inside? It made her seem, what? Powerful, magical, something like that. It sounds stupid to say it. But she asked for a cauldron of water to be placed over a fire and then she asked us about our father's condition, when we had noticed it worsening, and so on. She seemed to be listening, and we explained how worried we all were. She nodded, her huge dark eyes darting from one of us to another, as though she were assessing which of us she would eat first. When the cauldron was bubbling, she told us – in her stumbling Greek – that she wanted to show us something.

Where did the ram come from? She must have brought it with her, must have left it with the slaves when she was shown to our father's room. But somehow, she had an old ram, lame in his left hind leg, limping into the room. She told us to take a good look at him and asked if we thought he was a strong specimen or if he was old and ailing. We gave her the honest answer: it looked like a sickly old creature. She nodded gravely, and then the light glinted off something in her hand. It was so bright in the curtained room that we all blinked, dazzled as though we had been staring at the sun. And then suddenly she was throwing chunks of meat into the pot.

We don't know how she did it. Did she butcher the ram

while we stood there? None of us saw her do it, but the meat must have come from somewhere. There was no smell of butchery nor of cooking, something none of us realized until afterwards. There was a powerful stench of herbs and something we couldn't identify. But the hunks of flesh went into her pot and suddenly a bright young lamb leapt out. We cried out in surprise but there was no mistaking it: the lamb was walking and bleating before our eyes. Medea nodded at our astonishment, then she picked up the lamb and held it out to us. We felt its warmth, its vitality.

And then comes the part that we cannot endure. The moment where we asked her how she had done it, and she explained that she had made a special concoction which had rejuvenated the old ram. She would not give us the recipe – such a clever touch – but she would be glad to give us a bottle of this potion for our father. We protested at first: she could not be suggesting that we should chop our father into pieces? She could not be claiming that this would revitalize him the way it had done the ram? She shrugged, like a foreigner. If we didn't want the potion that was all the same to her, he was our father, not hers. She would leave us to discuss it, and we could send a message if we wanted the bottle. It would work almost as well after the full moon as it had today.

And we fell into her trap. Because who would ever imagine that a woman would want an old man dead, and dead in the worst possible way? Who would do such a horrific thing to her husband's family? Of course, if we had known then how she treated her own family, we would have been far more suspicious. But it was too soon for that news to have travelled to us. We believed her because she seemed to understand our love and our concern for our papa, and we thought she was trying to help us, in her strange barbarian way.

People asked us afterwards: how did you do it? How did you hold a knife to your own father's throat and drag it across? How did you catch his blood in cups that were made for wine? How did you chop him into pieces, how did you even find the strength?

These questions are not important. The only question that matters is: when.

When did you realize she had tricked you, that you had killed your father when you thought you were saving his life?

Medea

and my mistress – is

There were laws in Greece, and they were different from the laws in Colchis. In Colchis, the law was whatever my father said it was. Beyond that, we had customs and they were easily upheld. But for the Greeks, it was not the same. They had different customs when they were at home, sometimes opposite to the ones they had when they were in what they called barbarian lands. So, Jason saw nothing wrong with killing my brother in a place far from Iolcus. But the killing of Pelias in Iolcus was wrong. I asked him why, if I should have persuaded his cousins and uncle to sail away from his home before I acted. He said that wasn't what he was saying, but he didn't explain any more.

We were sent away from Iolcus, or asked to leave, I was not sure which. He would be allowed to return at some point, but until then his father Aeson would be king. I asked if I would be allowed to return, since Aeson owed his power to me, but that was not the kind of question a woman should ask, apparently. Other questions a woman shouldn't ask were why so many Greeks treated me differently – no matter where we went – from the way they treated Greek-born women. After we arrived here one man asked Jason when he planned to marry, as though I didn't exist. I knew Jason would be annoyed that I had heard this man and would tell me I had misunderstood, so I didn't ask what was meant.

Jason promised me – when we met, in Colchis – that the Greeks would treat me as a hero, a goddess, even, because I had saved so many Argonaut lives. On their journey back to Greece, I saved many more. But somehow, once we were here, all that was forgotten. I felt strange, foreign, unwelcome. I thought that might change when I gave birth to our first child, and when it became obvious I was expecting our second. But nothing changed. I was never a part of their crew, I was just on their ship for a while.

We never stayed anywhere for long, always moving from island to island, town to town. He said it was because we were not welcome in whichever place we had recently settled, so we always had to leave. I didn't ask him why, because I thought he would say that it was my fault. I tried to forge alliances everywhere we stayed: I had a reputation, after all, and I wanted to build on it. And often the women would come to me for help. It was usually medicine they wanted, or advice.

I wondered if it was Jason who didn't like staying in one place. He had set sail on a mighty voyage not so many years ago, and perhaps he needed to travel across the sea to feel like a hero again. He missed having men around him to command or persuade. He was a hero to our sons, of course, but that was not enough for him. When we arrived on one island, he seemed happier, at first. We were closer than we had been for a long time, and he had family friends there who gave us a place to stay, servants to do our bidding. I developed friendships with the local women, the boys had their own tutor.

But even as we flourished there, Jason still wanted two contradictory things: home and adventure. The first was not yet an option, he said. His father could not welcome us back to Iolcus while Pelias' daughters lived there. We had endured this conversation too many times for me to begin it again. They were the ones who had killed their own father: why should we be the ones to suffer? I would never understand his readiness to accept banishment. I had assumed he would have inherited Iolcus, since Pelias had no sons and Aeson had not been equal to the task of ruling the first time he tried it. But Jason was convinced we had to endure years away in exile before he could inherit his throne.

The longing for adventure was more difficult. He wanted to be full of his youthful promise once more, to capture the imagination of his peers as he had when he set out on his great voyage. He wanted goddesses to intervene in his affairs because they found him irresistible. I think he would have been happy to live permanently on a ship filled with men if he met different women every time he set foot on land. One of the boys once asked him if they could dress up in a finely woven robe they had dug out of an old chest, and he replied that it had been made for him by a foreign queen. I was in another room: he didn't know I could hear him. They were thrilled, of course, at this pedigree. Now they longed for adventures too.

He had been terrified for half of the time he was on the Argo, as I recalled. He had been afraid of the strange land-scapes, animals and people he encountered, he had been perpetually anxious that his companions would replace him as their leader. But he remembered none of that. He claimed to have preferred a life at sea to one on land, a perilous quest to a quiet life with a wife and children. And this was the truth of it, as I saw it: he wanted to be celebrated for his adventures everywhere he went, every day. And the longer we stayed somewhere, the less excited by him people were. He was a great Greek hero, certainly, but only when we had recently arrived, straight out of a rhapsode's song. After a few months in the same place, he was just an ordinary man with a foreign-born wife and children.

I still loved him, in case you are in any doubt about that. I saw his flaws more clearly, perhaps, than when we first met. But I didn't love him any less for them. He was still beautiful, even when Hera stopped enchanting him so that he seemed to be made of gold. He still spoke in that soft, conspiratorial voice when we were curled around each other at night. And when I heard him laughing with the children, I still knew that I would follow him to Oceanus and beyond, if he asked. He wasn't everything he wanted to be, but he was still everything I wanted.

It wouldn't be enough.

Part Four

Corinth

Medea

sharing his bed

I don't know why we settled on Corinth. We had been travelling for so long and I was tired of it, even if Jason was not. Corinth was a crossroads of a place, filled with people passing through on their way to Athens or Delphi, Argos or Tiryns. It was somewhere we could establish ourselves, we thought. Jason had friends who provided him with an introduction to the king: even a wandering hero can benefit from friendship, I reminded him. And it was also somewhere I could develop my reputation among the Greeks for wisdom and advice. Those travelling to and from Delphi were always in need of help, particularly if they received an oracle they couldn't understand.

We arrived there on a cool spring afternoon, and we soon found the home of Jason's family friends. I was uncertain about approaching them, but Jason always says I must lose my foreigner's fear of strangers. The Greek way, he likes to remind me, is to treat everyone as a friend until they prove otherwise. I always smile and ask him how he reconciles this belief with the knowledge that he landed in a foreign country and seduced the king's daughter before spiriting her away. His laughter is delicious.

On this occasion, though, he saw my point. He reassured me: the Corinthians were friends of his mother's side of the family. So they would not have vengeance for his dead uncle Pelias on their minds. He approached them with his usual ease, introduced himself to them and them to us, and then revelled in the pleasure of being greeted as a great hero and a family man. They were delighted to welcome us all into their home, and immediately they offered us beds for as long as we needed them, and a feast that night.

*

As we lay in bed together in the darkness, I stroked his chest, kissing him.

'How does a man who once singlehandedly fought off a battalion of earth-born warriors still have such soft skin? Anyone would think you had some kind of magic potion to protect you.'

He wound his hands in my hair and kissed me back.

'I found a beautiful princess to help me, she's the one you should thank.'

'Should I really? What if I'm jealous when I see how lovely she is? Or are you exaggerating?'

'I never exaggerate. She is glorious and you would be sick with jealousy if you even caught a glimpse of her. It's better if I keep you here, in the dark.'

'Your mother's friends seem kind enough, I think we could stay here for a while.'

'Kind, and desperate to impress the captain of the Argo,' he murmured. 'It's a good place to start, isn't it?'

*

We stayed with them for many days, and their kindness was unwavering. But as the days lengthened, they explained that they would soon be setting out on a journey to see the wife's family, in the mountains. Jason asked if they would like us to accompany them or if they would prefer us to keep an eye on their servants and livestock here in Corinth. I have no idea if they had been planning to ask us to leave, or if they were hoping we would stay. But as soon as Jason asked the question, they were desperate to lend us their home and we were content to stay. We waved them off a few days later and Jason turned to me with a grin. 'Finally,' he said. 'We have the place to ourselves.'

And he enjoyed it for a day or two, until his desire for an audience overcame it.

*

Corinth was always bustling, and Jason was never short of people who wanted to hear his stories. His crew had been drawn from across the Greek world, so wherever travellers had come from, they were bound to know at least one of the Argonauts. Reliving his adventures made him feel like he was still the captain of a ship of heroes, even though his comrades were now long gone. He was easily bored, and the life of a man who had once been an adventurer was not enough for him. I wondered if this was why he hadn't taken up the kingdom of Iolcus when Pelias died, why we'd found ourselves banished and always on the move. But we were in Corinth now, so it scarcely mattered.

But when his environment wasn't in constant flux, I began to see that he would create a shifting landscape from within. His mood changed dramatically from day to day, sometimes from hour to hour. I had first noticed this several years before, on the Argo. If the ship was in peril from any source, he might be anxious, but he was also quick and decisive. If the weather was calm and the ship was sailing, he might be happy for a short time, but it could never last: he abhorred constants. Jason could swing from tremendous self-confidence to absolute despair and it was not always possible to predict what would prompt the shift. The same event might provoke two contradictory reactions.

He loved to be welcomed home, to feel that no one was truly happy when he was absent.

'How's my hero today?' I asked him one day, hearing his footsteps behind me.

'I am everything you've ever dreamed of and more.' He smiled as he slid one arm around my waist and kissed the back of my neck. He had shared his stories with strangers and they had shown sufficient appreciation. He felt every inch the hero.

But then the next time he came home, I asked again, 'How's my hero?' And this time he was filled with remorse for everything that had gone wrong on his quest, full of melancholy for the comrades he had lost and guilt for the ones he'd left behind. But whatever mood he was in, he would usually be cheered by spending time with his boys.

*

'Guess what happened today?' he asked me, as we lay in bed one night.

'Everyone told you that you were brave and clever and handsome?' I suggested.

'How dare you? They said handsome first,' he said.

'They're trying to get you off your guard,' I replied. 'Don't trust them.'

'I received an invitation to visit the king,' he said.

'Creon?'

'Yes.' The pleasure came off him in waves. 'Someone has told him I am here, and now he wants to meet me.'

'He might be useful,' I said.

'I think so,' he agreed.

*

The first visit was a success. Jason could charm any ageing king, apart from my father. The royal household was small in Corinth: just the king and his little girl. My husband was ebullient when he returned home that evening, partly from the wine, he admitted.

'But partly because he wanted my advice,' he said. 'It is so good to feel . . .' He paused and searched for the word. 'To feel useful.'

'Is it?' I asked. 'How come?'

'You don't understand,' he groaned. 'Everyone comes to you for advice.'

I laughed. 'You do exaggerate.'

'Never,' he replied. 'I had to wait in a queue to get in through the front door yesterday. Someone asked me what I needed help with and I said, "I'm hoping if I wait in the queue long enough, I might one day meet my wife." He was quite sympathetic, actually. He was looking for a wife as well, I think.'

'Oh, I think I remember him,' I said. 'Tall, luscious black hair, beautiful muscles on display for all to admire?'

'He was balding,' Jason sniggered. 'With a paunch.'

'Oh, him. I told him he should try next door.'

The children were clambering all over him, as he tried to sit down at the table. 'How would you feel if your papa was adviser to the king?' he asked. They shouted their approval and his face shone as though in torchlight.

*

'They don't care what you do,' I told him later, after I had put the children to bed.

'I know,' he said. 'But they will care, one day. I want them to care. I want them to tell everyone that their father is Jason, captain of the Argo, winner of the golden fleece.'

I nudged him.

'I suppose they can say their mother helped with that. But only when they've finished talking about me,' he added.

'When are you going back to the palace?' I asked.

'Tomorrow,' he said. 'Or the next day. I said I could help him with some shipping routes.'

'And can you?'

He shrugged. 'Probably.'

*

The children missed him, now he was spending more time away at the palace. But he was his old self again: satisfied with the lot the Fates had given him. I carried on as before, dispensing medicine and advice to whoever came asking. When we were reunited at the end of each day, there was a thrill in seeing him again. I was missing him like the children, I suppose.

He sometimes brought them presents from the palace, toys that had once belonged to royal children: a little round horse on wheels, a terracotta dog with a plumed tail.

*

The first time Aegeus knocked at our door, I didn't know who he was. But he knew me. He was polite about it, in the Greek way: he introduced himself to Jason and asked if he could speak to me. Jason was always so gracious that Aegeus didn't notice that he had caused offence. My husband had promised me that my name would ring round the Greek-speaking world when the Argonauts returned home, but he didn't particularly like the attention he had brought me. He preferred – though he would never have said so – visitors coming to meet him, not me.

I had learned this over time. Jason would never have

255

wanted to imagine himself vain. Nor – though he was cheerfully competitive with other men – would he have believed he resented his wife's reputation. As a great hero, of course, he thought he had nothing left to prove. But he loved power, longed to have it or to be close to it. No wonder he had kept a cloak made for him by some long-lost queen years before. He would feel his own status rise every time it caught his eye.

So – when we were first married – I believed that everything I did would reflect well on him and I sought to build my reputation wherever we went. At first, he appreciated my efforts to ingratiate myself with his countrymen. So long as my name was always firmly after his, he was content. But as the years passed, his story was unchanging and fewer people wanted to hear it again. He had once been a hero, but what was he now? Whereas I was harder to push aside: I had once been the one who saved his precious life and won his precious fleece, but now I was known for my ability to help with all kinds of difficult problems. Jason's great fear – after the death of Pelias – was that the Greeks would believe him tainted by my barbarity. He used prettier words, when he explained what I had done wrong, but that was what he meant.

So – even though I saw myself as no more barbarous than him – I did not offer my assistance to those who wanted to be rid of an unpleasant relative. I didn't open my medicine chest at all. I simply advised women which herbs to pick and prepare if they wanted to be sure their pregnancy would last, that their baby would come on a propitious day, that he would be male. My own children proved I could achieve these things for myself, so why not also for them? I helped them interpret their dreams and distinguish which had been sent by a god and for what purpose. I let them talk and then I told them what they needed to know.

My reputation was steady while Jason and I moved around Greece, but it had really begun to grow when we were in Corinth, where someone always needed help with something. When men wanted my help for themselves rather than for their wives, Jason grew irritable about them seeking me out. If I kept my advice in the domestic sphere, he was happy. But when Aegeus arrived, it tested his patience.

'I'm looking for the woman they call Medea,' said a white-haired man. 'I am Aegeus of Athens.'

'She's my wife,' Jason replied. 'I am Jason, of Iolcus.'

'Ah, so I have come to the right place!' The old man was delighted.

Jason nodded. He was waiting for the man to ask him about the Argo, about the fleece. But Aegeus was consumed with his anxiety to have a son, an heir. He was travelling to Delphi, and had been told to ask me to help him formulate his question and advise on the offerings he should make to the god. He ate and drank with us, and showed some interest in Jason's stories. But – like so many men – his primary concern was for himself.

As he was leaving, I told him to come back when he had consulted the oracle, and he agreed. Once he was out of hearing, Jason was full of contempt for him: a self-centred old man who knew nothing about the world beyond his own city. Only then did I discover that Aegeus was the king of Athens, and that his lack of interest in Jason was a snub. I explained that people who long for children are often unable to think of much else, but it was not enough to improve Jason's temper.

'I am a friend to the king of Corinth,' he said. 'The king of Athens should want to know me too.'

'I'm sure he will,' I said. 'He is just thinking about fatherhood today. As soon as he comes back to talk affairs of state, he will want your help.'

Jason shrugged and walked away.

Glauke

with royalty,

'Do you like him, Papa?' Glauke's expression of careful nonchalance almost made the king laugh. But he knew his daughter, and he did not want to hurt her feelings. Still, he could not resist teasing her.

'Like who?' he asked. He was examining a new wine jug, and pretending to give it almost all his attention. 'The boy who delivered this?'

His daughter pursed her lips. 'No, not the messenger boy. You know who.'

'Oh, you mean our newest neighbour,' Creon said. 'What was his name? Heracles?'

'You're being deliberately annoying,' Glauke replied, and her father could not deny it.

'He seems a very impressive young man,' he said. 'All those adventures at such a young age. He made me feel quite old.'

'You are quite old,' his daughter said. 'Otherwise, you'd have remembered his name.'

'Even I'm not old enough to forget the name of Jason and the Argo,' Creon smiled. 'We've heard enough songs about their adventures, I assumed they must have taken place over many years. I was just astonished he could still be so young after doing so much.'

'I think he must have set out when he was my age,' Glauke said.

'Unless a god has bewitched him to appear young when he is really a hundred and three,' her father murmured.

'You aren't funny,' she said, and her father laughed.

'He caught your attention, then?'

'Oh, yes,' she replied. 'I can't imagine what it must have been like, to face down those monsters on his own. Fire-breathing bulls, a snake that never sleeps, flying bird-women! He must be the greatest hero there has ever been.'

'I would think so,' Creon said.

'Will you invite him back?' she asked.

'So he can tell us about even more monsters?' the king replied. 'You will start having nightmares if we aren't careful.'

She folded her arms and stared at him until he stopped laughing and promised to invite the young man to visit again.

*

'When were you most afraid?' she asked.

Jason smiled and rubbed his jaw as though he was thinking of the answer, and had not been asked this same question many times before. 'I'm not sure,' he said. 'When we were trying to get through the Clashing Rocks, perhaps? They dwarfed our ship, we felt like playthings of the gods. And it seemed out of our control, too. You can't fight a rock the way you can fight a giant snake.'

'Of course.' Glauke wanted their visitor to believe she had seen enough giant snakes to know their weak spots.

'How did you shake off the Colchians?' asked Creon. His tone was mild but the young man was startled, nonetheless.

'We out-sailed and out-rowed them,' he said, the words tumbling into one another. 'They aren't seafarers, like we are. So they were never going to be able to keep up with us.'

'And anyway, your ship was better,' said Glauke. 'Because the goddess Athene helped you build it.'

The smile spread slowly across Jason's face. 'Exactly,' he said. 'No one but a barbarian would ever imagine they could outmanoeuvre a ship built by a goddess.'

She nodded. 'And then you decided to come to Corinth.'

'Where else would I be able to continue this life of constant adventure?' he asked.

She laughed prettily, she hoped.

Medea

marrying

Jason came home from the palace in a playful mood and I thought he was joking when he first mentioned it. Because that is what anyone would think, if her husband came to her and told her he was wondering about getting married. I laughed. I said, 'You are married.'

'I know I'm technically married,' he said. And he was laughing too, as though the whole idea was absurd. 'We're married in a way, aren't we? But we're not legally married.'

I stared at him. 'We were married with the gods' blessing, in the land of the Phaeacians. Your comrades were our witnesses. We live as husband and wife: we share a bed. We have children. How is that not legally married?'

'Well, if you were Greek, we would be legally married,' he said. 'But you aren't.'

'Do you really believe that?'

He shrugged and smiled. 'It's not about what I believe, darling girl. It's about what the Corinthians think, isn't it?

'Is it? Not if you tell them they're wrong.'

'Their laws are their laws,' he said.

'I don't understand why you're saying this. What has happened?'

'Nothing's happened,' he said. He moved closer to cup my chin in his hand, but I backed away from him. His face became a mask of sympathy. 'Stop,' he said. 'Don't be like this. I thought you'd think it was funny.'

'Why would anyone think that was funny?' I asked him. But I let him put his arms around me, and press my face against his chest.

Glauke

the daughter

'I don't see who could be a more suitable husband than the captain of the Argo himself,' she snapped.

Creon sighed. 'I know you don't, my dear. But I don't know if I want you to marry a man who claims to feel most at home when he is far from home, in mortal danger. You would be a widow before you were twenty.'

'He is the gods' favourite!' Glauke replied. 'What better prospect could I choose for a wedding? He has survived so many trials and still he continued to travel until he came here, to Corinth. To me. And now, he is content to stay, because he has found what he was seeking. It wasn't the fleece, it was me.'

'That's what he said?' her father asked.

'He didn't have to say it. He shows me in countless ways every time he comes here, every day. When did he last go for a day without visiting me?'

'Well, he is a man residing in a foreign land,' Creon reminded her. 'He lives within our borders with my permission. He wants to nurture the connection with us, he's trying to keep himself and his children secure.'

'He wants to marry me.' Glauke could feel tears scratching to escape her eyes. 'He will be king of Iolcus when his father dies.'

'And king of Corinth when I die, if he marries my daughter,' Creon said. 'So his future is assured, one way or another.'

His daughter stormed out of the hall.

Medea

of Creon,

There was no more talk of marriage. For a few days, Jason didn't go to the palace. He stayed at home, playing with the children, drinking wine, making ostensibly polite remarks about the people who came to consult me. After a small flurry of local women had visited the house, he came up behind me and kissed the top of my head.

'You're so clever,' he said. 'I love how everyone now realizes how clever you are.'

'Clever women aren't always popular,' I said. Even in their own homes, I thought.

'You have all the right advice for these women,' he continued. He was pulling at my hair to free it from its pins. I heard them bounce on the floor as I felt my hair slide down to my shoulders. I wanted to bend down and pick them up, in case one of the children stepped on them. But his hands were on my waist now, and he was tugging at my tunic as he turned me to face him.

And I wanted him more than I ever had, this beautiful, deceitful man. People would ask – in later years – what we could have seen in one another that was so potent it could precede such a terrible unravelling. And I couldn't always give them the answer, because it was not always appropriate to explain that sometimes I wanted him so much, I could think of nothing but him until the desire was sated. Armed men could have threatened to take my boys, to enslave them in a distant land, and if the alternative had been that they would take Jason away from me, I might well have said to have my children and wished them the best of it.

It was not proper to love a man this way. It was certainly not proper for a Greek woman to feel such things: that's why I don't often answer the questions. This desire – one that pushed everything else aside – was apparently another sign of my barbarian nature. I long ago stopped trying to explain to people who didn't know us then – who never saw Jason when he resembled a golden statue of Apollo, gleaming and perfect – how things were in our marriage. Of course they can't understand: they didn't know him then, never saw the way he padded watchfully through the house like a mountain cat, never heard the soft music in his voice, never felt the urgency beneath his languid appearance. What I would like to say (but never do) is that very few people experience such desire, and even fewer find it reciprocated. Jason was always on the lookout for more, it is true – more power, more fame, more women – but he wanted me enough to drive those things from his mind, for a short while.

And there is never more than that, for him. He will never be satisfied with anything – any person, any situation – for long. He doesn't know how to be content: he only knows how to slew between wanting something and getting it, then immediately wanting something new. I know this now; I didn't know it then. Then, I thought there was a way of keeping him, and it just needed to be calculated, like the correct dose of a remedy or a poison. I needed to be clever but not too clever, to fit in but not too well, to be popular but not more than him, to be Greek but never Greek enough, to be his wife but still out of reach. I believed I could change and adapt sufficiently to hold him, and it never occurred to me that this would not – could not – be enough.

Glauke

who rules

The princess was beautiful, she knew. And she was her father's only child, so she also knew what it meant to be loved. She had heard plenty of stories of ungrateful old kings failing to appreciate their daughters, but her father was not such a man. Creon had believed he would never be a father by the time his daughter was eventually born, and he had adored her the moment he saw her. His wife had died a few days after giving birth, and he mourned her greatly. But he was no less besotted by his daughter because of the price the Fates had extracted.

Glauke's nurse had asked – teasing, as the little girl took her first stumbling steps – how her father would ever see her married.

'Who could ever be good enough for your grey-eyed girl?' she said.

Creon smiled. 'Only a god of the sea could hope to match her,' he replied.

'Well, now I know who to pray for,' the nurse said.

And the household watched as the little girl became bigger, and her father only loved her more.

*

There had been no suitor for Glauke before Jason. Many men looked at her ageing father and concluded that the throne of Corinth would be available to whoever married his daughter. But Creon did not welcome young men into his home, precisely because he didn't want to lose his only child to a man who failed to appreciate her as much as her father did. He took no risks that his daughter might set her heart on an unsuitable man: if she never met any, she would never fall in love with any.

He had made an exception for Jason for several reasons. Firstly, he wanted to meet the captain of the fabled Argo and learn about his quest from the man's own words. Secondly, he assumed that someone who had undergone so many adventures would be scarred by them. Fire-breathing bulls caused terrible burns, surely, and a never-sleeping snake must have sharp fangs. And yet the man who arrived in his palace was young and handsome. Creon sensed the danger Jason posed as soon as Glauke set eyes on him, but it was already too late. Still, Creon was comforted when he discovered Jason was married, with children. But he had failed to consider his daughter's determination, and he had not yet known that this charming stranger was as ruthless as anyone he had ever met. And when he realized that there was an irresistible bond forming between his daughter and this young hero, he still thought the situation could be much worse. Jason had nowhere else to call home, so even if she married him, Glauke would stay in the palace. Her husband could join her, and her father would never lose her. But he still felt something was wrong.

*

'Tell me about your wife,' the king said. Jason looked uncomfortable for only the briefest moment, before his assured smile returned.

'She isn't my wife in the legal sense,' he said. 'She's from Colchis.'

'You have sons,' Creon answered.

Jason shrugged and the older man nodded. They both knew how things were. Jason's children by Glauke would be true Hellenes, in a way that those by a foreigner – even a princess or a queen – never could be.

'I hear she is clever,' the king added. 'She will understand what's best for you, then.'

'She will,' Jason replied. 'I'm sure she will.'

Nurse

If only the Argo had sunk to the bottom of the sea rather than winging its way towards the land of Colchis, through the dark Symplegades; if only the pine trees in the glades of Mount Pelion had never been chopped down; if only those mighty heroes had never picked up their oars, the men sent by Pelias for the golden sheepskin. For then my mistress Medea would not have sailed to the towers of Iolcus, stricken with love for Jason; nor would the daughters of Pelias – persuaded by her – have killed their father; and she wouldn't live here, in Corinth, with her husband and children, pleasing the citizens to whose land she came in flight, helping Jason in everything. That is the greatest help: whenever a wife doesn't disagree with her husband.

But now, everything is hostile, and the things she loves most are harming her. For Jason – betraying his own children and my mistress – is sharing his bed with royalty, marrying the daughter of Creon, who rules over this land. Medea is wretched, dishonoured like this. She cries out about the oaths he swore to her, she cries for the greatest pledge he made, when they bound their right hands in marriage. She calls on the gods to witness what Jason has now given her in exchange for their vows.

She lies prone – unable to eat a thing – surrendering her body to the pain. She wastes away the days with tears. Since the moment she heard about her husband, she hasn't lifted her face, or even raised her eyes from the ground. Her friends have offered her advice, but she doesn't hear them. She's like a rock or the waves of the sea. Only once has she moved at all, and then she turned her head and wept for her abandoned father and her homeland. She betrayed them both when she came to Greece with that man, the one who holds her now in such contempt. Poor Medea, she has learned the hard way what it is to be cut off from your home and your family. She even hates to see her children, and takes no pleasure in them. I'm afraid she is planning something. She's a strange woman. No one starts a fight with her and takes an easy victory.

Medea

Oh gods, how could you allow this? How is it possible that a man could pledge himself to me and swear his oaths by every god, even Zeus himself, and every goddess, and it could count for nothing? How can I have been betrayed by so many?

He didn't seem false. Of course that is a stupid thing to say, to think, but he didn't. He took my hand and told me we were married and the nymphs brought flowers to our wedding chamber. I didn't imagine these things; they happened. He asked for my help and I gave it. And I didn't demand marriage: he offered it. No one forced him to make any vows. He was a free man and he entered into solemn promises of his own volition.

And yet. The promises he made are ones he has decided not to uphold. He could have taken his pleasure anywhere – I have no doubt he has done, over the years. He has lied when he felt guilty but I never expected him to be faithful. I am not a fool, I am not a child.

But I thought our vows meant something to him, I thought our children meant something to him. I thought – at least – that we were married. And now? Now he says we are not. That I have imagined things he didn't say, or if he said them, he didn't mean them. How could I have been so naive as to imagine that a man like him was bound by promises made to a foreigner like me? He didn't even – he reminded me – make any pledge to my father. So could I really have expected that words spoken in the heat of adventure, in the anticipation of battle, in the aftermath of victory, can I really have believed that these words bound him to me?

I tell him I trusted his words, and he laughs and says he doesn't believe me. I tell him I loved him then and I love him now, and he tells me not to be ridiculous. How can love be ridiculous, I asked him. And he said, love isn't ridiculous, you are. The tears pour down my face in torrents and he says, stop crying, why would you cry, don't look at me that way, don't stare at me with such anger.

It isn't anger, it is pain.

But he never accepts he has hurt me, he cannot believe it of himself. So instead, he believes that I must be angry, that he is the one being mistreated. You're angry, he said, because you think I don't love you any more. But you are the one seeking to put boundaries around my heart. I love you, I love our children, I love our family. That has nothing to do with the way I feel about her.

The pain looks at him and he looks away.

You are marrying her, I said. It has everything to do with us, we are your family, I am your wife.

You won't stop being my family just because I am married to someone else, he said. And I feel as though everything is sliding past me, as though I am at sea in the middle of a lurching storm.

You're throwing us away, I said. Cast aside, like jetsam. Where will we live, have you even thought of that?

And he says, you will live here, you idiot, no one will throw you out. I will move into the palace, of course, to fix my place with my new wife and the king. And you can stay here, in this little house.

He says this as though it were completely reasonable. Perhaps I am mad.

I don't know what he said after that. I was screaming and then there was black.

Nurse

Children, listen to me. You must keep out of your mother's sight, until I say. Do you understand? She is not angry with you, precious, she is angry with everyone, and you are nearest to her. So you must keep away from her for a little while, until her anger subsides. Don't cry, my darlings. We must be as quiet as we can, when we are inside the house. But I will take you outside to play, and I promise that once we are far enough away that your mama cannot hear us, you can make all the noise you like.

I know you miss him. Your mother misses him too. I don't know when he will come back. No, he hasn't gone on another big adventure, don't worry. Your father isn't lost at sea or battling monsters. He isn't far away and he'll be back here soon to see you, I'm sure. Please don't cry. Or – if you must – do it quietly.

Glauke

Glauke walked beside her father, trying to keep pace with his longer stride.

'Are you happy, dearest?' Creon usually tried to pretend he hadn't noticed when his daughter wanted to discuss something with him, but she had been trying to have this conversation with him for several days, before changing her mind at the last moment.

'Almost,' she replied.

'You will soon be married to the man you said you wanted to marry. I have made him welcome in our home. What is left that is impinging on your happiness?'

'I don't want her in Corinth,' Glauke said.

'You don't want who in Corinth?' Her father tried to think who his daughter might mean. Surely Jason had been wise enough to keep the details of any other dalliances to himself.

'That woman, the foreigner.'

Creon turned in surprise. 'Medea?'

'I hate hearing her name,' Glauke snapped. 'The women are always bleating on about how she saved someone's baby

278

or whatever. She's always doing something, apparently. As if I want to hear about her. I hate her.'

The king shrugged. 'Tell them they're not to speak of her. You're my daughter, she's just some foreign refugee. Why would anyone be discussing her at all?'

'I don't know.' His daughter looked so petulant that he realized she had been asking all these women about the mother of Jason's children.

'I'm sure you can bring yourself to ignore her,' he said.

'I can't,' she said. 'I don't want to have to, I want her to be banished from here so no one even remembers her.'

'Has Jason agreed to this?' Creon was surprised. The man had conveyed to him that the Colchian was simply a trophy from his quest, but he hadn't seemed to bear her any ill-will.

There was a pause.

'We haven't discussed it,' his daughter said.

'Why not?'

'Because he says he loves his stupid children with her, and I don't think he'd want them to be sent away.'

'I doubt he would,' Creon said. 'I wouldn't have agreed to be separated from you, no matter who asked me. But that isn't relevant, is it? You just want her sent into exile, not his children too?'

He glanced over at his daughter and saw her looking studiously at the ground.

'We will have children of our own,' she said. 'He will never think of them when our first child is sitting on his knee.'

Creon slowed his pace. 'He will, my love. A man doesn't just forget his sons.'

'Whenever he looks at them, he'll be reminded of her. I don't want it.'

'So what is it you want, my dear?' The king stopped and turned to face his daughter. 'Are you saying you want his wife and children thrown out of Corinth? How will you explain that to him?'

'I'll think of something,' she said.

And she did.

Medea

I cannot stay inside the house any longer. Everyone tells me that I must pick myself up from the floor and welcome the women I have befriended here. The children's nurse says they are asking for me, and that they are worried about me. I cannot afford for them to think me rude or ungrateful: I am a visitor here, I am from a distant land. I am – as Jason never tires of reminding me – not Greek. I must be careful that I don't alienate these women, after I have worked so hard to gain their support. Though I don't know how much use that will be to me; they are hardly going to speak up for me when my rival is their beloved princess.

But I must try. If I am going to be abandoned by my husband – in the teeth of every promise and vow he made, to Zeus, Themis, Hera and every other god – I will need every friend I have. A refugee like me can easily offend without realizing: our customs are different from yours. So, I will go out and meet with the women I know, I will thank them for their concern, I will accept their good wishes. And I will hide the strength of my feelings from them; I will not let them see how much I long for death.

I have lost everything I cared about. People will tell me that this is an exaggeration, that I love my children, that I am lucky they are healthy and growing up to be strong and well. I do love them, of course I do. But everything is bound up in him: without a husband we are no longer a family. We are bereft.

I don't know what I did wrong, that is the thought that plagues me, circling and returning to its carrion. I bought my husband with everything I had: I gave him my skills, my knowledge, my goddess. I saved his life and stole his fleece. I gave him myself, and none of it was enough.

Except it was, I know it was. I speak to women every day about their hopes and fears, for their husbands and children; I have heard the intimate details of hundreds of lives, since I left Colchis. I know that Jason had what he wanted: I can see further and deeper than most people ever will, and I learned how to thrill him from the very first night we spent together.

Did you really have sex on the fabled golden fleece, people used to ask, if they were brave enough. The fleece was less than we were that night, it was – it is – enhanced by everything we did on it.

So, yes, Jason was happy, more than happy in our bed, in our home, with our family. He always said that I kept him from boredom, and I did. I knew he thought of himself as an adventurer, so I gave him the adventure he needed. There were days – many days – when we abandoned our plans, our friends and our children so that we could be alone.

And I do not accept that my charms have weakened over time. I am still young, I am still – so they tell me – beautiful. When men come to ask my advice, I see their veiled appraisal: they do not find me wanting. And yet, my husband has decided that our marriage is nothing to him. That there is nothing here he wants that he cannot have elsewhere. I don't have that option, naturally. If I had wearied of him, I wouldn't be able to look to other men to alleviate my boredom.

What would my new friends do if their men treated them in such a way? If a Colchian man had behaved like this, he would already be dead at my father's hands. Or my brother would have killed him. But I am orphaned, I am stateless. I abandoned and betrayed those who would have protected me, and I did it all for him, for that worthless, fickle Greek. I believed him when he said he loved me and I believed him when he told me we were married. And so I exchanged everything I had – my family, my homeland – for a man who did not value them, did not even acknowledge my sacrifice. All he wanted was to carry the fleece away from Colchis, and he knew he couldn't do it himself. Was all of it a pretence? Can he have lied to me for so many years, even as our children were born and growing? Wouldn't I – who can see so much – have seen if his heart were false? I can read men, I can read him. But I didn't ever guess he could do this.

So, here I am. I cannot undo what he has done. I thought he would come back to me once he tired of her young body, but he is too cunning to insult the daughter of a king. And besides, it is already too late. Why would I allow him back into my bed now? His behaviour has been witnessed by all of Corinth, and that is already more than I can bear. If I allowed him to return to our family, I would be confirming the image he has presented to all: that I am a woman so I count as nothing. All the work I have done to build my reputation has been undone by him in a few sordid acts. How will I survive now, if anyone knows that he can rob me and cheat me and there will be no reprisal? I am a woman alone; I cannot afford for this to be my reputation.

I must find a way to make Jason regret his decision. I need to punish him in a way that will humiliate him as he has humiliated me. I want him to come crawling along the ground to this door – that used to be his but is now mine – and I want him to beg me to allow him back inside. Even Jason would not be so stupid as to try and force his way in. And when I have done whatever it takes to bring him back to me, I will stand and watch as he grovels his apology and pleads with me to be his wife again.

And even if he is bewitched by Hera herself, even if she makes him gleam golden as he crawls towards me, even if Aphrodite appears beside him to make me love him more than I already have, I will say no. You could not be trusted with my love, Jason. You will never have it again.

Nurse

Children, you must choose your favourite toy: one each is all we will be able to carry. Very well, two each, but that is all. There is no point crying, because it will not change the truth, which is that we cannot leave here carrying all our household goods on our backs. I know you don't want to go, my loves. I don't want to go either. This had all the potential to be a happy house, and you were a happy family when you arrived here. But the king has banished your mama, and you are banished along with her. I cannot change his mind, darling boy, because he is the king, and I do not have the power to challenge him.

I don't know why a king would want to banish children, no. And, no, you haven't done anything wrong. It isn't your fault, none of this is your fault. The king has decided to punish this family for no good reason.

No. I don't know where we will be going: your mama is trying to find someone who will receive us into their homes, she is working hard, my darlings. She will not leave it to the Fates to decide where we go; she will find you a new home.

Perhaps you will get on a boat, yes. I don't know. When

we know, we'll tell you. But you must be patient: it won't be for long. We don't have long.

No, your daddy won't be coming with us this time. Please, don't cry. Don't cry over your papa, because he is not . . . No, I won't say that. It isn't for the likes of me to be offering my opinions on a man like your father. But I will say that I am surprised any man could see his children carted off into exile on the whim of a young girl who should know better. What kind of future will she have, knowing she is marrying a man who won't defend his loved ones from attack? It is difficult for the young to imagine they will ever be anything but young, I suppose. She believes their marriage will make him the man she wants him to be. But part of her will always know that she asked him to act against his children's interests, and that he agreed.

So pack up your treasures, my loves: be sure you have your best things and a bag in which to carry them. If we can take a cart, or a mule, we will. But otherwise, you must not take more than you can carry.

No, we cannot just pretend to leave and then hide, my darling. The king's men will come to ransack the house, I have no doubt of it. They will search everywhere, and we must not be found inside the boundaries of Corinthian land, or they will take our lives as well as our possessions. I don't mean to frighten you, I am sorry. But no, we must leave as soon as we can. And let the gods witness what is being done to her, and to us all.

Medea

What kind of man is he, the man I married? If I can even call him that, if I can say he is the same man as the one I met in Colchis, all those years ago. Because that man would not have allowed his children to be sent out into the world with no defence but their poor mother. He would not.

I sent a message to the palace, asking if he knew his bride's father was casting us into exile, and there came back a brief reply, saying only that if they had their mother to protect them, he was sure they would be well. What man would say this, or even think it, but him? I can imagine his face, as he gave the message to the boy: mock serious, voice so grave, laughter dancing in his eyes. I kept him safe from monsters and giants, I can certainly keep our children safe from bandits or hunger. He takes the credit for my bravery, and then abandons his children to my care.

But does he really not want to see his sons growing into manhood? They are so like him already. You would have thought vanity alone would have made him want to be near them: who is not beguiled by the echoes of ourselves we see in our children's faces? And yet, he is content to see them disappear while they're still young, trusting in my power to keep them from harm, and his reputation to bring them back to him one day, when they are men.

I will not let this stand. I will not allow his simpering wife to drive us out of our home, the first real home our children have ever known. I must be revenged on her, and it must be soon, if we are to be exiled from this land.

So I will do something that shames me almost more than I can bear. I will ask the king – their king, not mine – to give us a few more days before we have to leave. It pains me to ask the hateful old fool for anything, but I must give us the best chance of having a haven to escape to. I have sent messengers where I can, but nothing has come back yet. It will, but not yet.

So I must throw myself on his mercy: the very words sicken me. I will remind him that I am an abandoned wife, a mother trying to do the best for her children. He is a doting father, so he cannot approve of the way their father is treating them.

But I must set this anger aside. I must not let him see how I despise Jason, or we will be in a worse predicament than we are now.

Glauke

Glauke sang to herself as she brushed her hair. She had only a few more days of unmarried life ahead, and she intended to enjoy them. Nothing pleased her more than imagining the moment when the marriage hymn was sung and her friends cheered her on in her new life.

She wanted to be a bride, she wanted to stand beside Jason and have everyone remark on how beautiful she was and how well-suited they were. And now – she experienced a small shiver of happiness – she would be standing there in the full knowledge that his foreign whore had been thrown out of their kingdom. Nothing would pollute her perfect day. Not even his children, who would be gone along with their vagrant mother.

She heard Jason's footsteps before she saw him, and she smiled: she loved how quickly she was becoming accustomed to having him nearby. And – when he came through the doorway, she smiled more broadly – he was wearing the tunic and cloak she had given him, instead of the awful ones he had before. He looked like a proper Corinthian now.

'Darling girl,' he said, as he bent to kiss the top of her head. There was something so assured and confident about the way he did this, she thought. As though he had been saying it all his life.

'Good morning,' she said.

'It is now,' he laughed, and lifted the brush from her hand. He placed it carefully on the table in front of her and – holding her by her shoulders – he turned her around to face him. 'You look so beautiful today. Even for you, and you are beautiful every day. You fill me with delight.'

'Thank you,' she said, marvelling again at her ability to make him feel such joy. It was so lucky that he had never loved the foreigner, even if he'd had to pretend he did to escape her violent father and complete his quest.

'I want to ask you for a favour, my love,' he said. 'And I need you to promise that you won't be angry with me for asking. If I could avoid saying anything that might annoy you, you know I always would. But I do need this one thing.'

'Anything,' she smiled.

'I want you to beg your father for a favour,' he said, kissing her cheek as he did so. 'A favour for me. Will you? Please?'

'Of course,' she replied. 'You know my father will do anything I ask him.'

'I can't blame him,' Jason said. 'I feel exactly the same way.'

'So what is the favour?'

'I want you to ask him if my sons can stay behind,' he said. 'No, don't frown. Don't spoil your perfect features with an expression like that, it is cruel to treat them in such a way. Most girls will never know the satisfaction of watching a man become actually speechless when they smile, but you have that effect on me eleven times a day, at least. So please, I beg you, don't let that little line appear between your elegant brows.'

'I don't want you to be remembering your old life when we're together,' she said. 'You will be my husband.'

'Darling, I cannot wait to be him,' Jason replied. 'Your husband will be the luckiest man alive, and he will be me. There will never be a moment I think about any other woman, I guarantee it. But, this is the problem. If my sons are off in exile somewhere, I will be worrying about them. I can't help it. They're mine, and I have raised them. I promise you that when we have our first child, you'll be amazed at how much babies adore me. And our sons will be so much happier with older brothers kicking around the place, keeping them company. Imagine how much fun it is to have an older brother. I wish I had been so fortunate when I was a boy. And I bet you would have enjoyed having a sibling or two. Please, don't be cross with me, dear girl, you did promise.'

'Your children don't belong in Corinth,' she said. 'I thought we'd agreed that this would be the life you'd always wanted, the one you couldn't have before because that woman held you to promises you had to make to keep your men and yourself alive.'

'This is going to be the life I've always wanted, you silly thing,' he said. 'You are the life I have always wanted: nothing has changed that. Nothing will change that. But I don't think I can sleep well beside you when I don't know where my boys are. You do understand, don't you? I can see you do a bit, even though you don't want to. Beautiful girl, you are the kindest person I have ever known.'

And she looked into his brown eyes pleading with her, and knew she could refuse him nothing.

'You promise that you won't let them ruin things?' she asked.

'They are incapable of ruining anything, I promise,' he said. 'You just need to meet them and you'll see what they're like. They are beautifully behaved – excellent manners like their father, naturally – and they won't trouble you one bit. You'll scarcely know they're here: they have a tutor, a Corinthian man, he's wonderful. He will be looking after them during the days. You will have my undivided attention. And, of course, the nights will be just for you and I.'

She shivered a little, imagining it. She made one last attempt to refuse him, but they both knew it was futile.

'Won't their mother mind, if they stay here?'

He shrugged, cheerfully. 'It doesn't matter what she wants, sweetheart. She won't be here.'

Medea

I have two things I didn't have before.

For someone who thought she had lost everything, these things must be counted. The first is that Creon has given me a few days to make arrangements for our departure. And the second is that we have somewhere to go. The Athenian, Aegeus – who came to consult me on his way to Delphi – visited again on his return. As I suspected might happen, he had received an oracle he could not interpret without my help. I did not especially want to use his ignorance and childlessness to my advantage, but I have found myself in intolerable circumstances. So I offered him a bargain: I said that I would uncover the meaning of his oracle (as though I hadn't done so already). But I could only do so when my own position was secure. I explained that I am to be exiled from Corinth and he was shocked that Jason could have allowed such a thing to happen to his wife.

What a phrase for him to use, after Jason had claimed no Greek would ever treat marriage to a foreigner as a real marriage. This man – this king – thought of me as Jason's wife. I explained that my husband was marrying the daughter of the king of Corinth, and Aegeus was astonished. His first question was why Jason would abandon a woman who had given him sons, to which I could give no answer. The second was why Creon would allow his only daughter to marry a man who couldn't be trusted. I had no answer to that either.

But – because of his pity for my predicament and his desperation for an heir – I extracted a promise that he will give me sanctuary in Athens. This is exactly the offer I needed. Now I can leave Corinth in the knowledge that I do not have too far to travel with my children, and that I have a haven waiting for me in the court of King Aegeus. And all he wants in return is a child.

But there is more news, and it is terrible.

Should I have known that Jason would not see his sons sent away from him? He once told the children they might have an older brother, yet he has never mentioned this child to me. Certainly, I would know if he had met this child since he and I have been together, and he has not. So I suppose I assumed his attitude to his children was similar to his attitude to his wife. Because there was no evidence to the contrary.

But now, my exile has taken a more agonizing turn. Because Jason has ordered me to send my sons to the palace. I must leave, but they must stay. No one can help me, of course. They expect a man's sons to be with their father. None of the Corinthian women I have spoken to thinks it is unusual for a woman to be thrown out of her home and her children taken from her in this way. They agree that it is cruel. But they tell me this is only to be expected: that the boys are not mine, they are his. The older ones say that my sons might

– might – come to find me, when they are grown. It is not such a long way to Athens from here. They are old enough to remember my name, old enough to understand that I am being sent away.

One thought plagues me above all others: what if they believe that I chose to leave them behind? Jason has lied to me, he will not hesitate to lie about me. And this – above all – is what I cannot bear. If I am cast aside and my sons stay with him, he will choose what to tell them. And there will be no one left to defend me: who is going to contradict the man who has the ear of the king, who has banished his own wife and stolen her children?

Every time I find the answer to one disaster, two more have appeared and are as intractable as the last. I lie here weeping all night, unable to sleep, and I wonder how it has come to this. It is not too many years since I was a woman with so much power that Jason and my nephews were begging me to save his life. I was a priestess, I served a mighty goddess. I was the daughter of a king. And somehow, I have been reduced to a woman with nothing but my own wits.

But then, I think: wait. How am I diminished, if all I have is my wits? I no longer have a father who acknowledges me, but that is because I was strong enough to defy him and survive. In Colchis, I spoke to Hecate and she would heed my words. I may no longer be her priestess, but I still have the knowledge of magic she instilled in me, and I still have power. I have lost my husband, it's true. I can't do anything about that: I won't deign to perform spells to make a man like Jason love me once more. What do I want with love that isn't freely given?

And I am not merely the daughter of a king. I am the killer of a king, the woman who made a man's own daughters chop him into pieces while they imagined themselves his saviours. How has Jason forgotten his uncle's death so quickly? And how had I forgotten it? He was so ashamed of me, of what he said was not the Greek way to behave. And I have been trying so hard, for years, to make myself — What? More Greek? More ordinary? Less Colchian? I have been trying to be the ordinary woman he wanted, once he arrived back in Iolcus. Trying to become anything other than the woman he needed when he sailed the Argo across the seas, who did not fit into his Greek life.

I have failed. And I have failed because it was never possible for me to succeed: I couldn't become Greek. I couldn't change my accent, even as I learned his language. I couldn't stop being cleverer than him; I couldn't pretend people didn't want my advice when they had long since stopped listening to his. He has made me feel small and weak, because I couldn't hold on to him. But a mountain isn't weak, and the water of a river still flows down and away. I am not the one who cheated and lied to his loved ones. I am not the person who doesn't know whether to keep her children or throw them out into the streets.

It is time to change my plans. I have somewhere to live, and I will make myself invaluable to Aegeus when I arrive there. But before I leave, I will show everyone there is a price for cheating a Colchian woman. I am not the negligible woman he believes me to be. If he were not a fool, he would never have made such an error of judgement. And I – who allowed his estimation of my worth to dictate my own – I will make him regret his treatment of me. And I will make this royal family fear me, just as the daughters of Pelias do. Just as my own family do. My enemies shudder when they hear my name.

Now Jason is my enemy, he will do the same.

Nurse

Darling children, you can unpack your bags. Yes, I mean it! You are going to stay here, in Corinth, where you have been so happy. It is true, it is all true. You can keep all your toys, and you will be looked after by the same tutor you have now. Isn't that wonderful? The gods have answered our prayers.

Some of our prayers, at least. You have done so well to keep quiet in here, I am proud of you both. Yes, your daddy was here. He came to talk to your mama, and she was glad to see him, she really was. He has explained to her that he has arranged matters so that you two can stay here, with him.

What's that? No, my dears, I'm afraid your mama will not be able to stay. Don't start crying again, please. Please. I know it is very difficult for you to be separated, I know it is sad. But I am afraid that your mama is no longer welcome in Corinth, so she must leave. Whichever parent you stay with, you will not see the other one for a while. And your daddy has decided to keep you here with him. So you will not have to travel to a distant land, you will not lose the friends you have made since we arrived here. It is better for you both, I promise.

I know you will miss her terribly, my darlings. She will miss you in just the same way. But you will be with your daddy and your tutor and your friends. So you mustn't be sad.

No, I cannot stay with you: I must go with your mother. She needs a friend, just as you do. So when you leave, we will say goodbye. I know, I will miss you too. But you know that your mama needs someone to take care of her and I am the person who does that. You would be frightened if she was going off on her own, and this way, you know that I will look after her and she will be safe.

Now listen, and I will tell you what is going to happen tomorrow: your tutor is going to take you to the palace, the big house on the far-away hill that we have seen lots of times when we go out to play. That is where your daddy lives now, and you will go to visit him. Your mama is preparing gifts for you to take to the princess who lives there too. You'd like to meet a princess, wouldn't you? Of course you would. So tomorrow you will take a small box with you, and you must promise to carry it very carefully as you go. You mustn't drop it or leave it behind somewhere. Your mama promised Daddy that there would be gifts and that you would take them. He is so grateful to her, and so pleased you are going to be taking them. He said you would charm the princess in no time, and that she loves to receive presents.

I know you like to have presents too, and I am sure your daddy will have some treats waiting for you in the palace. Yes, I think he will take you exploring, I'm sure it will be exciting for you to learn your way around a new home.

Medea

I knew he would show himself to be weak. He has known me so intimately, for so many years, but he still doesn't know me. And yet, I know him. He is feeling unsure of himself in the company of kings: he did not grow up in such a world, the way I did. He believes that his position might be insecure, that Glauke might decide he is not the hero he has promised her, that she might end their engagement at the last moment. And then, he would be as stateless as I am: unable to stay, unable to go home. And he has done far less to earn favours and make friends with other Greeks than I have. My name has already reached distant lands, and once I arrive in the house of Aegeus, it will extend further still.

He was bound to agree – after the most minimal protestations – to my suggestion of the boys taking presents for his bride. He has used up too much good will, he thinks, in arranging for them to stay with him. His precious wife is not used to sharing anything: why would she not resent two boys coming to live in the palace with her? She wanted a handsome husband, not his family. Not when they aren't her boys, anyway. She has heard the same stories as other women: men favour their first children and their interest fades by the time they have the younger ones. She has seen how easily Jason's affections can be lost, and she doesn't want any competition for his attention. So of course she didn't want his sons to stay behind. And yet, Jason is always so persuasive. Never more so than when you are in love with him. He tempted me into betraying my entire family; he can certainly persuade a spoiled girl to allow his sons to visit.

Not for the first time, his weakness makes room for my strength. Because now I have a route straight into the heart of his palace, and he has opened the gates. The gifts my boys take will be beautiful: she will find them irresistible. I will send a dress, I think, that was one of my great treasures, woven with golden thread. And a small golden circlet with delicate leaves. She will see them and she will long to wear them, she won't hesitate to try them on. They will fit her to perfection.

Glauke

The princess sulked in her bedchamber, wishing she had never agreed to meeting these children. She didn't want to spend time with any children. She wanted her husband to embark on a new life with her, not to drag the old one into their home. She put on her least pretty tunic, because she could see no point in wearing one she liked more. Her servants fussed around her, and she snapped at them all to leave her alone.

After a while, she heard voices and bustle and she knew that Jason must have arrived. She was certain no one would dare to come and disturb her after she had sent everyone away. And she was right: it was Jason who came to her door, all charm and golden confidence.

'Darling, you look glorious. You're actually radiant: how do you do that? How do you make it appear as though all the light in the room is emanating from your perfect face? And what a lovely dress, too. I don't know that I've seen it before.'

She tried to maintain her quiet fury in the face of this assault, but she was struggling.

'Now look, I have brought the boys to meet you, which they're thrilled about because they have never met a princess before and they are certain you will be the most beautiful thing in the whole of Hellas. And they're right. So will you come to greet them? It will only take a few moments and then their tutor will take them somewhere to learn — I don't know. Whatever it is they need to learn, I suppose.'

Glauke pouted.

'My beautiful girl, if you do that, I will lose interest in anything but closing this door behind me. Come and meet them. They have brought presents because they are so keen for you to adore them.'

She stood slowly, as though reluctant to leave her couch and walk into his waiting arms. He kissed her and murmured into her ear, 'You will love them, darling, I'm sure of it. As sure as I've ever been of anything.'

And she allowed him to take her by the hand and walk her towards the grand hall.

*

It helped that both children looked like miniature versions of him: his face leapt from theirs, and she knew instantly what he had looked like as a child. The boys were shy when they saw her, the open expressions they had for their father closing when she met their gaze. They looked at the ground and she felt a moment of pity. An old man stood a few paces behind them: their tutor, she supposed. He muttered a few words, and the boys lifted the handles of the small wooden box that sat on the ground between them. They walked forward – the younger one turning to check with his brother that he wasn't making a mistake – and placed the box in front of her.

'This is a present for you,' said the bigger boy. 'Thank you for inviting us to visit you.'

They stepped backwards until they reached their tutor.

'Well done,' Jason said to them both. 'You did that wonderfully.'

Glauke was conscious that he was waiting for her to respond, so she thanked them politely.

'Open it,' Jason said. 'I'm sure you'll love what's inside.'

Glauke would much rather have opened the box in her bedchamber, without this audience of strangers. But she couldn't see how to explain this to Jason without them hearing her, and she didn't want them to know how uncomfortable they had made her. So she reached down, undid the catch and opened the lid.

For a moment, she thought the box was full of molten gold. Then she saw it was the finest cloth she had ever seen, so delicate that opening the box had made it shimmer in the light. She gasped, but could not speak.

'I think you've chosen well, my darlings,' said Jason proudly. 'Go back home and say your goodbyes: I'll collect you in the morning.'

The two boys scurried away behind their tutor, but Glauke was paying them no attention. Spellbound, she reached into the box to touch the magical cloth.

'What is it?' she breathed.

'I think it's a dress,' Jason said. 'But if we took it to your room, you could try it on and be sure.'

She smiled. 'Wait here,' she said. She nodded to her maids who picked up the box and carried it ahead of her to her chamber.

*

She did not want anyone else to touch the glimmering material and she brushed aside the maids' offers to help. The idea of anyone else's hands soiling the dress was unbearable. She reached into the box and as her fingers sank into the fabric, they felt warm as though the dress were somehow alive. But it was so delicate between her fingers, it almost slid away. She lifted it from the box and it draped perfectly: she could see that it was the right size. She shrugged off her old tunic and slipped into the new one. The delicate cloth stroked her skin, and she already knew this would be her wedding dress. She could scarcely imagine that she had ever planned to wear anything else.

'There's something else in the box, my lady,' said one of her servants, and she looked down to see that − nestling beneath the dress − there was a delicate crown, made of thin golden branches, twisting round one another. She picked it up and found it surprisingly heavy, though when she placed it on her head, it felt light. Laughing, she took the skirt in her hand so she didn't trip as she ran back to the hall to show her husband.

*

Glauke hurried through the doorway, knowing that she must look like a comet, blazing through the night sky. She saw the wonder on her husband's face as he gazed at her in all her finery, and she knew she was perfect. She smiled in delight as she took another step towards him, opened her arms to embrace him, and felt a sudden searing pain around her skull. She staggered under the new weight of the crown, wanting her hair to be flowing freely to ease the agonizing tightness. She raised her hands to lift it off her head – all thoughts of protecting its delicate beauty were gone, she tried to hurl it to the floor – but it was stuck fast, as though it had melted and solidified once more. She shook her head, frantic, trying to loosen it, but she could not.

Then she began to shudder, as her complexion lost its dewy glow. Her face was now white with livid purple marks forming beneath the crown, as though it was burning her. Her mouth gaped and frothed as the servants who had followed her into the room watched in horror. One old woman pushed a chair forward, and Glauke collapsed onto it. Her eyes rolled up into her head and she screamed as a second agony made war on her tormented body. Now the dress began to eat into her skin, and as she clawed at it to try and free herself, she tore her own flesh instead.

She slid to the ground, her heels drumming as she moaned in pain. She felt as though every part of her was ablaze and no one could help her. Glauke could no longer see, but she heard the screams from everyone around her. She wanted to call out to Jason to help but – though she didn't know it – she had bitten through her tongue and silenced herself. Her maids were crying their prayers to Asclepius, begging him to direct all his healing powers towards their mistress before it was too late. But Glauke was now unrecognizable, and even the gods could not have saved her from this poison that had set her alight from within.

Creon had heard his daughter's scream and rushed into the hall to see what had happened. He was not deceived by the change in her appearance, but cried out as he ran to hold her in his arms.

'No,' he shouted. 'My girl, my lovely girl.' He sank to his knees beside her, wrapping his arms around her to try and ease her pain, or at least to show her – so far past language – that she was not alone in her final moments. 'My poor child,' he wept. 'Which god has taken you from me, depriving me of you in this terrible way? Who can I have offended who would do such a thing to an innocent girl? Why not take me instead? I am old, I have lived as much as I needed to and more. I would have given my life to save my daughter, if any god had asked.'

Glauke's body convulsed one final time, and her father howled.

'Let me die here with her, my only love,' he cried. 'There is no reason for me to live, orphaned of my child.'

No one dared to approach him. After a few moments of silent grief, the old man tried to raise himself from the ground. But he found he could not separate his body from his daughter's shattered form, and he did not have the strength to lift them both. He tried to pull away from her, but his flesh too was stuck fast to the toxic dress.

'Help me, help me,' he moaned, but no one watching knew whether he spoke to them or to the gods who were robbing him of his daughter and his life in one awful day. 'Please,' Creon said. But as he tried to free his arms, his old flesh was pulled from his bones just as Glauke's young flesh had been torn from hers. The king did not struggle or scream as his daughter had done. The poison was not intended for him; he simply sank back down and closed his eyes. The poison took him anyway.

*

Creon's servants had watched the destruction of their royal house and they had no idea what had caused it. They prayed frantically to every god, hoping this raging sickness would spread no further. The women produced sheets and sheets of cloth while the men built a pyre just outside the palace gates. No one wanted to touch the bodies of the dead, all feared that the contagion could take them too.

The conjoined bodies of the princess and the king were dragged from the hall using old leather straps that had once held huge chests shut. The fire was soon blazing, and the living withdrew to try and avoid inhaling smoke from the ruined corpses. The courtyard was soon stained black and the royal household had been wholly consumed by fire. And only then did the servants begin to hope that they might themselves not be killed in this cruellest fashion. As they huddled together inside the gates, they tried to understand what had happened: which gods must they appease to avert this curse from the rest of Corinth?

The sun was dropping below the hills before anyone thought to ask what had become of Jason.

Nurse

Oh children, you're back! We have been looking forward to you coming home again. Did your father want you to spend lots of time with his new family? She must have liked the gifts you took. What? You were sent away after you handed them over? You didn't stay at the palace today? But then, where have you been? Didn't the old man bring you back . . . ? And why are you covered in dirt and twigs?

Someone chased after you and your tutor hid you in the trees? What do you mean? Boys, you know lying is not allowed. Not to your parents and not to me. Tell me what happened and tell me plainly.

You gave her the box as soon as you arrived, like you were told? Good. And that's when your father said you should leave? Straightaway? Before she'd even spoken to you? Well, I suppose he wanted her to focus on the presents your mama had sent. So we don't even know if she opened the chest. She did? You saw her open it as you left the big hall with your tutor. I see. But you were only in the palace those few moments.

Well, they say no one can look upon divinely wrought

309

gifts and be anything but delighted, so we can assume that the princess was thrilled with the box. What happened next? Don't say nothing, because something must have happened next, or you'd still be standing right there outside the palace gates. Wouldn't you? So you must have set out with your tutor to come back here.

Very well. You walked to the carriage and the mule wanted something to eat and went slowly because you didn't have anything. Yes, I know that mule, I can well imagine it. What next?

What kind of noise? Shouting of one person or many? I am glad it was only in the distance, my loves: I would never want you to be where people were angry, if I could help it. Well, what did they sound like, if they didn't sound angry?

No, I don't know why they were afraid, darling. Something must have scared them, I suppose. If you're sure that's what you heard. Is that when you hid?

Not until you heard the men chasing you. Your tutor told you to hide in the woods, I see. And you both stayed hidden and silent until the men had gone, and then you waited a while longer, to be sure? That is brave: I'm proud of you. What happened to your tutor?

Please, don't cry.

Medea

Things have become complicated, and I must think fast. Punishing the princess for taking my husband has proved satisfying. She died as agonizingly as I had hoped she might. In a few short moments she experienced the same quantity of pain that her actions have meted out to me over many months. Everyone is so shocked, it seems, by what that kind of torment looks like. They should have been looking at the woman who lay prostrate in their midst, day after day, believing her life was over. If she had ever given a kind thought to me, she might still be alive.

Killing her rancid father as well was an unexpected pleasure. Even I did not imagine that the old man would be such a fool as to embrace someone whose flesh is melting from her bones. Everyone else knew to keep their distance, except him. Ha, I would have given a great deal to stand there and watch the man who has treated me so cruelly die in such a way, fused to the body of his dead daughter.

So Jason's attempt to marry into respectability is at an end and the royal family of Corinth is at an end. I could not be more delighted with how this has worked out:

everyone got exactly what they deserved. If Jason really did love his precious princess, he will now be sorry he ever laid eyes on her. Perhaps one day his grief will rival mine. And if he didn't, if it was all just a way of improving his status, as he once claimed? Well, then he should have discussed this with me and only acted upon it if I agreed to it. He disregarded my feelings and my name, and now he is justly punished. The gods know the vows he made and broke. He once had the favour of one goddess after another: he cannot doubt that they have all abandoned him now. No man can commit such perjury and expect to prosper.

And my revenge will not only be felt by him today, but in months and years to come. Who will ever agree to marry his daughter to Jason now? No king, no hero, no one. They will all remember what happened to the last man who was stupid enough to try and marry off his daughter to my husband.

It is not enough, but it is something. Nothing has grieved me more than knowing that Jason has insulted me and rejected me and that he has been seen to prosper because of it. No one should be able to behave in this way and continue to thrive. Jason was very quick to forget that his success was dependent on me, on my wits and my talent. He owed me a debt and he failed to pay it. So now everyone is aware of what happens when someone treats me in this way. Perhaps they thought I would simply accept his behaviour, and that of his princess and his king. Perhaps that would be the Greek thing to do, I don't know. But it is not the Colchian way. Jason saw my father, he knows what kind of world I grew up in. The gods know we talked about these things in the depths of the night, when our marriage was new and our greatest joy was to lie entwined in one another, telling the stories of our pasts. He took me away from Colchis, but part of me will always remain there. And if he had thought about me at all, he would have realized I would never accept his diminishing of me. I deserved better from him. I deserve better from anyone.

But my revenge – successful as it is – has brought me new difficulties.

The Corinthians want vengeance for the killing of their royal house. I thought some of them at least would be grateful for the removal of a tyrant. If my father and brother had died suddenly, there would have been plenty of men jostling to replace them. My many conversations with the women of Corinth led me to believe the same might happen here, but some men at least demand vengeance. This does not concern me for myself: sanctuary waits for me in Athens, I need only travel there. But there may be complications in leaving Corinth. It would have helped me if the princess had delayed a little while before she opened her gifts, but I cannot regret anything that has happened.

The nurse tells me that they killed the boys' tutor. How does the death of a Corinthian man repay me for the death of their princess? I asked her. There will always be other tutors. But he was loyal: she said they tortured him to discover the whereabouts of my children, and he refused to say where he had hidden them. Some Greek men have honour, at least.

This means they will pursue us when we leave Corinth. Will they follow us to Athens? I need to plan: the quickest route may not be the safest. It would be easier if I could travel alone, but I cannot abandon the children. They were the most effective way of delivering the poison straight into the hands of Jason's princess, but I had a second reason for sending my gifts with my sons. I have no right to keep them with me: now I know that the law in every part of Greece says that sons belong to their fathers. But Jason cannot separate them from me any more. He must know he would not be able to keep them secure from retribution.

So – I must send a message to Aegeus, reminding him of his obligation to me. And I must pray to every goddess who has abandoned Jason, and ask them all to help me in my escape. In the meantime, I will find somewhere to hide my children. They cannot stay here, it isn't safe.

Hera

The temple of Hera stood high above Corinth, and the only path wound its way steeply uphill until it reached the great rocky outcrop. The temple was encircled by walls with large gates where they crossed the path. It was one of Hera's favourite temples, primarily because it had been built on an area that was sacred to another god. Acrocorinth offered the perfect view out across the isthmus, as well as the city, and the Corinthians were rightly proud of it: no one could take them by surprise while they held Acrocorinth.

The gods prized this place no less than the Greeks. In a past so distant even Hera could only just remember it, two gods had fought for possession of the huge rock. Poseidon had wanted it for its expansive views of his beloved sea. How could any god deny him the right to call this place his own? They could not. He had struck the ground with his trident and the earth had shuddered beneath them all.

But then one god did make a rival claim. Helios, the sun himself, rode across the sky every day and had noticed Acrocorinth for a very different reason. It was so lofty he could see every boulder and pebble as he flew past. The rock should belong to him because it was almost as high as him, so was surely in his territory rather than Poseidon's. The two gods argued, and Hera had the strongest memory of finding the entire discussion both pompous and dull. This was – had she thought about it for a moment – usually her view of both these gods, but she couldn't spare them that much attention.

This was a widely shared feeling. The wrangling between the two eventually reached the ears of Zeus, who decreed that someone else should arbitrate between their competing claims, so that he didn't have to hear any more about it. The decision fell into the hundred hands of Briareos, the giant. There were three hundred-handed giants: this Hera did remember, because they had fought alongside the Olympians when the Titans rose up against them. She tended to remember who had taken her side and who had opposed her in anything from a squabble to a war. No one especially liked the giants, nor were decisions usually delegated to them. But this was a judgement that could not fail to alienate a powerful god, so Briareos' primary qualification was that he had not moved out of the way quickly enough to avoid Zeus' gaze.

The hundred-handed giant tried his best to listen to the two cases presented to him. Poseidon spoke forcefully enough, but Helios dazzled him. After hearing them out, Briareos furrowed his gigantic brow and tried to think. Poseidon, he bellowed, should have the isthmus of Corinth. It was surrounded by his great seas, and it only made sense for the god to hold this tiny strip of land as well. Poseidon nodded gravely: the giant only spoke the truth that all could see. But then came the rest of his decision. Acrocorinth was not the isthmus, it was merely next to the isthmus. And it was extremely high up. So this mighty crag would go to Helios, who could pause and rest his horses on it, if he chose.

The sun shone more brightly, to reflect his delight. Poseidon retreated beneath the waves and growled for a while. The other gods thought Briareos had made a fair judgement and Zeus thought he should make more decisions this way, removing himself entirely from the process so that any discontentment was directed elsewhere. Hera did not waste a moment on congratulation or consolation: she went straight to Helios and told him her temple must have pride of place on his mighty rock, or the crag would lose its claim to be considered a sacred location. And Helios knew that Hera had many more temples than most gods or goddesses (perhaps Zeus had one or two more, she conceded). She would give Acrocorinth the reputation it deserved.

Helios ensured that his priests erected two grand altars to him at the top of the path. Facing them was a sanctuary to Necessity, so that everyone who came to this pinnacle remembered that it was sacred to the all-seeing Sun, and that Poseidon had been compelled to relinquish his claim. But Helios knew better than to refuse the queen of the Olympian gods. If she had asked for something directly, he could not pretend ignorance of her request. It was simply easier to concede rather than avoid the many variants of revenge she might employ against him. What could Poseidon do to him, when he flew too high for the Earthshaker to touch?

So beyond the sanctuary and the altars, at the rock's very highest point, was the temple of Hera Akraia. The women of Corinth came here to make their offerings to a goddess who would protect their families. They dressed her statue in finery, and once a year they paraded her through the streets. Hera loved this temple more than almost any other, because of its spectacular views and the way it infuriated Poseidon that it was hers.

Corinthian Women

It was dawn when Jason arrived at the place he had once called home. He was out of breath and the children were not there. He had not expected to find his wife, so he was unsurprised to discover that she was missing. The children's nurse had also disappeared. He hurried out of the house again, his expression dark.

His neighbours watched from their doorways, this treacherous man with a sword in his hand. He had always had a casual air. More than one of the women had asked Medea how such an unhurried man had ever battled monsters and claimed a magic fleece, and she had simply laughed and said Jason's great heroic talent was making the right friends. But now they saw him rushing through the house, hunting for his erstwhile family, then searching outside for any trace of where they might have gone.

'Where has she taken them?' he cried, and ran to the closest house. 'Did you see where she went? Did she have my sons with her?'

The woman looked at him for a moment, then nodded.

'Tell me where she went!' Jason shouted. He reached out

as though to shake her by the shoulders, before changing his mind.

'I heard you didn't want them any more,' the woman replied.

'That's what I heard too,' called one of her neighbours.

'Didn't want your wife or your children any more,' shouted another. 'Did you expect her to wait for you to change your mind again?'

'Whatever you may think of me,' Jason said, to the nearest woman, 'you must believe me when I tell you my children – her children, if you prefer – are in terrible danger, and it is all down to her rabid temper and vicious nature.'

'Down to her?' asked the second woman. 'She's not the one who went off without them, is she?'

Jason turned to address her, his easy charm now a ghost. 'She has killed your king. Your king and his daughter, his only heir. Do you understand?'

The woman looked at him again. 'I don't see much royalty around here,' she said. 'But I'm sure you're right to be angry.'

'They are coming for her,' he hissed. 'They are coming to kill her, and they will kill my children because they are her children. Listen to me, I am begging you. The king is dead, they will demand retribution.'

'Who will?' The woman shrugged. 'You said his daughter was his only heir. So who is demanding retribution, if he hasn't got any heirs?'

There was a pause. 'I don't know!' Jason replied. 'He must have cousins or something, mustn't he? Or allies. His allies will take their vengeance out on my children.'

'What allies?' The neighbouring woman had left her

house and was now standing nearby, watching his discomfort when he looked over at her and was dazzled by the low sun. 'You were the one marrying into the family, weren't you? So you're probably the closest thing to an ally they had.'

'Please stop this,' he begged. 'Please stop obstructing me because you think I behaved wrongly. I assure you Medea is far from the helpless little wife she has led you to believe. She is a powerful witch; she has poisoned the king and his daughter.'

'When did she do this?' asked the first woman. 'Why haven't we heard about it?'

'Yesterday,' he replied. 'She killed them yesterday.'

'You're lying,' said the second. 'Medea was with us yesterday. The whole day.'

'I'm telling you: she poisoned them. She sent poisoned clothes to the palace with our children, so she could be far away when the princess was dying in agony.'

'Poisoned clothes?' The third woman had now walked over to hear more. 'What are you talking about?'

'She sent a poisoned dress and crown,' Jason said. 'Everyone knew they were from her; she didn't even bother hiding it. I can see you find the whole thing confusing—'

'I'm not confused,' said the first woman. 'You seem confused. You think Medea killed people when we're telling you she was here with us. And when you've been told she couldn't have, you start talking about her delivering poisoned crowns. I think you should go and sit down somewhere, and try to sober up.'

'I'm not drunk.' Jason was trying not to shout. 'There are men, armed men, who are very angry with her.'

'You, for a start,' said the third woman.

'Men who will kill her and my children,' he pleaded.

'If she's a powerful witch, like you say,' said the second woman, 'they won't be able to do her any harm, will they?'

Jason looked from one face to another, seeing nothing he could use to help him.

'She will have taken them to the temple of Hecate,' he said. 'Where is that?'

'We don't have a temple to – who did you say?' said the first woman.

'That huge temple up there,' said Jason, gesturing up at the rock that towered above them. 'Whose is that?'

'That is to the queen of the gods, of course.'

Relief broke out across his face. 'Hera! Finally, some luck for me.'

The first woman looked at her neighbours. 'I don't think it will be good luck for you,' she said to his retreating back. 'The queen of the gods is unlikely to help a man who lived here all that time and never even knew where her temple stood, is she?'

Nurse

For so long, it has been women who have a reputation for treachery. That is what men say, of course: never trust a woman, they'll always betray you. This is what all the old songs and stories say. But that isn't what I see.

Jason betrayed Medea and his children, when he decided on his marriage to the princess. Medea reminded him of all the oaths he had sworn, of all the gods by whom he had pledged himself, and he didn't dispute one of them. He never told her she was lying. He accepted the list of gods, he simply questioned what it meant that he had made these promises. He claimed he had done everything he'd offered her: rescued her from her Colchian family, taken her onboard his ship, shared a bed with her, given her children. This, he said, was the sum of his promises to her, and she could not deny he had carried out his words.

She hurled a cup at him, and he ducked so it smashed against the wall behind him. She said that he promised her marriage, and he said that wasn't his to promise, because she was a barbarian and they had come to Greece. If they had stayed in Colchis, he acknowledged, he would have married her legally. But in Greece – which they had to flee to, because of her father's men demanding her return – she could not be married. It was hardly his fault that she had misunderstood him: they only half-shared a language when they first met, he said. Her Greek had come on so far, she had forgotten how difficult she had found it at the beginning. And then he told her that his greatest gift to her – aside from their children – was that he had brought her to Greece. Because now, he said, her reputation was growing across the Hellenic world, and this was far more valuable than being a witch at the ends of the earth. He had enhanced her name by involving her in his quest. And then he had allowed her to achieve renown here – in Corinth – and she should be grateful to him for that. Being in Greece had given her the opportunity to live with civilized laws, not under the whims of a savage tyrant. But what good were those laws to her, she asked, if they allowed him to cast her aside like dirt?

Late that same night she walked out into the moonlight, and she called on the goddesses that dwell beneath the earth, pleading with them to walk alongside her and punish Jason for his wrongs. Did her dark goddesses respond? I don't know. I crept away when I heard her chanting. It wasn't right for anyone to overhear. But she was determined to call the gods to witness Jason's betrayal of her: she was certain that the gods know what marriage is, even if Jason does not. If his own honour did not compel him to treat her fairly, she thought the gods should force him to do so.

And now, we have come to the great rock above Corinth, where there is a huge temple to Hera. I thought we would hide in this temple as Hera's suppliants: that is what Medea had planned, when we set out. But when we reached the acropolis, she saw the shrines to Ananke and Bia, which stand in front of the temple to the queen of the gods, and she asked me what they were. I explained to her that the Corinthians have this dual sanctuary to Necessity and Force. She asked me if these are goddesses to the Greeks, and I said yes, but they don't have temples and priestesses like Hera or Aphrodite, only these shrines. And Medea was pleased because that meant we were less likely to be discovered while she waited for a reply to her appeals.

So we are hiding within the walls of the sanctuary, and the children have been told to be as quiet as possible. The boys understand, I think: they are afraid of the men who killed their tutor, they know they need to keep out of sight until we can flee. Medea says she has a place for us to go – in Athens – but we need safe transport if we are to avoid the Corinthians who are bent on killing us. So we hide here, and we wait.

Medea

He is coming. I can sense him approaching us, I have been able to feel him since the first time I saw him. I can feel how agitated he is, and I am revelling in it. He was so panicked by the loss of his precious bride: I would laugh out loud if it wouldn't draw attention to my children's hiding place. And then to come chasing after me with his mind set on revenge. It is pathetic. He would have seen me exiled, but he will avenge the death of a girl he scarcely knows? Of course not.

He is simply trying to ensure that the Corinthians hold me responsible for the death of their precious royals, and not him. But why should they blame me? They don't know me as a sorceress or witch, or whatever he will try to persuade them I am. They know me as the quiet, kind young woman who saved their youngest daughter from birthing pains, or kept their baby alive when the fever had him in its grip. To them, I am someone who saves lives, not takes them. Whereas Jason, what do they think of him? The handsome young men of Corinth must dislike him, I assume. Arriving in their city as an outcast from his own, then suddenly about to marry their princess, with an eye to becoming their king: who would not find that unbearable?

And now, the princess and the king are dead, and it was Jason who killed them. Jason who stood by and watched it happen. Jason who did nothing to save the life of Glauke or Creon. Jason who ran away from the palace before anyone could interrogate him about what he knew and when. No wonder those men chased after him. And how typical of Jason that they almost found his sons, but didn't find him. He has always known to protect himself before anything else. And I should have thought of this, when I used the boys to try to incriminate him. Blame never sticks to him: he would deflect onto a child in a heartbeat.

So, what happens now? Jason is on the run from the Corinthians, and he will be searching for me and the boys. Will he think to come to the temple? I believe so. He will think Hera still cherishes him, the way she used to, forgetting that when he abandoned me, he insulted her. Only Jason could imagine the goddess of marriage could still love him.

Hera

The statue of the queen of the gods sat in her temple, her sceptre in her hand and a cuckoo perched on the arm of her throne. Her face was made of the palest ivory, and her golden crown glittered in the early light. And when Jason stood before her, the goddess looked down from her darkest ox-eyes, and wondered if he had really been worth the trouble. She had put so much effort into his quest, and yet he had done so little of interest since he won the fleece.

He was still very handsome, she admitted. His eyes had not lost their remarkable brightness, and his curling brown hair was no less delightful than it had once been. His arms had barely a scratch on them, despite his many adventures. She smiled to herself: she really had done an excellent job of keeping him safe. And he had killed Pelias for her, had he not? Jason's head was now bent in prayer, so he did not see the small furrow that appeared between the statue's arched brows. No, he hadn't.

It was the girl who had killed the old king. Oh, and she had done it wonderfully. The goddess smiled to think of the ruined daughters of Pelias, standing around a cauldron containing the wreckage of their father. It had been precisely the kind of revenge Hera would have exacted upon a man. Perhaps Jason had disappointed her, but Medea had been well worth her efforts. Hera realized that Jason had been talking to her for some time, and she had not heard a single word.

She decided to listen for a moment, because it seemed that he was intent on injuring someone, and that often caught her interest. He wanted her dead, apparently, and Hera could understand that: she had often wanted someone dead herself. Someone had killed his bride and her father? Well, that was a shame, Hera thought. She had just remembered Medea and now it turned out she was dead, and her father too. But then more words came, and the names were different: Glauke was a Greek name, and so was Creon. The goddess wondered if Medea had died in childbirth: perhaps she had missed it. Women usually prayed to her when they were struggling to give birth; they usually prayed for months beforehand. But now she thought about it, that didn't seem right either. Hera recalled Medea praying for her own babies and those of other women. So she had children and yet Jason was no longer her husband. Ah, he was one of those men.

Hera felt a sudden, sharp rage. They were all that man. Every one of them. The king of the gods himself set them their example, and they followed him in every way, so eager to mimic whatever Zeus did. But why should they flourish when they did exactly what he did? Why? She could not punish her husband, though she had certainly tried every possible method to make him regret every goddess, girl and nymph he laid his wandering hands upon. But she would not let his behaviour become the norm among men, not when she could act and make them wish they had chosen to respect her values over his. She was the goddess who protected wives against their husbands, and here was her chance to do that. Jason wanted her help to kill Medea, did he?

No, Medea was not the one who would die today.

Medea

I would not have believed it if I hadn't heard him say it.

Is that true? I would have believed most things about him. He was a liar with no concern for anyone but himself. He cared about his children to a degree, but we both knew where the limit was. He would have let them rot in exile beside me, that was his first instinct.

But isn't it reasonable to believe that a father will love his child's life more than his own?

The children were out of sight at the back of the shrine to Ananke, with their nurse. She has been loyal to us in a way Jason could not even begin to understand.

I was gratified to see that I had guessed correctly when I saw him appear on the acropolis, panting from the climb. But something about his posture was not as I expected. Jason was desperate for something, but not angry, something else. Something I hadn't seen before, or not for a long time. I watched him as he stood for a moment, catching his breath, trying to place what I could see. He would not be able to recognize me. I was dressed as a priestess, with my head veiled, walking through the outer colonnade of

Hera's temple. He paid no heed to the women who move around a temple: when did Jason ever notice a servant of a goddess? Once, when he needed her help to survive. Otherwise, his eyes sought the young and impressionable, like his dead princess.

I watched him hurry towards me and my breath quickened, but I was right: he wasn't paying any attention to me. He walked into the sanctuary and came out again, moments later. He was looking for his family, but I would have thought even Jason would have the sense not to enter a temple for a purpose other than honouring its goddess. Betraying our marriage was insult enough to Hera: now he was willing to ignore her too. I murmured my prayers to her from the colonnade, so she would remember who honoured her in a moment of need, and who disregarded her.

Jason was hunting round the acropolis, his gaze darting back to the path he had climbed, so he could see no one from the palace was closing in. He was walking back to Hera's temple when he saw something – someone – that scared him. He rushed inside the sanctuary where her statue was kept. My children were still out of sight and I issued another prayer to Hera, this time giving thanks.

And then I heard what he had heard moments earlier: the sound of men, armoured men, guards, I supposed. I was standing close to the sanctuary, but I was shielded by a pillar. So when they came stamping towards me, they saw even less of me than Jason had done. I thought of the way I had felt, when Jason first announced his marriage: as though I had become invisible, nothing more than a voice that no one even heard. I had felt the injustice of it, and now I revelled in it. These men could not see that the person they sought – the killer of the king they should have guarded – was standing undefended nearby.

Inside the temple, Jason was praying for my death, begging the goddess he had so recently ignored to kill his children's mother. Perhaps this shouldn't have surprised me; I had prayed for him to die many times. But couples argue when they have grown to hate one another: this is nothing new. Still, he was asking Hera to kill the wife she had chosen for him; even saying those words aloud seems blasphemous to me. If a goddess intervenes in your life, you accept the consequences gladly, don't you? You make offerings to Hera every month to thank her for the good fortune of your marriage and your family. You don't tell her she made a mistake and ask her to rectify it.

But of course – like so much of what he did and does – this was a performance. He didn't care what Hera heard or did, he cared that the armed men who were now entering the temple heard his ardent pleas for the killer of Creon to be struck down. The men had found their quarry, but they did not know he was a great deal more cunning than most. I couldn't see him at that moment, but I heard him say, 'No one wants to use violence in a temple, surely? It would be the worst kind of sacrilege to raise your swords against me here, with the goddess as witness.'

Their uncertainty was audible, although Jason could offer no man a lesson in avoiding blasphemy. I listened as the men muttered to one another and then their leader said, 'You're a wanted man. You poisoned our king and our princess. You should die here, but we are agreed it would be better to kill you in front of the palace, so our fellow-citizens are witnesses.'

'Ah, I see the mistake.' Jason was almost smiling now; I could hear it. He often disguises his fear this way. 'I was present for the awful death of your king, and of his daughter, whom I planned to marry. It was utterly horrific: nothing in my days voyaging on the Argo could have prepared me for such a terrible scene. But I am not the perpetrator, I assure you. I wished your royal family nothing but happiness; I intended to join my own name with theirs. Your king was mine, and he was to have been my father-in-law also. My loss is yours.'

'Oh?' The armed man sounded a little less sure. Jason almost always had this effect on men. 'I thought you'd given them the poison.'

'That's what we heard,' said a second man. 'I heard you'd taken the poison to the palace, and that's how they died.'

'That's not strictly true,' Jason replied. 'I accompanied the people who took the poison there, but I did so unknowingly. And so did they. The guilty party in this dreadful affair was a woman, and that is why you find me here.' His tone was exactly what it would have been if they had ambled into one another over a cup or two of wine. 'I am here begging for the assistance of the goddess in finding this woman. Perhaps you might be her answer to my prayers?'

This was Jason's great skill, as I have always said: he could make friends anywhere. Moments ago, these strangers were accusing him of murder, and now he was beginning to persuade them they were his divine intervention.

'A woman did it? Killed the king and the princess? Why?' asked the first man.

Jason would have given them an eloquent shrug. 'You know women,' he said.

There was further muttering from these men, who could believe a woman guilty of anything.

'But what do you mean, unknowingly?' said the second one. 'You said you accompanied the poisoner unknowingly?'

'I did say that,' Jason replied. 'I know it is hard to imagine, but I took my sons to meet the princess. They were going to live with us, of course, and she needed to meet them before our wedding day. She loved them the moment she set eyes on them, which only makes what followed more wretched.'

'You're saying your children poisoned the princess?' The first man was outraged.

'They're just children,' Jason said. 'They had no idea what they were carrying to the palace. I know it is shocking that anyone – let alone a mother – would use her boys in this way. But that is the kind of woman she is. Well, I cannot say "the kind of woman" because she is uniquely monstrous. But she is who we are searching for: the foreign woman who used to be my wife.'

The men did not notice how easily he had recruited them to his cause. Now they were all engaged in the same quest.

'A foreigner? That would explain it then,' said the men's leader. 'No Greek woman could ever do something like this, she wouldn't even imagine such a heinous crime. Murdering the royal family, using her own children to carry poison to the palace?'

And now it was Jason who did not notice what he had done.

'She did. And we will find her, and I will kill her, my friends,' he replied.

'We will kill her,' said the man. 'We are the bodyguards

who should have protected our master, we are the men she has shamed with her deceit. You can escort us to her and identify her for us. But we kill her.'

'And her children,' said the second man. The others shouted their assent. And only someone who knew Jason well would have heard the panic behind his words.

'I don't think it would be necessary to kill them too,' he said. 'These are my sons, after all: they would have been adopted by your royal family in just a few days.'

'Our royal family didn't have time to adopt your sons,' the second man said. 'And now they're dead and they never will. You said the foreigner was the poisoner and she used her children to help her. So now we kill them, and the honour of Corinth is restored.'

'I would prefer to take my vengeance on her and her alone,' Jason replied. But the men would not shift.

'No better way to punish a woman than to kill her children, is there? We kill them first, of course, so she watches them die. You will have sons with a Greek woman one day soon, and they will be proper Greeks like these ones never were.'

'Yes, I see.'

Was Jason pretending to agree with them? After everything that had happened, it was difficult to be certain. I know what he would say if I could stop time, and ask him what he was doing. He would say that he was about to be killed by the Corinthians for a crime I had committed. That he would have been dragged from the temple by his hair, begging for mercy as Hera watched over this sacrilegious act. Oh, I would have thrilled to see that: the man who has taken my life from me, kneeling on the ground as

336

his throat was slit in revenge for the woman I killed. I would have licked the spilled blood from his skin, I would have grown drunk on it.

But I hadn't stopped time, so I couldn't ask him if he had really just agreed with an armed gang that they would be justified in killing his sons, that he would stand by, or even help them as they did it.

'So, where do we find them?' asked the men's leader.

'I don't know,' Jason replied. 'I thought she might bring them here, that's why I came. But there's no sign of them anywhere.'

'Don't try to protect them, son.' The man's voice had taken on a sharp edge. 'Your foreign whore will die today, and so will her bastard offspring. The only question for you is whether you join them or save yourself. You've said you came here to take your vengeance, so tell us where she is.'

'I really don't know,' Jason said. 'I went straight from the palace to our house. Well, the place that used to be our house. She's not there: few of her belongings remain. Creon had banished her, you know? So it's possible she is already beyond our borders.'

'No.' The leader was certain. 'No one has seen her travelling, and there are only a few roads from the city she could take, with children in tow. Our scouts have gone in every direction, but none has sent a message back.'

This was valuable information. I needed to avoid the roads however we were going to escape. I would have guessed this, but it was useful to have it confirmed.

'She could easily have gone across country,' Jason said.

'She grew up in a wild landscape, she would trust herself to take the children on that journey.'

He did not know that I could hear him; he cannot have known. But was he trying to protect my children now? Had he guessed they were nearby? Was guilt finally taking its toll on him? He had been so quick to lay the blame at my door – to make me the one the Corinthians wanted to find and kill – he didn't even think about what he was doing to my sons. I won't say our sons, I will never say those words again. But – thanks to his cowardice, when another man would have died before giving up his sons to their enemies – getting the children out of Corinth had become almost impossible.

'Hmm, I don't think she would have outrun our scouts,' the man answered. 'Not unless she had help.'

Alert to the danger, Jason agreed with him. 'Then perhaps you would accompany me back to her home?' he asked. 'Perhaps she has hidden with a neighbour or friend. They will be far more willing to confess to you than they were to talk to me.'

'Very well,' the man said. 'We will search the houses of those nearby. Come on.'

Jason has never accepted the blame for things he has done; he didn't even accept it when he killed my brother. He preferred to implicate me, keeping everything at a distance from himself. Only now do I understand why he was so angry when Pelias died, and he and I were blamed for the killing. He wanted Pelias dead, but he wanted to be far away when it happened. So he denied wanting it (blamed my foreign ways) and did everything he could to avoid responsibility. And we still ended up in exile because – for once – no one believed him.

And if he is quick to shun responsibility, he never hesitates to accept credit for things he has not and could not have done. The fleece would still hang in a Colchian grove if it weren't for me. He has spent years now snatching the credit for my brain, my skills, my work. He wanted to be the hero, so no one could see that his wife was the one doing the heroics. I remember when he promised me my name would ring out across all of Hellas as the saviour of the Argonauts, before doing everything he could to keep me quiet. Where did that man go, I wonder.

The men began to leave the temple, Jason bringing up the rear of their gang: just another man with his sword drawn. I exhaled my relief as I saw them go. I was drawing water, ostensibly to take inside the sanctuary, but none of them was looking in my direction. I could have pushed my veil back and stood there in plain view, and I don't think they would have noticed me, even then.

Whether by accident or by design, Jason had led those armed men away from my children, and I had one plan – not one whose success I could guarantee, but a plan nonetheless – to take us all away from here. But just as I turned to go back to the temple of Ananke, I heard the worst sound in the world.

My younger son had caught sight of his father amid the pack of men. He had been told – by his nurse and by me – that we would not see Jason again, that we had to flee Corinth and hide until that moment came. So the poor little boy must have been thrilled to see his father once again, when he thought he was lost to them for ever. And though he had been told and told again that they had to keep quiet at all costs, the excitement was too much for him.

'Daddy!' he cried, and ran out from behind the temple. Jason flinched and tried to ignore the dear familiar voice, but it was too late, and a wall of blades rose to greet my child.

Nurse

She always begged the gods to take pity on her, because she only lost sight of him for a moment. A moment, but it was enough. The nurse had turned her attention to the older boy and suddenly the little one was out of reach and calling for his father. And the woman was hissing at him to be quiet but he was too far away to hear. She ran after him, which was foolish because then the older boy followed her and they were all facing the Corinthian soldiers with their swords.

But a priestess in her veil was closer to them than the armed men, and she rushed to pick up the little boy, embracing him as she turned to face them all. She held his head against her chest so he would not see what was happening. The other boy was now next to her, and she whispered to him to hide his face in her dress, because it was important that the bad men couldn't see his eyes.

The men were strangely still, as though something held them on the spot.

Medea

I was praying to Hecate and to Hera, to Ananke and Bia. I needed the help of my goddess and the strongest magic she had ever given me to hold the men back, even for as long as it took to run to my boys. I cursed them with all the force I had: do not allow their muscles to move, nor their sinews, their bones, their blood or skin. I prayed that Necessity and Force would help me if my Hecate was too far away. And through all this, I prayed to the queen of the gods: you keep children safe, keep mine safe, I beg you; I was your child once, the girl you chose for Jason, the girl he chose and then rejected, I have been faithful to him and to you, and I have borne him three children; you kept them safe from fever and sickness, please don't abandon them now, keep them safe, keep them safe, keep them safe.

I prayed so hard, the words jumbled as they fell from my mouth. I prayed in Colchian and Greek, tongues mingling because I could no longer remember which was which, I only knew that I must save my boys. I begged and bartered and pleaded and promised, I would do anything these goddesses required of me, anything, they could take my life and I would not fight if they would just keep the children safe.

And the power of one or all of the goddesses flooded through my body and held the murderers back from my beautiful children, my perfect boys. I was concentrating so hard to maintain the spell – no potions or herbs available to me, they were boxed up with my other belongings – and it was draining my strength fast, too fast. There were so many of them – I could not even pause to count, I just had to hold them all still in time and place for as long as I could. But it would not be much longer, I could not hold it for very long. I felt as though I was carrying the weight of every man, of his heavy bronze armour and his sharp bronze sword, and I felt my legs buckling under the strain. I gasped and straightened my back. Not yet, Medea, not yet, hold on, hold tight.

And somehow, through all this, I could still hear him in my mind telling me it was my fault and that I must accept the inevitable, that the boys would die but that he and I could live, that we could have more children, more sons, who would take the place of the lost and fill our hearts anew and I realized that this was his plan, to sacrifice the boys and save ourselves, and I wondered how I could ever have loved a man who had feelings like this, and how I could ever have had his children when he didn't know how to love anyone, anyone but his own worthless heart, and I prayed to Hera that she would forgive me because I could never return to marriage with this man who valued his children's lives less than his own, and she did not answer me, nor would she ever, because now I had betrayed her with my disdain for Jason, the man she had chosen, and she had understood my jealousy for him and then my rage, but she could not forgive this, and I knew I could do nothing to placate her so I prayed to Hecate again and begged for her to stand beside me in my battle as she has stood beside so many men in theirs, and I reminded her that I worship her as the nurse and foster-mother of the gods, and pleaded with her to raise my children as her own if I died today, and I prayed to my grandfather, Helios, who sees everything, and asked him if he would really shine his cleansing light on the death of his own descendants, the children of his granddaughter who was begging for his help.

And he heard me, and the sky was filled with golden light.

Nurse

The nurse was never sure if the gods had heard her own prayer, but they certainly heard Medea. She always said her father was the son of the sun god, and the nurse had never doubted her, exactly (because it was a strange thing to say if it wasn't true), but it did seem to stretch belief. And then she watched her mistress hold off a small army of men, alone, and she wondered how she had ever questioned that Medea was touched by the divine. And that was before the chariot arrived.

The huge golden vehicle was drawn by dragons, even though the nurse was sure the Sun's chariot was pulled by horses, because she had heard it in stories when she was a child. But these were giant golden snakes, and they drew up alongside Medea, as though they had been waiting for her call. The nurse thought she should be afraid of them, but it would be like fearing the sea or the sun itself. She was too small to matter to them, if they even noticed her.

She saw Medea's body convulsing from the strain of the

spells she had worked, and she ran towards her mistress, though the dazzling brightness of the chariot held her back. She closed her eyes to protect them, and she held the baby closer to her.

Medea

One mistake.

I made one mistake and I could not repair it. I had told the gods what Jason was, and they turned from him in disgust, as I had. But they would still support me. And when Helios sent his blessed chariot to transport me, I cried out with relief because I knew I could not hold on for a moment longer.

But then he told me that Jason's sons could not come with me, because they would sully the divine things they touched.

I begged my grandfather to reconsider, and he said no. The boys had carried my poison to the princess, and they had placed the box in her hands. There was no ambiguity here: they were murderers, they were impure.

I said I was the murderer, it was I who killed her and killed the king.

But the gods do not debate these matters.

Flee with the baby, Helios said. Or all your children die.

And I knew it was all my fault and that I had done it.

I could not let my beautiful boys be cut down by the cruel swords that faced them, that faced us all.

347

So I took my knife – my priestess's knife, the one I've had since I was a girl, for sacrifices – and I killed them both.

The younger one first, in my arms. He didn't see it, he didn't feel it. He was alive in my arms and then his blood was spilling, warm down my front.

The older one screamed and I stabbed him once, in the throat.

After

Eriopis

What do you mean, you didn't see me there? Well, of course you didn't. It's not a trick, it's grammar. Greek uses the masculine and the feminine, but it prefers the masculine (I know). So no matter how many girls were in a room (just one, in this instance), if boys were there too, the word 'children' takes the masculine ending. And the girls disappear. But yes, in case it's unclear, Medea and Jason had three children, two sons and then a daughter. I was a baby when Jason left my mother; Medea fled Corinth holding me in her arms.

People are surprised when I tell them that. Which I don't, unless they're asking me, because why would I? I don't want to spend all my time talking about my parents, and nor would anyone. But if your parents are as renowned as mine, it's hard to avoid. So let's start with the first question everyone asks me, because I bet it's what you want to know.

What was it like growing up with the worst parents anyone has ever had? Well, that's a tough one, because I only have experience of my own parents, don't I? The same as everyone else. Although when I say my parents, I mean my mother: I don't remember Jason at all. I wasn't even a year old when we left Corinth, so of course I don't. He didn't follow us to Athens, for whatever reason. Scared of my mother? Perhaps. Not interested in his daughter? Certainly. He didn't ever care about me: it was only my brothers he tried to save from exile, not me. That wasn't grammar, that was just the way it was.

And then, a few years after we left Corinth, he was dead. Not by his own hand, although plenty of people assume that. What else would a man do when he has lost everything? Almost everything, I say, correcting them quietly. They don't usually notice, they just go on to list the horrors: dead uncle, dead father-in-law, dead fiancée, dead sons. He himself had survived, but he had nothing to live for. He didn't stay in Corinth either, he went back home to Iolcus, only to find it was no longer home. His parents were dead and his comrades long gone. Jason – the man famed for his friends – had no one left. He found his consolation in the bottom of a wine cup.

My mother predicted his death, when he left her: she shouted it at him during an argument. How do I know? My nurse told me. She said, when Jason and Medea were fighting, she told him he would die alone, no matter how many wives he tried to marry in the meantime. He told her she was mad, because he was marrying once not twelve times and – as Medea herself had pointed out – his fiancée was years younger than him, and would certainly outlive him. Was that where my mother got her poisoning idea from? I don't know, I've never asked her. Probably. She always can sense a sore spot in your heart or mind, she knows exactly what hurts if you press it like a bruise. No, not so that she can hurt you: not to hurt the ones she loves, anyway. She just knows where people are hard and soft, where they need protection and where they're strong. She calls it magic, and I suppose it is.

When it was Jason though, she says herself, she would wound him with her words when he hurt her with his actions. So she told him that he would die alone, not as a warrior or a hero, in the heat of battle. There would be nothing heroic about his death at all, it would be pathetic and banal. And so it proved. My father sat drunk beneath the prow of the Argo, which had long since fallen into disrepair. He leaned back against the splintering planks that had once been the golden toast of all Hellas – just like him – and he misjudged the distance, hitting the ship harder than he had meant to with his shoulder blade. It was enough to dislodge a large chunk of wood above him, which landed on his head and crushed his skull. My mother used to say that she felt like this when she first saw him, like she had taken a blow to the head from something heavy. And now her fate was his.

Perhaps you think I sound cold-hearted about my father, and perhaps I am. It is hard to know how I would feel if I were telling this story about someone else, someone who wasn't Jason. I think I would feel the same: sympathetic for the tawdry and depressing death of a man I didn't know.

If people are disappointed that I don't remember Jason and can't tell them what he was – hero or villain, both or neither – they are sorrier that I don't remember my brothers. Because surely, they think, the loss of both siblings must be seared on my memory, no matter how young I was. But no one remembers things from when they were a few months old. Why should I be any different? They think I must have been spattered in fraternal blood, that I must have watched their small bodies crumple, abandoned, to the ground. And here, I have to correct them: my mother killed her two sons, but she didn't leave their bodies to be despoiled by the Corinthian soldiers. She took them onto her chariot – their uncleanness now gone, in the eyes of Helios the Sun – and she carried them away. Her nurse helped her lift the boys, which is why she was my nurse: she came with us. When my mother buried her sons, the nurse stood beside her. They lamented together as they scattered the earth over each body.

And so that brings my questioners to what they really want to know, which is (of course): what happened to Medea? What was she like as a mother? How did it feel to be the daughter of a woman who'd committed the most unforgivable crime? And wasn't I afraid of her, growing up?

I say, no, of course I wasn't afraid of her. My mother was an imposing woman – she was sharp-witted and she could be sharp-tongued – but rarely to me. They find it hard to believe that a woman who had killed her two sons could have ever loved them, and could have loved her other child too. They assume she was a monster, inhuman. But it doesn't matter to me what they believe, the only thing that matters is what I know. And I know this: my mother sang to me when I was scared in the nights. She would pick me up and carry me, and she would sing stories of Colchis and her childhood there. And – night or day – she would tell me stories about my brothers. She never lied to me, never pretended they hadn't been born, never pretended she hadn't killed them. She told me about Tisander, the oldest, and how he would never sit still, not even if she bribed him. About how he had the same smile as Jason, and how she couldn't stay cross with him for more than a moment, because he would look up at her through his long eyelashes (like an ox, she would say, and then the next day we would go and look at a farmer's oxen, and she would point to their eyes and say, see!), and she would smile because she couldn't bear him to be sad, and then he would smile back and everything was forgiven. When he died, she said, he had a gap between his two front teeth, and he would push his tongue through it to try and make Pheres cry.

Pheres was a quiet baby, she used to say, and he looked like her brother, Apsyrtus. All watchful eyes and a serious expression. Unless he was laughing, he always looked like he might cry, but then he didn't. He just watched everything very carefully, as though he'd been asked to memorize it. And then when he was old enough to talk, he would ask about trees and animals and birds and everything, and she found it hard to imagine he had ever been quiet. Was he like Apsyrtus in other ways, I asked her. And she said yes, and cried for a while, and I held her and said I was sorry, and she said it wasn't my fault.

I asked one day who I looked like, and she said I had both of my brothers in my face, and she put her hands on my cheeks and smiled, and I put my hands on hers and we stood together like that until I squashed her cheeks together and made her look like a fish. When you're a child, your home is the only one you know. If Medea wasn't like other women – like other mothers, I suppose they mean – I didn't notice it. She told me she had killed my brothers to save me, and that she would do it again every day for the rest of her life. Once, after I'd broken a plate by throwing a ball at the wall, she shouted at me and I ran away and hid. She found me later, crying in a cupboard. I suppose one of Aegeus' servants had told her where I was. She asked me what was wrong, and I told her I was scared that one day she would decide she'd made the wrong choice, killing the boys to save me. And she said no, she would never do that, because she hadn't explained it properly: she hadn't chosen between me and them, she had chosen between losing all of us, or saving me. So I would always be the most precious thing she could imagine. And she had seen many magical things, from bronze giants to golden snakes, so I would have to trust her in this matter.

As to what happened to her, she went to Athens, just as she had planned. She arrived – with me in her arms and blood all over her tunic – on a golden chariot pulled by snakes, and the people of Athens were not sure at first whether she was mortal or divine. People still feel this way about her: she knows so much, and she guesses so much more, that they sometimes think she can read their minds. And then they marvel that a goddess would appear in the guise of such a small, thoughtful woman.

Aegeus married her, of course. Did you not guess that he would? Or did you just think no man would choose to marry a woman who had treated her former husband the way Medea treated Jason? Aegeus – like many Hellenes, it transpired – valued my mother for her medicinal skills, her magic powers, her priestly knowledge. He loved her, I think, and if he was also a little afraid of her, he concealed it. Two years after we arrived at his palace, she gave birth to my brother, Medus. Everyone loves him, except me, sometimes, when he is being especially irritating. But mostly I do too.

We left Athens in a hurry (not by my mother's standards, I suppose), many years after we arrived. Something to do with a suspected poisoning which people attributed to her. It probably was her doing, if I am completely honest with you. My mother never did think it was worth engaging with people she wanted dead. But surely I was afraid of her then? Again, no. She didn't ever want me dead, she didn't ever want my brothers dead. If she wanted some obnoxious young Athenian out of the way, I can't say I don't understand. I have felt the same way myself, from time to time.

And after that, the Greeks were not quite sure where my mother went. They used to mutter that Aegeus should have kept her in Athens: he died a year later from a broken heart. Medea left Hellas for good. Most people stop asking questions at this point: it never occurs to them that a life outside Greece could be a life at all. They think when I say that she left Greece, I mean she died. But she did not. She returned to Colchis at the invitation of her father. She was cautious at first, of course, but Aietes suspected one of his courtiers of attempting to poison him. Who better to help him find a poisoner (and an antidote) than his youngest daughter?

Aietes soon disbanded his inner circle, because he was sure they would plot against him. He had no wish to die in a palace intrigue. He placed increasing responsibilities in Medea's hands: she was more than equal to the challenge. When he died, the Colchians asked her to be their queen, and she agreed.

And now, she is old. She has ruled Colchis for many years; her mind is sharp, although her memory fails her sometimes. Sometimes she forgets she ever left for Hellas, forgets her whole life in Greece, thinks I was born here (I don't know who she thinks was my father on these days). At other times, she talks about Tisander and Pheres as though they are still alive, and come to visit on festival days, like good sons would. A few days ago, she caught sight of two young men in the palace courtyard. Younger than me, but it didn't affect her sudden belief that these were her grown sons, and she called to them. The two men approached her cautiously – she was not using their names, of course, but she was still their queen so they came when summoned – and she held out her hands to them. They looked their questions at me (I am always by her side) and I nodded.

This is who I think of, when people ask me about my mother. A beautiful old woman, small and sharp, like a little bird. She is reaching out her hands – still deft, even with her swollen knuckles – and these two young men are holding her hands in theirs. Tears are streaming down her cheeks and she whispers that she still loves them, and she always will.

Author's Note

This essay is going to play fast and loose with spoilers, so ideally don't read it until you have read the novel. And yes, I know there can't really be spoilers in myths, but there are in novels, so do me a favour and read the book first. If you are not interested in authors telling you about their books, feel free to skip over it. Lots of students ask me about my novels when they have an essay due, and I never have time to reply to their questions. So this is really for them.

This is a novel I have been preparing to write for most of my life. Euripides' *Medea* was the first Greek tragedy I saw performed (with Diana Rigg in the title role: a performance which gave me the unusual sensation of knowing my life was being changed for ever as I watched it), and it was the first or second play I read in Greek. I sat an exam on the differing depictions of the character in Pindar and Apollonius at the end of my second year at university; the year after, I wrote my dissertation on the heroics of infanticide in Euripides (I don't have children, before you think about composing your sternly worded letter).

And when I came to start it, at the beginning of 2024,

I had no idea where I wanted to begin. This isn't unusual: it tends to mean I haven't done enough preparation for a novel to know where it starts. But I've been reading and thinking about this play for the best part of thirty years, and I have probably seen it performed twenty-five times: how much more preparation could there really be? I decided that the thing I needed to do was translate the Euripides, longhand. This is – in case you were wondering – weapons-grade procrastination. It took me a few weeks (and I would like to take this opportunity to apologize to Professor Whitmarsh of the University of Cambridge, for stealing his green-and-yellow edition because it was more up to date than my ancient copy of Page. Sorry, Professor). I'd like to tidy it up and publish at some point, and I hope one day to see it performed.

I realized within the first few pages of writing that I had found the title for the novel. It is not – as I think many people will assume – a phrase that refers to Medea. It is in a conversation between the Nurse and the Tutor, in which the Tutor reluctantly reveals that Creon has decided to banish Medea and her children. The Nurse can't believe it. Surely he wouldn't do that, she says, surely Jason wouldn't agree to it. The Tutor is unequivocal.

κοὐκ ἔστ' ἐκεῖνος τοῖσδε δώμασιν φίλος.

That man is no friend to this house.

And so I realized that the novel I thought I was going to write – about Medea and her encounter with Jason – was not exactly the novel I would write. The title would refer to Jason, not Medea. And the novel would be about the cumulative damage caused by a blank space where a man should be.

The story of the Argo is a classic quest narrative, but it is also a tale of many women whose lives are touched by men hunting for the golden fleece. Most of these women are marginalized: at least nine different names are offered for Jason's mother, which doesn't suggest a hugely significant role in the story. Aeson is always his father. Sometimes the marginalization is modern: Hypsipyle had plenty of stories told about her in antiquity, but she's not very well known now. I had the pleasure of translating/adapting Ovid's poem in her voice – from the collection known as the *Heroides* – for performance a few years ago. If you think she sounds good when I write her, you should hear how she is when Olivia Williams performs her, and Tom Littler directs. But sometimes a character was marginalized in antiquity too: we meet Iphias, the priestess of Artemis, very briefly in book one of Apollonius' *Argonautica*. She approaches Jason to speak to him, but can't. Whole academic papers have been written on what she may have intended to say. But, of course, we can't be sure (I left it for you to decide).

And the voyage of this divinely wrought ship is a story filled with lost children, onstage and off, from the children of Ino (who the chorus mention in Euripides' *Medea*), to Helle, and the children of Hypsipyle (who – in other accounts – is enslaved after Lemnos is invaded by men who discover there are only women there, and separated from her sons. She becomes the nursemaid of another child, Opheltes, who promptly dies in a freak encounter with a snake). Childhood was a dangerous time in antiquity: perhaps a third of children didn't survive to adulthood. But this does seem an especially perilous myth for the young.

So many abandoned women, and so many children who cannot survive in the face of murderous or absent parents. The first part of this book I wrote was the section on Chrysomallos, the golden ram. The sources for this part of the story are not well known, but I knew I wanted to include a character who is remembered so much less often than the object he becomes. A bonus fact: this makes it the first of my novels where a sheep is killed (in fact, two sheep). Usually I manage to make a sacrificial knife fall elsewhere, but this time it was unavoidable. The first quarter of the book takes its inspiration from the first two books of the *Argonautica*. The section in (and immediately after) Colchis owes a great deal to books three and four.

The section in Corinth is, of course, inspired by the Euripides play. The lines in italics – at the beginning of many of the chapters – are my translation of the opening of that play, with the Nurse's monologue. Much of Medea's thinking is taken from (my interpretation of) her depiction in this text. I made some major changes – because this is a novel, not a play – and regret none of them. I love Medea's two monologues in Euripides – more than any speeches made in any other play – but I didn't want to replicate them here. The debate over killing her children is one I will very much enjoy writing if my translation of the play is ever performed.

The essential conundrum of Medea – within her myth – is the shift between super-powered witch and helpless abandoned wife. She is the former in some of Apollonius, and in Pindar's fourth *Pythian Ode*. She's approaching the latter at the beginning of Euripides' play, though she turns out to be far from helpless, of course. Ovid tries to combine multiple versions of Medea in the *Metamorphoses*, but she becomes rather pedestrian along the way. Hesiod lists Medea in his *Theogony* – the origin story of the Greek gods – implying she belongs in divine company, rather than being a mere human who loses her husband to a younger rival. How can one woman be so many contradictory things?

One of the elements of the Euripides play that most frequently puzzles directors is how to reconcile the killing of her children – an act of supreme self-harm – and the way she appears onstage at the end of the play: in a divine chariot, apparently immortal and untouchable. The usual solution to this unsquareable circle is to make her mad in the final scene. Surely only a mad woman could feel so little after murdering her own children, and surely a mad woman might easily imagine herself riding in a chariot belonging to a god. It's an ostensibly attractive solution, but a frustrating one: if she is mad, she is not quite responsible for her actions. But the whole point of her extraordinary monologue, in which she wavers over whether to kill her sons before deciding she must (because her anger overwhelms her reason), is that she makes a decision to do something unbearable, because the alternative – allowing her ex-husband to have humiliated her and paid an insufficient price for doing so – is more intolerable. It may not be the decision you or I would make, but it is the choice Euripides' Medea makes.

Jason is also a shifting figure in his different representations. His myth is set relatively early (the Argo makes its way through the Symplegades before Odysseus and his men set sail in the *Odyssey*, for example. Apollonius makes references to the *Odyssey* throughout his *Argonautica*, creating a pleasing tension between the chronologically earlier myth and the historically later poem). But Jason's character in the *Argonautica* is complicated: heroic in his ambitions, but not especially in his powers. Jason is always persuasive and attractive. Men – like the Argonauts – flock to him. Women – Iphias, Hypsipyle – are drawn to help him, at the very least. When Eros shoots Medea, in the third book of the poem, it almost seems unnecessary: why would she resist him when no one else ever seems to? The only people who are impervious to his charm are supreme alpha males: Heracles wants Jason to remember that he is the greater hero, and Aietes is very much not in the market for a shiny new son-in-law.

But goddesses queue up to help him, particularly Hera, Aphrodite and Athene. And don't forget that Artemis was offering advice at the very front of that queue, when her priestess tried to speak to Jason before he first set sail. Even the reluctant Circe gives him her assistance when he comes asking for it; Hecate too is willing to contribute to the success of his quest. In *Stone Blind*, I tried to ask (and answer) the question of what it means to be a hero if you need the help of multiple gods and goddesses to complete your heroic task. Jason is a more successful man than Perseus, I think – he can inspire a huge crew of demigods and heroes to share in his quest. But he is still (as Erato slyly mentions) a man who sees most of his crises resolved by goddesses.

In Euripides, he is clever, persuasive and morally repugnant. It is one of the great delights of the play that an actor can choose which aspects of his character to accentuate, because he is so well drawn in so many different ways. For me, the most successful productions are those in which the fantastic debates he has with Medea feel like a substitute for the fantastic sex they used to have. She is cleverer than him, certainly, but he is no slouch. When you watch Clytemnestra and Agamemnon debate at the centre of the Aeschylus play *Agamemnon*, it's like watching a cat playing with a lost sock. There is nothing Agamemnon can do to affect the outcome of any conversation with his wife, he is never more than a passenger. But with Jason and Medea, you know that where she has her wits and her witchy skills, he has charm and persuasiveness in abundance. They are far more equally matched and – while their rows must have been catastrophic – their make-up sex must have been spectacular.

Medea and Jason have varying numbers of children (with varying names, according to the sources). Sometimes she also has children with Aegeus. Her later life is not widely attested but she has a reputation for founding cities (as does her son, Medus), and ruling them. Herodotus takes her to what we would now call Iran. The return to Colchis – sometimes at the request of her father, sometimes at the request of the Colchians – is one that dates back to antiquity. Diodorus Siculus says that the reason we have so many contradictory versions of her story is because tragic poets are drawn to talking about marvels. It is certainly a story filled with those, whichever ending we prefer. It's also worth mentioning that any character who prompts different versions of their story is one who was popular in antiquity. We have contradictory elements in the Medea story (and indeed within her character) precisely because so many storytellers wanted to talk about her.

If you want to read more about Medea, I spent many happy hours with *Medea*, a collection of essays edited by James J. Clauss and Sarah Iles Johnson. If you want to know more about the extraordinary physical violence that accompanies love spells in antiquity, Lindsay C. Watson's *Magic in Ancient Greece and Rome* is bloodcurdling. Her essay *The Violence of Amatory Magic* was particularly helpful. Medea's status as an outsider, a non-Greek, is discussed brilliantly by Edith Hall in *Inventing the Barbarian*. Please don't write in and ask to read my undergraduate dissertation (*The Heroics of Infanticide: a comparative study of Euripides'* Medea *and* Hecabe), because I'm afraid no copy survives. Nor should it: I'd write a much better one now. There is a chapter on *Medea* in *Pandora's Jar* if you'd like a detailed discussion of the Euripides play. My monologue for Hypsipyle – a loose translation of the Ovid poem – appears in the collection *15 Heroines*, published by Nick Hern Books.

I am never averse to a talking crow, so it is a happy accident that Apollonius features one in his poem. I don't only include talking birds in my novels because I know I'll be reading the audiobook, but I would be lying if I said I didn't derive some glee in writing this chapter, knowing I would get to perform it. Although – full disclosure – the first person I read it to fell asleep during my performance. Twice. Feel free to go back and check how many pages it is.

Acknowledgements

First of all, I'd like to thank everyone at Pan Mac who works so hard on my books, and especially the Mantle crew: my editor, Maria Rejt, Maddy O'Shea, Rosa Watmough and Michael Davies. Elena Richards read the book under instructions that she should always assume I am an idiot (which she politely pretends is a stretch). Thanks to Susan Opie for her thoughtful copy-editing. The gorgeous cover is thanks to Emma Pidsley, and the illustrations are by Hemesh Alles; I am always thrilled to finish a book these days, because it means the contents of my scrambled brain will soon become a beautiful object. No one would know the book was coming out if it weren't for Elle Gibbons and Emma Finnigan: thank you so much for all the work you put into the marketing and PR. Lydia Thomson is the audiobook producer and, given that she can run a hundred miles in one go, she must want to be.

Peter Straus: you are the best of agents and the best of men.

Thank you to Pauline Lord, who runs my live schedule and my life; to Xn, who runs the website and the half marathons; to Matilda McMorrow, who runs me.

Thank you – as always, and never enough – to Dan Mersh for being my first reader.

This year marks the end of an era: Mary Ward-Lowery and I have made ten series of *Natalie Haynes Stands Up for the Classics* for BBC Radio 4. I don't know how I'll cope without her. We'll do something else together soon, I hope. Thanks to Beth O'Dea for picking up the reins.

I often thank Roz Bell and Tim Parkin for their help with my work, but this time I mean it more than ever. Without their attentive kindness, this book wouldn't exist (and neither would I). Thank you also to Larissa Tittl for all your help, and for taking me for mango sorbet, and to Frederick Vervaet for bringing me a book when I had none.

Thank you to Tim Whitmarsh for his unending patience with my Greek, and my many (many) random questions about Apollonius and Euripides. One day I will ask him something for which he doesn't have a learned article to send me, but this novel has not claimed that day.

Thank you to my magnificent friends: to Helen Maus and Philippa Perry; to RDF, my daily touchstone; to Jo Walters, Carey Weich and everyone at TMAP (special mention to Sarah Perkin for her wildly encouraging texts last May). Thanks to Neil Broadbent, who built me back to full strength. Thank you to Amber – I'm so glad you mailed.

Thanks to my family: to Helen and Lottie, Chris, Gem and Kez; to my mum, Sandra, and my dad, Andre. And thank you to the wolf in my story: you got here just in time.